The Poets' Magic Sanctuaries

by

Dana Furgerson

To Shelley
Enjoy the read,

Dana Furgerson

All events and characters in this novel are fictional.

Halfway, Oregon

A town in northeastern Oregon at the base of the Wallowa Mountains

1978

Cover photo generously provided by William Sullivan: Eagle Creek,
Halfway, Oregon.

To Keith

Chapter 1

Halfway Wasn't on the Way to Anywhere

An olive green, 1957 Ford pickup pulled up in front of my store. A wooden framework extended the bed's height a good two feet, and a frayed, orange, plastic tarp covered a load that bulged against the tie ropes confining it. I figured that the contents of that load were the sum of the possessions of the folks riding inside. They had to be newcomers; Halfway wasn't on the way to anywhere.

A man, woman, and a little boy climbed out of the cab and sauntered in. They commenced sightseeing, looking intently at every part of the store as they wandered the aisles, picking up beer, pop, and chips.

The adults wore jeans and T-shirts. The logo on his shirt read "Pennzoil, all you need to know about oil" while hers had the words "all killing is wrong" wrapped around a red peace sign. He was a big man, his hair in need of a cut, and his beard showed a day's stubble.

She was regular size with long, straight, brown hair and no makeup. They had their arms looped around each other, and like two oversized doves during mating season, they nuzzled and cooed as they shopped.

"Damned beautiful place you have here, sir, lots of thundering streams," he said as he slapped a ten-dollar bill next to their purchases on the checkout counter.

"No need for the sir," I said. "My name's Joe."

"No offense intended," he said. "I did a stint in the military some time back, and it gave me the habit of using sir and ma'am a fair amount. My name's Harold." He stuck his hand out for me to shake.

I hesitated over whether I should tell this man that heavy snowfall was the reason we had them tumbling, boulder-rolling streams. Come winter, we never saw below our hips for all the fluffy white stuff. But in the end, all I said was, "Yes, Halfway is our own piece of sweet heaven."

She gazed longingly out the window at the Wallowa Mountains; they rose up, close in, just north and east of town. Sheared off beds of warped rocks lay jammed at crazy angles, as though they'd hit something hot and reared back to get away from it.

She sighed, and confirming my assumption that they were moving here, she said, "We hope to snag a little bit of this heaven for ourselves."

She extended her hand for me to shake. I'd never shook hands with a woman before, but this lady left me no way around it. Her hand was nearly jabbed into my groin. "My name's Magdalena Brown. This is my our boy, Sean." I extricated myself from her hardy clasp only to be once again grabbed into Harold's vice-like grip.

They were smitten. Halfway was the ticket for folks running from a nightmare and for folks running to a dream. Their souls were feeding on wind while their rosy futures were flashing before their eyes.

"Pleased to make your acquaintance, Mr. and Mrs. Brown,

Sean," I said as I yanked my hand out a Harold's. "As I said, my name's Joe, Joe Mobley, owner of Halfway's only grocery store. If it's happening, I know about it," I bragged and pressed my lips together, flashing 'em my best kindly proprietor look. I couldn't help myself. Business was business. I didn't want these folks driving to Baker City to shop.

I bagged their groceries, and to make conversation, I said, "So you folks are planning on settling here." Just wait until winter or your money runs out, I thought.

"Yes sir, that we are," Harold said. "I'm opening up an auto repair shop right across the street over there." He pointed to the rundown, closed up service station, the one that had gone broke under three successive owners within the last two years. He grinned first at Mag, then at me, and added, "Already paid six months rent." The two of 'em nearly sickened me; they were so damned proud of themselves. He shook his head and wagged a finger at me. "I won't be operating the pumps though."

Surprised at the man's arrogance, thinking he could make a living just by fixing vehicles in Halfway, I inquired, "You planning on lasting past your six months deposit? It's hard to make a living in a small town like this without diversifying." Yeah, the co-op sold gas, but folks liked a choice.

Harold brushed his nose with his thumb, a gesture that looked as much like a swagger as if he'd strutted like a haughty rooster, and he smirked. Obligingly, he filled in the gaping hole of my ignorance. "Mr. Mobley, I am a superb mechanic. I can fix anything with an engine."

"You sound confident of your success." I chuckled and shook my head in what was meant to be a skeptical way.

"Sir, I am," Harold said, and he and Mag beamed at each other.

"And as soon as we find a place to buy," Magdalena said, "we'll be building a greenhouse. I'm going to grow rare houseplants and medicinal herbs to market wholesale." She could barely contain her boisterous feelings. "Joe, we're in for one hell of a good time." She squeezed her hubby and son.

Harold spoke over the shoulder of his hugging wife. "In the meantime, we're looking for a place to rent, sir. You said you know of the goings on in town. Have you heard of anything?"

Damned my showing off. Now, I had to let 'em know about Jack's little brown house. The question was, though, how would I let 'em know? "The only place vacant is a square, tiny, two bedroom thing with a tin roof. It sets not three feet off Main Street, a block east of here."

I didn't tell 'em it was vacant because it had little insulation, and in the dead of winter, with the propane heater going full-blast and the oven on, a diligent person might keep the temperature up to 35 degrees if he was lucky. I glanced at their big eyed, little kid and felt a tinge of guilt, but I still didn't let 'em know.

Hell, they were new to town; how was I to know if they'd even make it to winter? And the guy who owned it, Jack, now there was a fellow who'd walked ass-backward into a deal if there ever was one, had to find someone more foolish than himself to rent the damned place. He was broke.

"The only place?" Mag asked. I suspected that she doubted me. "We'd kind of wanted a place out of town, but I guess that'll have to do for a start." She smiled uncertainly, refortifying her wind feeding soul. "What's the owner's name and phone number?"

I gave 'em Jack's number, guilt still nudging the edges of my brain. There might a been one other place available, but Jack was in desperate straits.

"We'll give him a call," Harold said, sounding a bit crestfallen, like Mag. "Where's the nearest public phone?"

"In front of the post office. That's the brick building next door." I didn't elaborate. I was finished exchanging cheerful patter with these folks.

Harold fumbled with putting the piece of paper with the phone number in his wallet, then asked, "How's the fishing and hunting in these parts, sir?"

Despite myself, I offered, "Best you'll ever get. There's trout in the streams, crappies and bass in the reservoirs, and deer and elk in the hills. You a hunter, Mr. Brown?"

"I damned sure am. Maybe we can go on a hunt together this fall, sir." He raised his eyebrows in expectation of an answer.

"That might work." I tried to sound as noncommittal as possible.

Harold shook my hand once more, picked up their bagged groceries, and said, "We'll get out of your hair, Mr. Mobley." He touched the fingers of his right hand to his forehead in a casual sort of salute.

"Bye, Joe," Mag warbled and grabbed my right hand in both of hers. "I'll be looking forward to doing business with you," she said. "You might even be interested in a little barter, groceries for plants, once I get my nursery set up." She winked, released my hand, and waved to me over her shoulder as she strode toward the door.

Their boy Sean waved too. He was just a slip of a boy, four or five years old, skinny and leggy like a meat-starved dog. He'd been quietly watching and listening, looking like he was evaluating the situation and me. He stopped just shy of the exit; his folks were already out the door.

"Yup, I think I'm going to like Halfway," he said. He smugly smiled at me, them big brown eyes of his staring right into the heart of things. "Don't worry, Mr. Mobley, I won't tell my parents that Jack's house wasn't the only place to rent."

He skipped out before I could corner him. The little twerp, not that it wasn't true, but how did he get the notion? I huffed and sputtered and did a thorough cleaning of the front window display so's I could watch him and his parents go to the pay phone, make their call, and climb into their truck. They didn't give any indication that he'd told 'em.

Later that afternoon, the Browns went into Jolane's Cafe and Bar for supper. I saw 'em go in because I usually hung out in the front of my store unless I was butchering or helping a customer. Wanda filled me in on what they ordered. Harold got a Coors and a chicken-fried steak and ate inside at the counter. Out front on the curb, to get away from the cigarette smoke, Magdalena ate a salad, and Sean ate a burger. Mag's decision to eat outside rippled through town. First impressions were already forming, and they weren't good.

Mag had nearly finished her salad when Harold leaned out the door and beckoned her inside. I saw her tousle Sean's hair as she said something to him. Then she hurried into Harold's arms, and in they whirled. I had to wait to get the rest of the details until someone from there came into my store. That happened to be George.

"George," I demanded, "what happened? Why did Magdalena end up going into Jolane's when she refused to eat in there in the first place?"

"You'd never believe it," George answered. That was all he said. I waited. He looked at the magazines. Each time he moved, I got a whiff of the cigarette smell Mag had been trying to avoid.

"George, goddamn it, what happened?"

"I ain't never seen the likes of it in Halfway before. I can tell you that," he said and returned to browsing the magazine rack.

"Halfway's never seen the likes of how I'm going to pulverize your rotten carcass if you don't tell me exactly what went on with Harold and Magdalena in that bar." I could a killed the old fart on the spot, damn him, baiting me like that.

He held out his hands in a cautionary gesture and spoke. "All right, all right. But don't blame me if you're offended."

"I won't be offended. Out with it!"

George exhaled so long I thought he must a been pumping air

into his lungs on the sly. Finally, he said, "This is it," and paused. "It pains me to have to repeat this." He paused again. I wanted to strangle him, but I would've had to wait longer to find out what happened. "Harold had put a quarter in the jukebox, okay. We'd all seen him do that. He went back to eating, shooting the bull with the guys at the counter. Ten minutes passed. He was on his second Coors."

"Yeah, yeah." I could hardly breathe; George talked slower than a slug walked backwards.

George's eyes bugged out a their baggy sockets and he said, "The song he chose starts to play, Kiss You All Over or Kiss Me All Over, some fool nonsense like that. The music was real slow and booming with drums and bass guitars. Harold leaps off his stool and runs to the door. He yells for his wife to come on in, saying the jukebox is playing their song."

"Yeah, go on," I encouraged him, for he had stopped again.

He continued, "Magdalena Brown came in all right, and the two of 'em danced to that throaty voiced, throbbing song."

"Yeah so, what about it?"

"It was the way they danced. Like they were alone, and God had taken a holiday. Hands going up in the air and twining into each other's. Bodies rubbing and swaying to the boom, boom pulse of the music. And Harold kissing his wife's neck and face and arms. I believe he even licked her cheek once. Maybe twice. His leg wrapped around her backside, and her leg shimmied up his. I couldn't believe I was watching such obscenity right here in Halfway." George shook his head in dismay.

I was starting to feel a bit heated and secretly wished I could a seen that dance. I consoled myself by remembering that I knew which button to push on the jukebox when Harold and Magdalena were there. I said, "Mighty unsettling for you, I imagine."

"I should say. Old Mrs. Hampton got faint and had to be helped into the fresh air."

I figured that raspy, cane wielding old woman probably had an orgasm on the spot, but to George, I said, "Oh my, oh my."

"Well, I got to be heading home. The little woman will be wondering if I ain't fallen into the ways of Satan if she gets wind of these goings on before I get home. Bye, Joe."

"Good evening, George." Satan wouldn't have you.

The next day, Harold and Mag moved into Jack's place, and Mag unpacked the six crates of starter plants she had moved over from Portland. Harold put an ad in the paper that read "Ace Mechanic, I can fix anything with an engine." By afternoon, the three of 'em were over at Harold's shop, unpacking his tools. I saw 'em tidying up the grimy old garage. They were clearly unaware of all the juicy gossip flashing all over town about 'em. They'd made a questionable, if not interesting, first impression in Halfway.

Chapter 2

Slow Dancing in a One-Horse Town

We'd seen the ad for a shop to rent in the Rural Lands flier and had made a quick trip over to check it out. So I knew that Halfway was a small town, but on this second trip, with all our belongings heaped in the bed of our truck, its smallness seemed even more apparent. Small was an exaggeration in its favor. Main Street curved northeast through town, and along its two block length lay the town's entire commercial section. The expression "one horse town" danced inside my brain as if lit in neon, burning its unmistakable message of limits and limited into my cortex. But the Wallowa Mountains wrapped themselves around Halfway like the fingers of a giant's hand, and I lost myself as I gawked at their granite peaks, imagining the alpine meadows I would soon discover.

The valley itself was lush with vegetation of all varieties. Old Doug firs dotted the town proper and profuse blooms of flowers, wild and cultivated, filled gardens and pots. Cottonwoods lined the boulder-strewn streams we'd crossed just west of town. The sunny day pulsed with heat. Summer had intensity here; the growing things knew they had only a short span to live before winter eclipsed life.

Harold pulled up in front of Valley Grocery and pointed across the street to the garage we'd rented. Twenty or so old tires leaned against the street side of the building, and the two stall doors hung shut at peculiar angles, leaving spaces big enough for an adult person to slide through underneath. What I could see of the front office window, through a cover of weeds and filth, was intact, but the side window was broken out. Three large pieces of the rippled tin roof bent up, offering no protection for the surface below, and another hunk of tin swung out, unsupported, over the office.

"Harold, are we sure this is the only garage available?" He'd said the rent we'd paid was a great deal; I understood why.

"Hon, I know it doesn't look like much," he answered, his eyes full of dreams. He was already sitting in that office writing up a customer's bill. "But it'll spiff up fine."

"Can you really make it here, in this small of a town?" Who would he have for customers?

"There's only one other mechanic in town. He's on the verge of retiring, and what he does equates more to bandaging a critical wound with duct tape than to actual repair." He leaned over and kissed Sean on the top of his head and me on the cheek. "We'll tour the garage later when we get to that part of the unpacking. For the present, I need a cold one and maybe something salty."

As we climbed out of the truck, I called to him, "Remember your promise."

"Mag, a man has the right to celebrate. One little beer isn't going to hurt anything." He grinned at me and held the door open for Sean and me to enter.

I decided I'd talk to Harold later. Instead, I looked at the market where I would shop for the rest of my Halfway days. Its exterior was a combination of multicolored, patched tin roof and white painted, old, wooden siding. I smiled, said, "Okay," and walked in.

Once inside the store, Harold could barely contain his excitement. He talked a mile a minute, tousled Sean's hair, and kissed me. His business was sure to succeed, and my nursery was bound to flourish. In no time at all, I caught his fever and became as agitated as him. Halfway lay like a river before us, waiting for our futures to flow into its own.

We meandered through the aisles, following what seemed to be some kind of pattern in a maze, for the chest high, bowed wooden shelves were placed in a design that slowed shopping cart traffic to a crawl and gave the impression of a much larger store. Small signs, advertising that Joe, the proprietor, did his own butchering and made his own sausage and burger, were stuck to every possible surface where they might be viewed.

When we paid for our groceries, we introduced ourselves, and it turned out that Joe was the man behind the checkout counter. He seemed like a nice older guy. He sounded as disappointed as we were when he told us there was only one house for rent, but I noticed a certain edge to his voice when he talked about the rental and figured we weren't getting the whole story. He acted as though he would have talked to us longer if another customer hadn't come up behind to be checked out, but I think he was relieved by the interruption. We excused ourselves and let the man run his business.

While Harold called the owner of the vacant house from the pay phone in front of the post office, I went inside to rent a post office box. Mail wasn't delivered to your door if you lived in town. I was the only one in the building besides the postmaster, but he let me stand at his counter for a good while before he broke away from whatever the hell he was doing and came to see what I wanted. "Can I help you?" he said in a voice as dry as his brittle attitude.

"I'd like to rent a post office box. You see we're new to . . . "

"That'll be twelve-fifty for the year," he said. "No out of town checks."

No idle chitchat here. I filled out the required form, paid the man, and got out.

By the time I rejoined Harold, he had arranged to meet our future landlord at the rental in a half-hour. To kill time, we went into the Farmers' Co-op, a sprawling, shiny tin building stocked with fifty pound sacks of grains and seeds and an assortment of tin buckets, gloves, hats, horse tack, and other farm gear. Everything was covered with dust, and it appeared that the popularity of an item could be gauged by how thick the layer was. To be honest, some things looked as though they'd been there fifty years. Out back were tin outbuildings that held bulkier supplies such as fencing, gates, and feeders.

The stocky man behind the counter wore a plaid, flannel shirt that supported a very large, sagging belly, and he had on button-fly jeans, with the top two buttons undone. Harold and I greeted him and introduced ourselves. I thrust my hand forward to shake his.

"You're new in town," he said and turned one corner of his mouth upward, forming a lopsided smile. My hand hung in midair, not shaken; he seemed not to have noticed it. I jammed it into my jeans pocket. He didn't offer his name.

"Yes sir, we're moving in," Harold said. "We need a quart of oil for our truck. The old Ford burned a bit getting here from Portland. You carry oil?"

"Course we carry oil. Right over there with the antifreeze," the man said and pointed.

While Harold walked over to retrieve the oil, I tried to engage this reticent man in small talk. "Do you know where the name of this town and valley come from?" I asked.

"Where d'you think they come from?" he said. Harold and I

glanced at each other.

"I'd guess they didn't come from any dealings anyone had with you," I murmured. "No mercy evident here." His sour nature was pissing me off.

"Mag, watch it," Harold cautioned.

I kept my eyes on the man. He didn't blink; in fact, he didn't show any emotion at all. "Yes," he said evenly, "no mercy and no credit."

Harold cracked up, and I couldn't help but follow suit. The unnamed clerk observed us stony-eyed. "Harold, pay the man," I said. "I think he wants rid of us."

Harold plunked the exact change on the counter.

"Bye now," I called.

"Catch you later, sir," Harold added.

"Thank you for doing business with the co-op," our anonymous clerk said. "Do come back." We waited for him to say more, but he merely turned a key in the register, locking it, and retreated to a paper filled desk, his back to us. We rejoined Sean, who was playing with a dog out front.

"Can I get a dog?" he asked.

"At some point," Harold answered vaguely. "But I don't think the owner of the rental allows pets."

"We're in the country now, Dad. All the kids will have dogs."

Not paying much attention to their conversation, I gazed at the Creek Bottom Motel across the street, where we would most likely have to spend the night. It was made up of ten small cabins that had been trucked in from somewhere else; they still had support boards tacked on them. Placed on foundations and set end to end, they formed one long, narrow line of buildings. The stream to which the name referred, Trout Creek, was visible, about a quarter of a mile away, in an alfalfa field. I wondered where the cabins came from, and I wondered about the person who had gone to great effort to move them here but then hadn't bothered to remove the boards used for transit.

"That must be Jack's place," Harold said; he nodded in the direction of a plywood sided, tin roofed, very small, brown house close to the edge of the road. "We better drive over. We wouldn't want Mr. Hospitality here to have our truck towed." Harold climbed into the pickup and drove the hundred yards to Jack's rental; Sean and I walked over.

Jack, a short man with blonde hair, emerged from the house as our truck rolled to a stop in front of it. "Can my dog live here?" Sean asked simultaneous with us arriving at the house.

"No pets allowed. Too close to the road; they'd just get run over. You said you had no pets," Jack said and peered into our truck in search of the hidden dog.

"We have no pets," I assured him, "only a son who would like to have some."

"I want to move back to Portland if I can't even have a dog," Sean said. He kicked a stone and sent it skidding onto the road.

"Do you want to look at the place or not?" Jack asked. He looked strangely uncomfortable, and the same feeling I had gotten while talking to Joe flickered through my mind.

Harold must have caught his urgency too because he said, "Don't worry, partner. From what I hear, looking at your house is just a formality. We're going to rent it if you'll let us."

Jack appeared puzzled but then seemed to put two and two together. "Oh, right, right, right," he said. "I want first and last month's rent and a fifty dollar cleaning deposit."

With a slight hand gesture, Harold appealed to me for confirmation of a decision. "Let's take a walk through anyway," I said. "Jack, you can point out the house's finer features and inconspicuous flaws."

Jack got that uncomfortable look again and smacked his hands together. "Yeah, all right," he said and glanced at his watch, "but I'm going to have to make this fast. I have chores, you know."

Except for the gray flecked, floor tile, the house was as brown inside as it was outside. The kitchen and living room comprised the front half. The rear consisted of two tiny bedrooms, without doors, and a dimly lit bathroom with no windows. A propane heater stood at the very center of the living room, our only source of heat.

"There's the kitchen," Jack said and pointed, his tour patter proving somewhat limited. "There's the living room," another point, "bedroom, bedroom," point, point, "bathroom. Okay, do you want it or not?"

Harold sighed and said, "Mag, we'd better pay the man his money."

I counted out the amount Jack specified and handed it to him.

"You'll have to go to Halfway Power to get your utilities turned on. It probably won't be today," Jack said and handed us the keys. He scurried out the door. Through the house's tiny front window, we saw him head for Halfway Bank with our money; it hunkered just east of the motel.

"I still what a dog," Sean said.

"Be patient, son," I said and rubbed his back in an attempt to sooth him. "How about we stretch our legs with a little walk around town?"

Sean was eager to see how many children might be around, so the three of us set out to explore the town of Halfway. We came to Halfway Bank. Constructed of gray stone blocks, it was the sturdiest of all the town's buildings we'd seen so far, and since we had to transfer our personal accounts and set up Harold's business account, we went on in. The ceiling was high, and dust motes danced in the light the tall, narrow windows let into the interior. Walnut counters and leather, upholstered chairs gave the bank a substantial air that belied its inconsequential location. An ambiance of a bygone age made me feel as if Jessie James could walk into this hazy, brown and gray, hushed room and demand all the bank's money. But I imagined, just as surely, that he would not get it.

We accomplished our business in whispers. Sean, caught by the gravity of the place, asked if he could open a savings account. We deposited ten dollars to get him started and reemerged into the sunlight, all carrying our brand new, blue plastic bankbooks.

Beyond the bank was downtown proper. We stopped by Halfway Electric to arrange for them to turn on our power. Long, sweeping, maple counters contrasted with the baby blue paint on the walls and ceiling. Baby blue, tufted cushions topped sleek, maple chairs. A professionally dressed woman at the counter greeted us. "Can I help you?" she asked. "My name's Wanda. You folks must be new in town."

Wanda chatted amicably about Halfway. "You're going to love it here. Folks are friendly, and the air is clean. Your little boy is going to go wild at the Fourth of July festivities coming up."

"I want a dog, though," Sean told her, not relinquishing his campaign for a pet, "but Jack said we couldn't have one."

"Oh," Wanda exclaimed, and her mouth dropped, "you're renting from Jack, are you?" She raised her eyebrows halfway up her forehead.

"Yeah," Harold said. "Why? What's the problem?"

"Problem? Oh, no problem." Wanda was backpedaling furiously. "I just didn't know Jack was renting that place again, I mean yet. I'm sure you'll love it. You're all young. You can do wonders with it." Harold glanced at me with a what-did-we-get-ourselves-into look.

Wanda tittered and reached for the appropriate paperwork for opening our account. She gossiped as we filled out forms, running through the local happenings as easily as water through a hose. We learned why Earl, the clerk at the co-op, was out of sorts. "His wife ran off last week with the UPS man," she explained. "George, our service rep, is just the opposite of Earl. He's a real talker, preacher, is closer to it. You'll find that out when he hooks you up tomorrow. But watch what you tell him." Wanda rolled her eyes. "He'll spread rumors like there was no tomorrow." By the time we walked out of Halfway Electric, I felt that I knew most of the people in town.

"Remind me never to cheat on you," Harold said. "You'd know about it before I got home. Hey look here." He pointed to the rear of the utility company building. We saw that the front brick wall of the office was a facade; the rear of the building was weathered one by fours.

We were hungry and decided to have supper. Our choices were Jolane's Cafe and The Home Cooking Cafe; both doubled as bars. For no particular reason, we chose Jolane's.

"Whoa," I said. Spots danced before my eyes as they adjusted to the dimness of the dining room.

A dozen people stared at us. "Howdy," Harold said and clumsily waved in general to all the diners. He leaned close to Sean and I and whispered, "Let's find a seat fast." We looked around for a table, but none was empty.

The year was 1978, but in here the 1950's reigned supreme. Red Formica tabletops perched on stainless steel legs, and red Naugahyde chair cushions sat on curved, shiny steel supports. Worn, black and white tiles checkerboarded the entire floor.

The locals returned to their conversations, no longer observing us. Country western music blasted from a jukebox. Since no one offered advice on where to sit, Harold walked up to the counter and plunked down.

"I think I'm going to eat outside," I whispered to Harold.

"Why? Too many eyes on you?" he whispered back and laughed.

"No, babe. It's more like the cigarette smoke and greasy grill smell are getting to me." I glanced to the right of my husband and saw a thin, bald man listening to our conversation. I figured I had better get used to the shared, public life of a small town. "Sean, do you want to eat in here or out front with me?"

"Out front," he said. "I saw a dog I could play with tied up there."

"Don't give up the cause, partner." Harold chuckled and sucker punched him. We all laughed, happy to relieve the tension of being so noticed.

I sat on the curb and ate while Sean played with a black and white cow dog tied to a tree by the side of the cafe. He was slowly feeding the dog his burger, thinking I didn't see him do it.

Harold had chosen our favorite song, Kiss You All Over, on the jukebox, and he called me in to dance with him. I felt tired, and worry was working at the edge of my brain. But when I saw the need in his eyes, same as I knew was in mine, and when he reached his scuffed up, calloused fingers toward me, my body kicked into overdrive. I was hot for Harold.

We danced as we always danced. Harold and I, that's all there was, the music flooding into us and our bodies moving as one. Our dreams resurfaced: Harold's shop, my greenhouse, his metal sculptures, and my poems. All became real in the open spaces of Halfway. My body swayed, in sync with Harold's. "Love you, babe," Harold whispered.

Harold had promised to stop drinking when he got his own shop and we got our own home. He had his shop. All we needed was our own home.

Chapter 3

What A Relief

Old Lady Hoagland Up and Had a Stroke

Folks began testing Harold's abilities in no time at all. Small jobs at first, like the lawn mower that hadn't run in ten years or the kid's broken down go-cart. They figured it would be something to talk about over coffee, whether he bungled the job or actually fixed the relic.

But Harold didn't screw up. He for damned sure was an ace mechanic. In no time at all, he had cars, pickups, and tractors crammed into his shop and backed up against it outside.

I felt guilty when I dropped off my Chevy with Harold instead of Tom, our resident mechanic, but Tom hadn't been able to fix the compression problem plaguing it. I finally went to talk to Tom. Goddamn it, loyalty had to mean something. "So Tom," I said. "What do you think about all the folks taking their vehicles to Harold? Do you want me to talk to 'em?" I omitted the fact that I was one of them folks.

"Hell, no," Tom said. "It's a relief. Let him be the one they call when it's forty below and they can't get their vehicles started. I'm too old to be sliding under cars and trucks anymore."

That was a big load off my mind.

Summer slid into fall, and Harold still had more business than he could handle. When I realized that the Browns were going to make it at least into winter, I got to worrying more as the cold weather approached. If I told Harold and Magdalena how God-awful cold that little rental got, they'd know I had known about it from the start, and the whole town'd be on my ass if I pissed off the ace mechanic. It was a real dilemma. I kept my yap shut.

Snow fell, and as we edged our way into December, the thermometer dropped into below zero temperatures. Christ, I knew that little house must be cold, but I acted surprised when Harold and Magdalena came into my store and told me about it.

Harold said, "That little house sure is a frigid one."

"Is that so?" I said. Hang tough, I told myself; they'll be okay.

Magdalena piped up, "I'm afraid that my little boy will freeze to death in his sleep. I'm up all night, checking on him, making sure he's warm enough. He won't sleep with us, says he's too big." She looked awfully tired. Damn it, what was I supposed to do?

"To tell the truth," Harold said, "she dresses him in so many coats and hats and covers him with so many blankets, the real danger is he'll smother."

"Harold, this is serious," Mag told him, but she laughed as hard as we did.

I breathed a sigh of relief when Hoagland's old lady up and had a stroke in early December, and they decided to sell and move to Ontario pronto. Their place wasn't particularly outstanding, but it stretched over fifteen acres of south-facing hillside, and that trailer was warm. Magdalena and Harold made 'em an offer, kind a on the cheap side from what I hear, but old man Hoagland accepted. They moved out, and the Browns moved in.

That took a shitload off my mind. It was getting real hard to frown all innocent-like when granola-purchasing Mag told me her troubles as she checked out.

Chapter 4

My Best Friend Sylvia

When Sean started kindergarten in the fall, Harold was the one who took it the hardest, despite all his "our son is growing up" talk. We walked Sean the three blocks to school. We were anxious, but Sean wasn't. He was ready to be away from his parents and around other children. Kindergarten was a small class of twelve students, very cozy. Sean had learned the alphabet before he started school and was reading actual words soon after the school year began. He was eager to leave for school each morning, confirming that he was enjoying himself. He didn't even seem to mind our frigid little rental. Getting Lucy, his dog, in December after we moved completed his world. That he now had to take a bus to school was fine with him.

For me, moving into the Hoagland place meant warmth and the promise of fulfilling our dreams. An unpainted, plywood shell into which four rectangular holes had been cut protected the trailer and provided a snow-bearing peaked roof. Unfortunately, the openings in the shell didn't line up with the trailer's windows, and very little sunlight actually reached the home's interior. We lived in a bath of artificial light, but we were warm. In fact, we had to be careful to not build too big a fire in the woodstove, or it could get too warm.

This eyesore sat on a gentle, grassy slope with a million dollar view of the Wallowas to the northeast. At the center of this view the massive granite slabs of Cornucopia Peak angled into the clouds. The uphill half of our acreage was forested and backed the trailer in the other direction.

"Esthetically, the shell and second roof are shit, but they're substantial. They'll outlast the trailer." Harold smiled with satisfaction as he gazed at our new home. "The Hoaglands used manufactured trusses, and they anchored them to four by four beams. They actually built a foundation instead of letting their supports rot in the dirt the way a lot of folks around here do. And we don't have the merry breezes blowing under the plywood."

Sometime in the future, we planned to add more windows and studs to the shell, add siding to the plywood, install glass in resituated window holes, insulate, and sheet rock. By gradually removing the walls of the trailer, we would enlarge each room by about two feet and gain access to sunlight. But first, we wanted to get Harold's at home, welding shop functioning and my greenhouse built.

Even before that, we needed to rig the pickup with some kind of snowplow. The peaks around Halfway invited storms to dump their loads of snow before passing over them, and they did. We realized that we'd be four or five feet deep in snow in no time. When we lived in town, we didn't have to worry about the snow's depth. Harold had only to make it down the block to his shop. But at the Hoagland place, we were over four miles outside town, and unless Harold learned to ski, he had to be able to get his truck down our drive and into town, possibly before the snowplow got to our road.

Our driveway was long, and if we parked on the road, our vehicles were at risk of being buried in the morning if the snowplow came by at night. Neighbors might help shovel you out when they could get to you, but Harold had to be at work early, and hand shoveling the drive was wearing us out. Harold welded a mechanism to support a snowplow to the front of the truck and got to work on time. His business grew. I helped with the books and billing.

When children with sleds started showing up at our place, we learned that our front slope had traditionally doubled as a sledding hill. Sean thought he'd found heaven; he could sled with built in playmates. I periodically brought out hot chocolate and cookies, and Sean beamed. He was reluctant to leave the slope even when he was shaking with cold.

Once we were surrounded by snow, we decided we might as well learn to ski. And we did; well, we sort of learned. We made our first long treks into the mountains in this precarious manner; the summer had been too jammed full of work to do extended hikes. Snowy alpine meadows fringed by jagged rock and cut through by rivers of dwarf hemlock sparkled in the brilliant sun and too cold air. We stumbled, slipped, and fell. We got chilled and had to retreat to the truck or home to warm our freezing limbs. But we fell more deeply in love with the Wallowas and eagerly planned future summer hikes and packs.

Spring came in fits and starts; killing frosts followed warm days. Thunder boomed, and lightning flashed while rain worked at melting the remains of the snow. We worked like crazy fixing up Harold's shop and our home.

Finally, the weather the first week of May stayed dry enough to allow us to dig the trench for the greenhouse foundation. Harold and I worked in different sections of the trench. Every now and then, I would notice Harold break from his spading to take a swig of beer. We'd been in our house over five months, and Harold was still drinking. Yes, he worked hard and went to work every day, but he didn't stop drinking until he fell asleep, a sleep I equated more with alcohol induced unconsciousness.

"Harold, do you remember what you said about quitting beer when we got our own home?"

"Mag honey, it's a beautiful day, and we need to get the foundation dug. This isn't the time." He finished his beer and tossed the can in the box with the other empties.

Harold slung dirt out of the trench ferociously. I was not as far along in my section as he was. There was no way I could keep up with him unless I used a backhoe. Harold paused for a moment and arched his back. He opened the cooler sitting on the ground by him, popped the top off another beer, and saluted me with it.

He took a long swig and set the can next to the trench. "I better get back to work," he said, and as was his habit if he suspected conflict, he avoided it, this time by turning his back to me. "Can't waste this nice day."

"How many beers is that today?" I asked, despite having just convinced myself to let it slide. "You said you'd cut back."

Harold answered with his back to me. "Yes, I did say I'd cut back. I'm still upright, and I'm still working. I'd say I have just about the right amount of alcohol in me."

If drawn into a discussion he didn't want to be in, Harold agreed with whatever was said and then made a joke of it. He did this with my worry about his drinking. He didn't get angry unless I pushed my point, but he didn't change, a characteristic that at times irritated the hell out of me. His behavior left little room for confrontation or resolution.

Unlike Harold, I was the queen of reaction. No matter how much I told myself that I wouldn't get defensive, I did. I grabbed the bait every time he tossed it. Not that this tendency helped me; it didn't. I never won arguments with Harold because he always agreed with me or walked away. I blustered, stammering, "but, but, but . . . you're still drinking."

"You're right; you're right," Harold said and kept slinging shovelfuls of dirt from the trench.

You're working hard, I thought, but I won't really have my husband with me this evening. Oh, his body will be next to me, and he might speak to me. He might even be affectionate, but he will most likely not remember anything he says or promises because he will be drunk. I thought that, but I said no more.

We had become acquainted with the couple who lived on the next farm; their son Bill was Sean's age. Sean and he became fast friends. Jessica, his mother, pulled up our drive around eleven, about an hour after I had talked to Harold about drinking; Bill would be with us until evening while his parents did their errands in Baker City. Harold and I went over to greet them.

Sean was so exited with the prospect of showing off his latest pets to his new friend that he could barely contain himself. "I got gerbils this week. I'll show you them first," he said. "They're in my bedroom. Then we'll go to the chicken coop and play with the chickens. What was the name for our kind of chickens, Dad?"

"Buff Orphingtons, Son," Harold answered. "But Son, you have to remember that Bill is a farm boy. He might be sick of chickens."

Bill grinned. "I like chickens. I want to play with your chickens. Sean said that we can hold your hens. Mine just run away from me."

Sean said. "We'll collect the eggs too."

Harold winked at him. "Hey, are you going to show your friend the new tricks you taught Lucy?"

"Oh, yeah, the tricks," Sean answered excitedly, "Come on. I'll show you."

As Bill's parents said their goodbyes and pulled down the drive,

Sean introduced Bill to his gerbils. Harold returned to working on the greenhouse foundation, and I walked uphill to the trailer to make lunch. I was at the trailer door when an electric blue, Ford Fairlane turned into our drive, and a woman with a carrot red, bouffant wig leaned out the window, waved at us, and shouted, "Hello, hello."

She rolled to a stop in front me and emerged from her car as if she had springs strapped to the bottoms of her feet. She was dressed in a bright green mini skirt and black turtleneck sweater and had on black, high-heeled, patent leather, calf length boots. I couldn't help but stare at her.

She introduced herself. "A belated welcome to Halfway, Magdalena. My name is Sylvia. I've been out of town and just now learned about you all from Joe." She held out her hand for me to shake. "I hear you're into herbs. I think that's fabulous. Herbal medicinals and cooking with herbs eases the mind and mollifies the soul." She broke off her vigorous shaking of my hand. "Which herbs do you have, honey?"

I said, "I don't have as many herbs as I'd like to have. I had to cut back when we moved, and I lost a few more when we lived in that cold rental in town, but I'd be happy to show you what I do have." I waved for her to follow me inside.

"Well, my oh my," Sylvia said. "We'll have to remedy your dearth of herbs situation as fast as we can." I introduced her to Harold before continuing to the trailer.

"I've heard about you," Sylvia said. "You're the ace mechanic from Portland."

"For now anyway," Harold said and smiled. "At least until I screw up."

"From what I hear that isn't likely to happen," Sylvia said. "Well hon," she said to me, "let's see those herbs."

I introduced Sylvia to Sean as he and Bill were leaving the trailer on the way to the chicken coop. She already knew Bill. I showed her the measly collection of herbs I had on one windowsill in the extra bedroom that caught indirect sunlight through an opening in the shell. She looked over the collection and then spotted my writing desk. It was strewn with several hundred pages of finished and unfinished poems. Carefully picking up a sheet of verse, she asked, "May I?" and gestured with the papers in her hand to indicate a request to read them.

"They're just poems I've written," I responded, dismissing my half-baked efforts, "but sure, go ahead, read."

"I write poetry myself," Sylvia said, placing the hand without paper on her chest. Her silver bracelets jangled from the movement. A radiant expression came over her face, and she grasped my shoulder and announced dramatically, "We shall be sisters in verse."

"You wouldn't want to read my writing on a regular basis." I again tried to discourage her.

"I know I'll love your work. I'll read this one right now," she said and read a poem, mouthing the words. Upon reaching the end, she looked up at me. "I love it. I truly love it." She smiled. I didn't consider my poems to be even decent, but Sylvia's spontaneous enthusiasm was flattering. "I'm so pleased. I've found a soul mate." She hugged me. "Can you come by my place to read my poetry sometime?"

I surprised myself by responding immediately; I was usually much more cautious about making friends. "How about next Thursday?"

"Super! Come for lunch; you'll need a break from building anyway. Will Harold be at work?" I nodded. "Well then, no need to invite him. Will Sean be in school?"

"Only in the morning. The bus brings him home around noon," I said. "He's in kindergarten."

"Well, he's welcome, and bring your poetry."

"It sounds wonderful." I paused. "But for now, I need to get lunch ready," I said. "Come talk to me in the kitchen."

After lunch, Harold, Sylvia, and I walked out to the greenhouse foundation. Sylvia surveyed the trench and studied our plans. "Look what you folks are doing here. This is going to be one marvelous greenhouse. I adore greenhouses. I may have one built just like this if it works out for you." She smiled.

Harold said, "Then you'll have to track the progress of our building. Bring your husband by too."

With a flip of her hand, Sylvia answered, "Oh, he's not likely to make it over."

Harold quieted. "Oh, I'm sorry, is he ill?"

"Not at all. He's resting quite nicely. He's dead."

"Oh, sorry to hear that," Harold said, the color rising on his cheeks. "I didn't mean to bring up a sad subject. I should have thought."

"It's okay. It's been ten years. Don't worry about it."

I loved this brash lady. She strode about our work site, firing questions at us, as if she were a building inspector. She spoke in extremes. She announced that she "cherished" Sean. She "adored" what the trailer would someday be. She "marveled" at my herbs and my collection of old books.

About an hour and a half into our visit, Sylvia said, "I better be getting out of your way. I know you need to take advantage of this warm day. Bye, dear; bye, Harold." Harold saluted her with his beer. She hugged me again and dashed for her car.

"Good-bye, Sylvia," I answered and fumbled for more to say. I liked Sylvia and wanted her to know it. "I'm really happy to meet you."

"We'll do us both good," she said.

I raced to catch up to her so that I could walk her to her car.

Harold and I talked about Sylvia the next morning over breakfast.

"Why do you suppose she dresses the way she does at her age?" Harold said, and lifting his own hair to indicate Sylvia's bouffant wig, he added, "And what's with that wig?"

"I'd heard about her. Seems she's always dressed pretty outrageously," I said. "She has quite a reputation around town for being different."

"She's quite the character. I like her."

"Yes, she is. I like her too."

"Harold, before you leave for work, would you mind looking at that form for the west side of the greenhouse foundation that I've been working on and let me know if I got it right?"

"Be happy to," he said and smooched me on the cheek.

The next Thursday, I went to Sylvia's for lunch. Sean decided he didn't want to come. He asked, "Will I get to see Bozo's mom another time if I don't go?"

"Her name is Sylvia, Son, and she's not related to Bozo."

"What do you mean? She has the very same hair as Bozo."

"Sylvia wears a wig, as you did last Halloween."

"But it's not Halloween," Sean said, palms up, elbows bent, arms at his sides.

"Some people wear wigs all the time. They like them."

Sean looked at me as if he truly doubted my common sense. "I think I'll go see Daddy at work."

I dropped Sean off at Harold's shop and headed for Sylvia's. She lived in a tidy, old house a block off Main Street. Her small yard brimmed with flowerbeds, bushes, and trees. She met me at the door, brandishing a thick bundle of verse in one hand and a small book in the other. She wore her red wig. "I've recently had a small book of poems published," she announced, "locally, you know."

"May I read some of them?" I asked. She considered my request for a moment and then handed me the unbound poems.

"I think they're easier to read this way," she explained.

"I brought some poems, but they're not very good. I think they rate pretty highly as humor items, though."

"I won't laugh at your poems if you don't laugh at mine." Sylvia was straight-faced and somber-eyed.

"That may be difficult when you read my poems," I said, still wanting to joke. "Okay, it's a deal. We won't laugh at each other's poetry unless the humor is intended." We shook on it, and with that handshake, Sylvia visibly relaxed.

"We'll have gorgeous fun," Sylvia said and tittered. She enveloped me in a big hug.

Later we solidified our friendship as we read our favorite poets to each other. Sylvia dramatized her readings from Emily Dickinson. "I must express all the emotions lying subtly beneath the surface," she said. "Emily is somewhat understated, as am I."

I shot her a glance to see if she was serious. Her face appeared placid as she thumbed through her Complete Poems of Emily Dickinson, choosing poems to read. I was thinking, holy shit, what planet did Sylvia rocket off of, when I saw her sneak a peek at me.

She cracked up. "Had you going, didn't I? Mag, the last thing I ever want to be is understated. It's hard enough to get a person to listen to you, even when you're inches from his face and have him by the collar. If I'd been subtle all my life, I would have been emotionally dead just that long, and I wouldn't get to wear these cute clothes." She stood and pirouetted, showing off her orange and black, miniskirt jumper.

In a voice husky with awe, I read poems from Nikki Giovanni and Adrienne Rich. Then we talked about poetry and our lives. We drank herbal tea laced with rum and honey and swung from teary-eyed melancholy to hysterical laughter. Since I rarely drank, the rum quickly percolated into my system and slid my emotions into a frenzied search for grounding.

"Sylvia," I asked her, "do you ever feel like you're standing on the edge of a cliff with the wind blasting you in the face? You're hanging on with your fingers and toes, trying to figure out which way you should turn when all of a sudden, the rock you're clinging to breaks loose, and you scramble to make life saving decisions before you're smashed to smithereens."

"Honey, if your thoughts wander off Main Street and your body follows, that's the way your life's going to be." Sylvia patted my hand to comfort me. "Believe me, I know. I have windburn from standing on that same damned cliff for most of my sixty years."

We read our own poems and talked expansively about the ideas we were trying to express, where more words or different words were needed, and how we might change the effect of a line. In my heart, I knew that no one else would accept my poetry as wholeheartedly as Sylvia did. That maybe we were pretending, as children did. But whatever the reason, the fantasy charmed me.

Suddenly, Sylvia sat up straight and said, "I know calligraphy, and Earl usually has plenty of plywood scraps left over from his custom cutting business."

"I always meant to learn calligraphy, and I know who Earl is. What's your point?"

"It's a simple and natural outcome of our convergence," Sylvia explained and came around the dining room table to sit next to me. "We'll cut the scraps into exotic shapes and nail them to trees in sheltered locations throughout the woods behind your house. I'd suggest my yard but as you can see, there are no secluded spots." She clasped her hands together in glee. "They'll be part of our poets' magic sanctuaries. Safe havens from a rude world," she said. "What do you say? Are you with me?"

"I'll have to check with Harold. It's his land too." I was unsure what the hell she was talking about but didn't want to ruin our momentum. "But I wouldn't worry about it. The man's motto is: there ain't no future in being normal."

"Let's get started. You pick out five of my poems to put in

calligraphy, and I'll pick out five of yours." Sylvia grabbed a stack of my poems and began reading.

I took a sip of my alcohol-fortified tea. Sylvia noticed that my glass was nearly empty and poured our glasses full, letting a few ice cubes fall into each glass.

She cut into my thoughts, "Well, lazy bones, are you going to chose any of my poems?"

"I'm on it," I said. "Poets' magic sanctuaries, hmmm, sounds like a good idea to me."

"You bet, honey, we're right on top of this wild one, poetically speaking, that is."

Three days later, Sylvia arrived at my house with ten pieces of plywood cut into curvaceous shapes of roughly one-foot by two-foot dimensions. She had painted them vibrant rose, lime, yellow, orange and blue. Our poems, written in calligraphy with jet-black acrylic, stood out against the bright backgrounds.

"I went ahead and painted them myself. I have more time than you do right now," she said. "I hope you don't mind."

"No, that's great, but next time you'll have to let me help you." As I spoke, I realized I was planning on us creating more of these plywood renditions of our poetry even though I wondered if they would appear tacky, like a freeway tourist attraction, on our lovely forested slope.

Sylvia beamed and waved for Sean and me to follow her. "Come to the pickup I borrowed from Bob to haul all this stuff. Wait until you see what else I brought for our first sanctuary." Sylvia stopped in front of the truck and flinging her arms wide, called, "Ta, da!"

In the bed of her truck were four metal lawn chairs and a small, round, metal table; all were freshly painted bright red with prominent yellow and green sunflowers. Words appeared to be randomly written here and there all over them.

"Each piece of furniture has a poem written on it. You have to find the golden dot and begin reading there. Damned neat idea, don't you think?"

"Slick," I said as I examined a chair, searching for a golden dot. Where was all this headed? "I've never seen the likes of your motif before," I told her. She smiled, most likely dreaming of future poetic exploits. "Our sanctuaries may be taking on aspects of the surreal." I was warming to the idea.

"We can only hope, kiddo."

We scouted out a worthy location for our first sanctuary. Harold came home for a late lunch while we were looking and followed our voices into the woods.

"What in Sam Hill are you two cooking up now?" he said in greeting and saluted us with the beer he had in his hand. He touched my cheek with his grease-stained fingers and kissed me. The taste of his beer lingered in my mouth.

"We're making our first sanctuary." I grinned, slightly embarrassed as if caught by a grownup, playing a little child's game.

"Say what?" he said.

Sean jumped up and down. "Daddy, we're going to have tea parties in the woods! Pooh is going to get to come and Christopher Robin too."

Harold scooped him up and gave him a big hug. "Will you be having chocolate chip cookies at those tea parties, partner?"

"Yeah, and Lucy's going to have a milk bone."

"Well, you'll just have to save a cookie and a cup of tea for me, okay?"

"Sure thing, Dad."

While Harold finished his lunch and returned to his shop, Sylvia, Sean, and I cleared our chosen area of fallen branches and protruding limbs and cut brush away to form a path to the spot. Piece by piece, we carried our treasures to the sanctuary. We arranged the furniture in the opening we'd made and screwed our poem boards into the surrounding tree trunks. Sylvia hung tinkling wind chimes from the boards, and Sean contributed bright, multicolored nylon streamers, leftover from a wrecked kite. Our assemblage definitely had an air of carnival about it, but Sylvia's painting and calligraphy were well done, and the sanctuary nestled into a small space overhung by tree limbs.

Since the day was cool, I brought out a tray with a pot of hot licorice mint tea (no rum), glasses, honey, chocolate chip cookies, a glass of milk for Sean, and a milk bone for Lucy. We drank our tea, ate cookies, and read poetry while Sean drove his toy trucks and cars through our legs or pounded boards together to make roads and ramps for his vehicles and stuffed animals.

"Can Winnie the Pooh and Christopher Robin live here?" Sean asked. He placed his stuffed Pooh Bear on one empty chair and his Tigger on the other. A tea party in a playhouse in the woods seemed as likely as not to Sean. He thought it was great fun to have two grownups playing with him.

Through the tree branches surrounding our sanctuary, we could glimpse the mountains. A tiptoeing wind lightly touched the firs, swaying them. A hermit thrush called its ephemeral notes into the air. We talked in whispers or seemed to, the sounds of our voices absorbed by the forest and the soft needles underfoot. Slender, orange columbines caught beams of sunlight that filtered through the canopy. I was soothed and enchanted.

But after Sylvia left, I felt uneasy. Each person I had told about Sylvia and I being friends seemed obsessed with telling me about her oddities.

I recalled my mother-in-law's words, even though she was not one to whom I usually referred for guidance. She had been raised in a rural Indiana farm town. Her summation of small towns was,

"Everyone knows your business, and you know everyone else's business. That's what there is to talk about, so you do. You talk about everybody else's business, and they talk about yours. And if you try to keep your business a secret, folks get suspicious." People talked about Sylvia incessantly. I wondered if this was why she had conceived the idea of the poets' magic sanctuaries, a place to escape the prying eyes.

Then again those same people might be talking about me as soon as I was out of earshot, and there was the problem of Harold's drinking. They most likely talked about that too. Yes, he made it to work on time and worked long hours at his shop, but he drank from the time he left his shop until he slept. If he stopped at one of the two Halfway bars on the way home, he sometimes didn't make it home until very late, and he was quite drunk when he got here, meaning he'd driven home in that state. I hoped he would honor his commitment to stop soon. Surely, he loved Sean and me too much to risk our marriage.

Chapter 5

The God Awfulest Sculptures and Reefer Madness

When things were slow, which wasn't often, or when Harold was tired of working on cars, which was at least once or twice a week, he got rip, roaring drunk and fabricated the God awfulest sculptures this side of Pluto. He welded jagged scraps of car bodies to various engine parts until he had fashioned towering, weird-looking creatures. His welds were perfect, but his creations were shit. Problem was, though, he thought they were the prettiest things he'd ever seen.

Unfortunately for those of us who had to look at 'em, he felt the dangdest obligation to share his work. He scattered 'em all over the three hundred foot hillside between his house and the gravel road he lived on. He was damned proud of them hunks of metal.

A stray tourist must a carried word of Harold's mountain of metalwork to the outside world because by the end of the Brown's second summer in town, "art" lovers started coming from as far away as Portland and Boise to see 'em. Not many buyers came, but Harold said they would come later. He was sure he'd be recognized as a great artiste some day.

Mostly though, them longhaired, skinny-assed weirdoes were the ones who showed up. The men sprouted scraggly beards, and the women's legs fuzzed with unshaved hair while their breasts swung loose without bras to fetter 'em. Most of 'em wore the kind of sandals that had built in depressions for the toes, no matter what the weather was. A number of 'em needed a dose of deodorant real bad. A person can get too natural, to my mind.

They straggled through my store, saying peace brother and peace sister, shit like that. This sort of talk was enough to scare my regulars. They asked for feta cheese and miso. Christ, at first I didn't even know what them things were, let alone carried 'em. After a while, I did order that stuff; weirdo money spent the same as preacher cash.

Harold and Mag welcomed these bizarre folks, and that meant they were back in town again and again. This didn't make the Browns too popular in Halfway. People in a small town are suspicious of strangers, but Harold was a damn fine mechanic so he got plenty of business anyway.

I had a notion that some folks were coming to the Browns to get a certain illegal herb Mag must have growing somewhere in that big greenhouse. So, real smart like, I studied up on the stuff, pictures and all, in an article that I found in a brochure sent out by the school district. I cooked up the excuse of wanting to find the misses a plant that she could use to brew a tea to calm her stomach, and I went to see Mag and her greenhouse.

She had the dangdest plants in there. Some had leaves as big as hubcaps. Over in one dark corner were plants tall as me, all sickly white. Worse yet, in the hot room that was glittery white with light from five lamps, one plant blazed fluorescent orange, the whole damned thing, orange. It had round flowers the size of baseballs with spears of orange jutting out every which way.

She had me sniff at plants called meadowsweet, hyssop, dogbane, and wormwort. I didn't personally know whether what Mag told me was accurate since I didn't really know much about plants and only carried the basic spices at my store, but that greenhouse sure did stink! Each of them plants wafted waves of noxious smells smack into my nose. In no time I was dizzy and light headed.

Of course, I acted interested in everything Mag was yapping to me about "her babies," as she called 'em, and she showed me all over the damned place. I never did spot a marijuana plant, but with all them leaves and stems and smells, I sure as hell could have been looking right at ten of 'em and missed 'em.

I bought a tiny plant with purple flowers, as that was the one that Magdalena said would settle the wife's gut. Two-fifty, it cost me. I tossed it out the pickup window into some brush about a mile down the road. Shit, I worried that it might be psychedelic.

Mag proved as good at growing things as Harold was at mechanics. People began taking their sick plants to her, leaving 'em for a spell and picking 'em up a few weeks later when they were growing healthy. She was a regular Tom Thumb plant doctor, or was that a green thumb plant doctor. I get the two confused. She answered a few ads in her plant magazines, and pretty soon she was selling plants to commercial nurseries.

Sometimes after school, Sean went on home, and other times he hung out at the shop. He was the most self-entertaining kid I'd ever seen. He'd play for hours with a battered toy truck and a pile of dirt. He was into building things. I figured he got that from his dad. One day that summer between kindergarten and first grade, he told me, "I'm going to build a snow machine."

I told him, "Remember last winter. Just wait a few months and you needn't bother." But he persisted at constructing his machine for weeks. The contraption measured about four feet by eight feet and had a hose attached and boards angled skyward in every conceivable direction.

The co-op stocked nails, and he kept walking over there and buying 'em like he was building a skyscraper. Several times, my curiosity drove me to check over back of Harold's shop where he was building, just to see how he was fitting all them nails into that snow machine.

Truth was, in the back of my mind, I wished that machine would make snow, if only for a minute; he was so set on it. But it didn't. He kept trying, though, and didn't seem too discouraged when only water trickled from the very last board aimed at the high heavens.

"Needs more work," was all he said and got out his green Tonka dump truck and played in the dirt with his pal, Bill.

Chapter 6

Moving Cows and Hiking the Wallowas

"It's going to be a scorcher today," Harold said as he pulled our pickup down the drive. "I'm glad we're going to be high in the hills above it all." He steered and held his beer with his left hand, using his right to shift. Once he'd reached cruising speed, he reached over and tousled Sean's hair. "You volunteered to carry the tent, right?"

"Daddy, I'm too little to carry the tent," Sean told him.

"What does size have to do with it, partner? You want to be tough, don't you?"

"Daddy!"

I put my arm around Sean and hugged him to me. "Your Daddy will be sorry when he has to carry all those toys that you brought because you're carrying the tent."

"He will?"

"Well sure, your toys are heavier than the tent."

"They are?"

"You bet they are."

"I'm the strong one, Daddy," Sean proclaimed, beaming. "I'm carrying the heavy toys."

"Hands down, partner, you are," Harold said; he swigged the last of his beer and tossed the empty behind the seat. He let his arm rest on the back of the seat and stroked my neck as he said, "Hand me another beer, would you, babe?"

I did as he asked, but I got that familiar, queasy feeling in the pit of my stomach. We'd been in Halfway over a year, and Harold was drinking even more now than when we arrived, which meant he was drinking a lot. I kept telling myself that it didn't matter, that he was a good father and husband, but I was letting him drink and drive, with our son in the car, and Harold would most likely be drunk before we reached the trailhead. I wondered if he'd be able to walk down the trail at all today.

We hadn't gotten very far when we saw cattle on the road up ahead. A horseback rider and a pickup with its lights flashing kept the cows headed in the right direction. A cow dog like Sean's ran after strays. Lucy whined from the bed of the truck, wanting to get into the action.

"That's Whitey," I said, recognizing our neighbor. "No doubt his mother's driving the pickup." Seeing us, Whitey waved and turned his horse in our direction.

He touched his cowboy hat with his gloved hand, slightly raising it off his head, and said, "Hello, neighbors. What're you up to?" He looked every bit the stalwart rancher that he was, leathery brown skin, straight back, silver hair, a wiry tough body.

"We're planning on hiking into the wilderness at Little Eagle Meadow, packs on our backs," Harold answered and saluted him with his beer. "You folks need a hand?"

Whitey considered the question for a moment and then said, "We could use a couple extra bodies shooing these cows into that field over there." He nodded toward the next fenced pasture.

Frieda pulled her pickup to a stop alongside ours and climbed out. She was grinning and talking to us before her feet hit the ground. "If it isn't the Browns. Howdy," she called and ducked her head so that she could see in the window better.

"Hi, Frieda," Sean called back to her, leaning out the window and waving. "We're going camping."

"You are? Aren't you the lucky ones," she said as she removed her baseball cap and smoothed back loose strands of gray hair.

"And I'm carrying the heavy toys."

"That's because you're getting big," Frieda said.

Since Harold and I had gotten out of the truck already, Sean asked, "Can I help too?"

"Why don't you come on up here and help me steer this horse, Sean?" Whitey suggested.

Sean gulped for air; he was so exited. "Can I, Mom? Can I, Dad?"

"Sure, partner," Harold answered him and turned to me. "Right, babe?"

"Yes, you can ride with Whitey." I hoisted my jubilant son up to our neighbor. Lucy barked incessantly, frantic to get out. "Settle down, girl," I called to her. "You're not getting out. You'd have cows strung out from here to Baker City."

Seated in the saddle in front of Whitey, Sean said, "This is really high up." His joy had momentarily given way to fear.

Whitey told him, "You hang onto the saddle horn, Sean, and you'll be fine. Old Becky's never bucked anybody off in all her years of running cattle."

Frieda walked back to her truck. "And neither has old Chevy here." She swung her cab door shut but called out the window, "Harold and Magdalena, you two divide up and hug a fence line. If one of these cows decides to head home, turn 'em around." She started her truck and pulled forward to Whitey. I heard her call to him, "I'll go open the gate." He nodded to her, and accelerating slightly, she nudged her pickup through the milling cows toward the gate in advance of them.

Harold thumped his chest with his fists and said, "This job calls for a cold one," and winking at me, he tossed his empty behind the seat and grabbed another beer from the cooler. "My side," he said and meandered over to the left side of the road. I veered right, hoping that no cows chose to wander my way.

I saw Frieda stop her truck, hobble over to the gate, and swing it open. Whitey called, "Yah, yah," and I heard Sean's higher pitched, little boy "Yah, yah." The smell of cattle sweat, dung, and half digested hay hung in the air as the cows began to file through the open gate. Just as Frieda predicted, some cows swung back from the gate and headed down the road toward Harold and me. We yelled, "Yah, yah," and swung our arms while running in a zigzag, depending on which direction the cows were headed. Slobber dripping from confused bovine mouths and mooing plaintively, the docile beasts turned easily and trotted back to their herd.

After all his cattle were inside their new pasture, Whitey trotted his horse over to us and lifted Sean from the saddle. Harold reached for our son. "Here, babe, hold my beer for a sec." I accepted the can without comment, but my mind jabbered noisily again.

"That was fun, Whitey," Sean said. "Can I do it again sometime?"

"I imagine we could arrange that," Whitey assured him. "You folks have a good backpack trip and thank you." He tipped his hat in our direction.

Harold said, "Our pleasure," and motioned to Whitey with the beer that I'd just handed back to him. "You want a beer?"

"No thank you," Whitey said and nodded to him: reining his horse, he loped over to Frieda, who was in the process of shutting the gate.

He swung a leg over his saddle and jogged over to help her.

Sean was wound tighter than a ball of rubber bands. "That was really fun. Whitey let me steer the horse and everything. Did you hear me yahing cows, just like Whitey?"

"We heard you, Son," I told him. "It looked like you were doing a mighty fine job herding."

"Yeah, I was," he said proudly, "Did you hear Whitey say I can do it again?"

"Yes, I heard him," I said, "and I'm sure Whitey meant it too." I headed toward the driver's side of our truck. "How about I drive," I said and raised my left hand for Harold to toss me the keys.

Harold gave me a disparaging look but tossed me the keys and got in the passenger side.

We arrived at the trailhead about two beers, or a half hour, later. Harold was in great spirits, but when he got out of the pickup, I could see that he wasn't all that steady on his feet. A flash of shame heated my face. This man was my husband; he knew we were planning on packing. Why had he drunk so much beer?

"How about we camp here for the night," I said, "and hit the trail first thing in the morning." We were high in the Wallowas, surrounded by firs, with a creek about fifty feet away.

"My sentiments exactly," Harold answered; he grinned, and his eyelids drooped as he popped the top off another beer. "Is that okay with you, partner?" he asked Sean.

Sean looked around our potential camping site. "Yeah, it's okay," he said and began unpacking the toys from his pack.

Harold swaggered over to me. "How's my girl?" he cooed in my ear as he nuzzled me. He set his beer on the ground and embraced me. Alcohol definitely aroused Harold's libido, to a point. He became very affectionate and horny. "How about we get that tent put up pronto," he murmured, kissing my eyes, my cheeks, my lips.

His breath reeked of hops and alcohol when he kissed me. I loved Harold and was attracted to him, but I hated what alcohol did to him. Confused and repulsed by his drunken state, lowered eyelids, and clumsy fondling, I didn't know what to do. "Remember, we have a son playing right over there," I said, nodding in Sean's direction, and we both looked at him. He was busy gathering sticks for a town he was building to plays cars in.

"Oh, I don't think he'll even notice that we're otherwise occupied," Harold said as he got up from the boulder on which we'd been sitting. "Now, you just relax right here while I grab the tent out of the truck and put it up as fast as I can." I stayed where I was, and he planted big, sloppy kisses all over my face. "Think sexy thoughts, at least some of them about me," he said, and after one more hug, he dashed to the truck. Maybe he could have hiked today after all, I thought.

Harold hummed as he pounded in the tent poles, and every few pounds, he interrupted himself to kiss me, then stumbled back to the tent. In a short time, the tent was up, slightly lopsided and not pulled all that tight, but up. "Hang tight a minute longer while I bribe Sean and fetch the sleeping bags," he said and winked. He scurried over to Sean and whispered something to him; Sean nodded and grinned at me. Then Harold dashed back to the truck for our bags, yanking them from their stuff sacks as he walked to the tent. He tossed them inside, and then, the picture of serenity, he approached me. "My lady, your tent awaits," he announced in a husky voice and gestured grandly toward the tent.

"I don't know, Harold," I answered him. "How about we just enjoy the sun." I knew I would be accused of ruining our camping trip if I mentioned Harold's drinking.

"Sean thinks we're going to take a nap; he gets two bucks not to disturb us. He promised not to stray more that four feet in any direction, and I told him we'd be out in ten minutes." He pointed to his wrist. "I gave him my watch to time us."

"I don't know," It wasn't Sean outside the tent that bothered me; it was Harold's drunken state. This would not be a good time for me.

"Don't be that way," Harold said, and he held the flap to one side.

I knew what would happen and didn't really want to have sex with Harold when he was as drunk as he was. The angry accusations that would follow a refusal flashed through my mind again. I went into our tent, and he followed me, zipping the flap shut after entering. I lay on a sleeping bag looking at him: his never neat hair, his worn flannel shirt, and his worn, grease stained jeans. He smiled. The light passing through the green walls of the tent cast most of his face into neutral hues, but his brown eyes seemed to have snatched sunny glimmers from the brilliant day outside. I did love him. I just wished he didn't drink so much. I wished he wasn't drunk at this moment.

"Come here, sweet thing," he whispered and reached for me. He eased himself onto me. He kissed me hungrily as he unbuttoned my shirt and slid it from my shoulders. Then he kissed my bared shoulders and breasts as he worked my pants off my body. "Oh, you sexy lady," he said between breathy kisses.

Harold quickly sloughed off his clothes. We were both naked. "Now we're talking," he said and grinned. He pulled me to him, embracing me. He didn't seem to notice that I was less than enthusiastic.

Harold definitely was impaired. After those kisses bestowed as we undressed, he rushed to get a condom on, and our sexual encounter was over with many minutes to spare of the ten minutes he'd told our son to time.

Harold collapsed on top of me, already drowsy and ready to sleep. That was the other thing about his drinking. While it did make him horny; it did not make him a very good lover. My body tingled with an unsavory mix of disgust and unsatisfied desire. I'd allowed our sex, but somehow I felt violated.

I dressed and left the tent. Harold had fallen asleep, his needs met.

When I emerged, Sean said, "You guys are pretty noisy when you sleep."

Embarrassed, I told him, "Yeah, grownups never get their own beds like kids do, so they're noisy sleepers."

Sean gave his me a look that nearly shouted, you expect me to believe that, but he said no more about it. Instead he said, "Come here and see the town Lucy and I built."

The next morning, we struck camp early and got our packs ready to head into the Wallowas. Crater Lake was about an eight-mile, uphill hike. We had planned on doing three miles yesterday and the balance today, in consideration of Sean. Because of Harold's drinking, we would do it all today. The packs weren't that heavy, but the climb was steep, and Sean would need rest breaks.

Lucy bounced around us, happy to be a part of whatever outdoor adventure that was about to unfold. She licked Sean's face, his hands, and even his pants legs; she was so happy.

We shouldered our packs, and Harold said, "Why don't you go first, babe. Sean can walk in the middle, and I'll tidy up the rear."

"Sounds fine with me, and we can trade places later if you want to be the one getting a fresh view of things."

"Oh, I'll be getting a fresh enough view to suit me," Harold said eying my rear.

On the trail, I lapsed into my own rhythm. My pace lengthened, which Harold kept reminding me wasn't necessary; I outpaced him already, and a calmness enfolded me. The dangers here were fundamental, dangers I could sense and cope with. The joys were exuberant and natural.

The dew was heavy when we set out, and our boots and pants were soon slick with moisture from the plants we brushed.

Lumbering, cumulus clouds drifted south, blown by a mellow breeze.

In about an hour, we climbed over a slight ridge and entered Little Eagle Meadow; it sloped downward in a series of hummocks, to the creek bank northeast of us. Blue lupine blossoms dotted the expanse, their citric fragrance redolent in the cool, moist air. As we crossed the meadow, the sun warmed it, and lupine that had gone to seed used these changing moments between damp, cool night and warm, dry day as a trigger to spring their pods and fling their seeds. Snapping pings followed by the faint tat, tat, tat of seeds landing accompanied our steps as we sauntered on our way.

Cornucopia Peak sloped upward from the far side of the creek, the scars and tailings of old mines evident between the scattered firs. Gradually, we circumvented it as we ascended ever higher into the Wallowas. On the drier slopes, lupine gave way to pockets of sage and the large yellow flower heads of arrowleaf balsam root. Pearly everlasting's white clustered blooms found refuge here and there amongst the more dominant plants, along with red sprigs of Indian paintbrush.

"Stream up ahead," I informed my family, as if they hadn't heard it too.

"Oh boy, oh boy," Sean called. "Can I get a drink out of it?"

"Let your mom and I take a look at it first, Son," Harold said.

The splash of falling water grew louder as we drew closer. Lucy broke ranks and bounded for the creek. She ran straight into the frigid snowmelt flow and plopped down, drinking as she sat.

"Lucy," Sean scolded her, "you're all wet. Silly dog." Lucy wagged her tail from where she sat but didn't budge.

"That dog must have one thick hide," Harold said. "That water can't be more than forty or fifty degrees." Harold and I looked up slope to where the creek gushed from a spring on the hillside. "Seems safe enough. Wouldn't you say, hon?" he asked.

I nodded and told Sean, "Drink from this side, before it crosses the trail. Okay?"

"Oh boy, I get to drink raw water." He rummaged for his cup in his pack and finding it, scooped a cupful of icy stream water into it. He swallowed a huge gulp. "Yeow," he said, breathless, "it's cold."

Refreshed, we hiked the remaining miles toward Crater Lake. Basalt gave way to jagged spires of granite. Colossal, broken chunks of rock lay strewn down the steep sides of peaks, and mountain hemlock and heather found purchase in the pockets of protection they provided. Snow slept in every shadowed place.

"Couldn't be much further," Harold said. "We're pretty near as high as we can go."

Looking ahead, I saw what could be just another ridge or what I hoped was the end moraine of Crater Lake. "Could be our lake's behind that ridge."

"I hope so," Sean chimed in, "because Lucy's getting tired. Right, Lucy?" His dog pranced up to him and licked his hand. Weary Sean patted her. "See, Mom, how tired she is."

"We're almost there, dear," I assured him. "You've done a really good job, hiking this far and carrying your heavy pack."

Sean perked up. "That's right. I'm tougher than Daddy."

Harold, who looked as if he might sit down on the trail at any moment and call it quits, said, "I believe you are tougher, Sean. You may end up carrying your old dad if we don't get to that lake soon."

"I'm not that tough," Sean squeaked. "You have to walk."

With everyone getting tired, winding our way up the ridge seemed to take hours. At last we rounded a curve, and Crater Lake rested dead center before us. Nestled in the center of the pinnacles that surrounded it, the clarity of its blue-green waters rendered perception of its depth impossible. Beneath a jumble of boulders, a sheered off bank of snow edged it on its north side while hardy, sub-alpine firs struggled for survival around the remainder of the lake. Engelmann spruce grew in pockets among the firs. We were the only humans present.

We clapped and hugged each other. Harold began to undo his pack but thought better of it. "How about we pick a campsite first," he said. "I'd hate to have to shoulder this thing again today."

"I want to camp right there," Sean announced, pointing to a fire ring to the right of us.

"Suits me," Harold said. "How 'bout it, babe?"

"I'm all for getting these packs off," I said.

We set up camp and ate our dinner of hot dogs cooked over an open fire. Harold had packed in three beers, which he drank with dinner. Shortly after our meal, a peak obscured the sun, giving the day over to a luminous dusk. At length the darkness of night came, and stars danced close enough for us to pluck them from the ink black curtain that embraced us. The shimmering lake sparkled their reflections, full to its lapping brim with another universe of stars and planets. We conversed in murmurs, gradually lolling into the night, and finally shuffling into the tent and wiggling into our sleeping bags, we slept.

Chapter 7

The Wandering Vets

Harold had four vehicles in his shop and a parking lot full of cars and trucks needing repair outside his shop. He'd worked late, trying to make a dent in his workload. Mag wasn't around; she was off somewhere delivering plants. That was why Sean was at our after work bull session.

We were sitting around shooting the shit, tossing back a few, and wham, somebody whacked the door to the backroom wide open. It bounced off the wall. All six of us guys sprung to our feet; lucky for the intruder, our shotguns were in our trucks. Harold tried to spring up from one of those swivel jobbies, and he ended up belly-down on the floor. Ed choked on his beer and was coughing, sputtering, and turning in circles, trying to figure out what the hell was going on.

Then a split second before we nearly all shit our pants, due to the suspense, we saw a blur of silver jump into the room and heard the thud of cowboy boots landing on the unyielding cement floor. The cause of the hubbub had entered the room. From head to toe, he was dressed in shiny, I mean real shiny, silver: silver cowboy boots, satiny-silver clothes, silver cowboy hat, and silver gloves. Silver gloves, can you believe it? And the weirdest thing was, he carried a big silver guitar, with the electric cord hanging down. He stood there grinning and nodding and tipping his hat.

"Howdy, partners, howdy, you all," he intoned, melodic as some damn radio announcer.

We were gap-mouthed and bug-eyed. A smell like somebody'd peed his pants began filtering into the room. Harold looked up from a sort of squatting position on the floor. He said, "Howdy." Nobody else spoke.

The silver stranger looked down at him and said, "I'm looking for the owner of this here fine establishment. Who might that be?"

"That'd be me, sir," Harold said, real matter-of-fact like.

The silver man reached his hand downward to shake Harold's hand. "I'm looking for a vehicle to buy. I have an important gig to get to, pronto, in Reno. Are you the owner of that blue Chevy out front?" Harold nodded yes, so the guy added, "How much you asking?"

"Eight hundred dollars," Harold answered, quizzically surveying his customer.

Sliver man continued grandly. "My man, you probably recognize me. The Silver Streak, they call me. I'm pretty much a rock-n-roll legend around Reno. I'm called the Streak because my fingers move so fast when I play. You've probably already figured where the silver part of the name comes from." He gestured toward himself with the hand not holding the guitar. "You ever catch my act?"

"Can't say that I have, sir," Harold responded. He had by now gotten to his feet. All of us but Harold were edging our way toward the door that this silver man had just banged open.

"Hand me a piece of paper and a pen," said the Silver Streak.

Harold did, and Silver Streak, rock-n-roll legend, autographed it. He held it to the light and scrutinized it critically. "Now that there pretty little piece of paper is worth close to two hundred bucks as it is. Catch my drift? I get to Reno for the gig, and I'll wire you the balance. My word's good as silver." He touched the silver shirt over his heart.

"Did ya get the car yet? Can we leave?" a voice from outside the door asked.

"Oh my, oh me, excuse my manners. This here's my traveling companion, Lizard Man," said Streak. He reached outside and pulled in the strangest looking human I'd ever seen. We all gasped.

Goddamn it! I'd never seen the likes of it. First off, instead of clothes, he had on paper grocery sacks. For the top part, he'd split two sacks, one sack for each half of his body. The loose ends overlapped midway, and an armhole was cut in each of the squared off parts. He had wrapped his arms and legs in strips of brown paper, secured by tucking the ends under the wrapped paper.

He had on a hat kind a like the ones we used to make out a newspaper as kids, but his was brown paper. His feet and hands were bare and full of cuts, the scabs crusted over with dirt. His beard and hair had stuff stuck in 'um, and his face was as dirty as his feet. Not least of his problems was his God-awful smell.

We'd forgotten Sean was there until he piped up with, "Oh wow, wait until I tell the kids at school about this." He was grinning from ear to ear.

You had to notice Lizard Man was holding this gallon jug about half full of lizards and water. Most of the lizards looked drowned, but a few still struggled to get out. He held the damned jar clutched up tight against his chest. Sean walked right up to the guy, still grinning, and asked, "Are they your pets?"

Lizard Man took a step backward from Sean and wrapped his arms tighter around the jar. "No, " he said, shaking his scruffy head till I thought the last marbles he had in there would spill out his ears. "They're my food. It's the only food I can eat. It's magic. It keeps me alive. They're mine. You can't have them!" He turned to Streak and whined, "I have to get back to open country. I'm running low. I need more lizards."

Sean looked first at the fella, then at the jar, then back at the fella, "You really eat those?" He pointed at the jar.

"I have to. They keep me alive. They nearly killed me when they took my lizards away in that hospital." He shivered and moved closer to Silver Streak.

"Oh no," Ed whispered. He put his hand in front of his mouth and continued, kind a muffled like, "Loony bin, escapees from the loony bin."

"You boys been in Salem lately?" I asked the Streak. That was where the state mental institution was.

"We were both recently in the veteran's hospital there," he answered and added, with a sweep of his hand toward Lizard Man and himself, "We served our country in Vietnam."

"Vet loonies, escapee vet loonies," Ed said, once again speaking through his hand.

I had to admit. Ed was kind a annoying, even to me. What, like those two weren't gonna understand him if he spoke through his hand? They were mental patients, not morons. It annoyed Streak too, and he reached over and grabbed Ed by his shirtfront and real quick like pulled him smack up against himself. Speaking real soft and smooth, he said, "We aren't escapees. It was a case of mistaken identity. They didn't realize I was the Silver Streak. We were set free after two days."

"Okay, okay, no harm meant, mister," Ed whimpered.

Harold added, "Yeah, let him go. Ed's just a general pain. It wasn't anything personal."

Streak relaxed his hold and shoved Ed away from him. He

smoothed Ed's shirt. "Sorry I ruffled your shirt, friend. Just you remember whom you're talking to. The Silver Streak, rock-n-roll legend." His eyes got this real strange look. It's hard to describe. Sad, frightened, and lost, like for a moment he didn't remember where he was. He looked confused.

Sean had zeroed in on Lizard Man. He was walking, real slow, back and forth in front of the guy, sizing him up. He said, "I could take you to where there are bunches of lizards."

"You could! Let's go. Right back, Streak. Come on, come on!" he called to Sean and gestured with one hand, causing the water in his jar to slosh from side to side.

Sean called over his shoulder, "Bye, Dad!" and bounded for the door. Harold lunged after him and caught his shirttail.

"Hold on there! We'll think about lizards in a bit. Let's get this car deal settled first." He flashed Sean a watch it buddy look and spoke to Streak again, "Now, Mr. Streak, have you two got money or not?"

"Friend, I just gave you my two hundred dollar autograph, and I promised to wire you the balance from Reno. My word's good as..."

"Silver yeah. Sir, I hear you, but bottom line is, no cash in my hand, no car keys in yours."

"I got a get the lizards. Come on. Let's get the lizards," Lizard Man said in a begging voice and tugged on Sean's sleeve. Harold made a small hand gesture to Sean, indicating a definite no.

Sean pulled Lizard Man's hand off his sleeve. "I'll get 'um," Sean called and tore out the door before his dad could grab him, but Harold did stop Lizard Man.

"No, no, no, you stay right here, sir. Sean will bring the lizards to you," he assured him. He walked over and shut the door.

I nearly shit my jocks. What was Harold thinking, shutting our only means of escape? But, damn it all; Harold started talking to them guys like they were normal folk.

"So both of you were in Nam. See any action?"

"Lizard and I were in the same squad," Streak paused and ran his fingers over the strings of his guitar. They gave soft, dull pings. "They say we saw a lot of action." He paused and got that bewildered look again. "But personally, I don't remember. Lizard and I were the only ones of our squad found alive. And they didn't find us for three or four days. Seems our squad leader didn't have us where we were supposed to be. Lizard was shot in the legs and couldn't move so he'd been eating lizards and anything else that came near him. Me," he grinned, laughed, and looked at each man around the room, "I was shot up pretty good." He grinned again and shook his head real slow. "I'm a performer anyway, not a killing soldier."

"Don't you have a home you could go to, folks or somebody like that?" Harold asked.

"Folks? Oh shoot, you still don't understand. I'm a rock-n-roll star. I don't need to go home to no folks." He slapped his thigh, laughed again, and shook his grinning face from side to side. "Lizard here has a bit of a problem about having to eat lizards and about thinking real clothes make him sick, but I ain't gonna send him away or put him in no lock-up. I owe him. We're buddies. We stick together." He put his arm around Lizard Man and hugged him. Lizard grinned up at him and chuckled softly.

Harold smiled and real quick looked each of us in the eyes. He turned and faced Streak square-on. Real solemn like, he said, "I was drafted during Nam but didn't make it over. But there were guys in our squadron just come back, finishing off a tour stateside, maybe a few months to go. They were real different from us guys that hadn't gone over. I heard tales from them that'd curl your toenails and make your heart fly out a your chest from sheer misery. They had no time for us or any of that army bullshit."

He nodded to Streak. "So, you have to understand that I do sympathize with you. If we call the cops, they'd just put you in the vet hospital for more observation and send you on your way again after a couple days. But you'd be no closer to Reno. So boys," he paused and looked at us, "we have a decision to make." He sat down in his swivel chair and brought his beer to his lips.

What decision was he talking about? Shit, we didn't know. Stew asked the obvious question, "What the hell you talking about, Harold?"

Harold took another long swig from his beer, tossed it in the box full of empties, and popped open another. "Well, as I see it, what we have here are two Vietnam veterans who've seen some pretty heavy action. Either of you care for a beer?" he interrupted himself and held two beers toward them.

Streak took one and said, "Thank you, friend." Lizard shook his head no and cowered closer to Streak.

Harold continued, "There's probably a lot we should do for these guys, but there's one thing we can do. We need to see that they get to Reno."

"We could chip in for bus tickets," I suggested. I wondered how they had gotten out here from Baker City. Had somebody given them a ride or had they walked the fifty plus miles?

"The chip in part is right but not for the bus. They'd never make it. I figure Magdalena and I could drive them there. They could ride in the back of the pickup in our camper shell. And you boys could pay for the gas and food. How 'bout it?"

"Why the hell would we want to do that?" Ed whined, "Why not just call the cops?"

Harold got this real stern, shaded look on his face. His voice dropped a couple octaves, and he spoke through clenched teeth, "Like I said, the system ain't gonna do shit for these guys. They may not make it very long in Reno, but the least we can do is get them where they want to go. Hell, do what you want. I know Mag will go with me tomorrow."

Sean burst in just then, carrying a little cardboard box. "Here, mister, here's some lizards for you," he enthusiastically said to Lizard Man, and he held up his little box.

Lizard Man bent down, set his jar on the floor, and reached for the box. He unscrewed the lid of his jar and carefully tipped the contents, three very lively lizards, into it. "Thank ya, thank ya," he murmured reverently. He screwed the lid back on and straightened up, the jar again clutched to his chest.

"You gonna eat one now," Sean persisted. He was stuck on that lizard eating thing.

"Sean, Christ, get over here," Harold said, and he pulled his boy to him. "Mr. Streak, you and your pal can sleep in my shop up at the house tonight. Tomorrow, we'll drive you to Reno. Okay?"

"Thank you kindly, friend," Streak said and raised his can of beer to Harold.

I said, "I have t'be getting home, but here's ten dollars. That's all I have on me. I'll give you more later if you need it. Excuse me, fellas," I nudged past the vets and on out the door. It was getting a bit ripe in there.

After I left, Harold told me later, each man left between ten and twenty dollars. When Magdalena got home that evening, she and Harold made supper for the vets; Harold said Lizard ate very little. They offered use of their shower; Streak obliged. He wouldn't let Mag touch his clothes though. They said they even tried to get Lizard to wear regular clothes, but he wouldn't, so they gave him some fresh, paper bags. Harold said Magdalena worried about letting 'em loose in Reno.

Next day, Harold, Magdalena, and Sean headed south and drove the five hundred miles to Reno. Most everything went smoothly. There was just that one incident at the truck stop.

Sean had the damnedest fascination of seeing Lizard Man eat one of them lizards, and just as surely, Harold and Mag wanted to keep him from seeing it happen. They stopped for lunch at a truck stop. Lizard wouldn't go in, of course. I'd a said, "Thank God!" As if walking in with a man dressed in silver wasn't bad enough.

Sometime during the meal, Sean excused himself, saying that he had to go to the bathroom, but that little squirt snuck out the door to see Lizard. They didn't know it until a stranger came up to the table and told 'em there was a little kid outside puking his guts out who said they were his parents.

They ran out the door, and the manager of the restaurant ran after 'em a hollering to beat the band, thinking they weren't gonna pay. Sean was right outside the door, white as a ghost, vomiting every which a way. They found out that he'd gone to see Lizard have his lunch, and it wasn't near as cool as he thought it was gonna be. It was a while before they could get him calmed down.

By this time, the manager was getting worried. He knew he didn't want no throwing up kid by his front door. And since he was scared that it might a been his food that had done the damage, he offered free meals for all of 'em if they would get the kid away from the door. Mag agreed to the deal after the guy said he'd get a free Seven Up for Sean.

Sean was mighty under the weather after that. He asked his folks a lot of questions about what had happened to Lizard and Steak in Vietnam to make them so crazy. Harold said they did their best to explain to him that people can only stand so much hurting and killing; then their spirits curl up inside themselves, and they act like those vets.

Harold said that Magdalena told Sean, "I won't ever let anyone send you to war, Son. You can count on that. Silver Streak and Lizard Man saw awful things and had to do awful things, including killing other people who were called the enemy. They couldn't help it; they were ordered to. I promise you, Sean, no one will ever do that to my boy."

"Good," replied Sean, "Because I don't want to eat lizards."

Chapter 8

Surviving Life

After Sean's experience with Lizard Man at the cafe, he lost his enthusiasm for the trip. At dusk, when we pulled into a casino parking lot, he wouldn't even get out of the truck to look at the blaze of neon lights.

"Had enough, Son?" Harold asked him. Sean nodded. "Don't worry, we won't be long." He leaned over and kissed him. Then he looked at me. "Well, are you ready to release the cargo, babe?"

I took a deep breath and glanced over my shoulder at our wayward vets. "I brought a bag of food for them and a supply of grocery bags for Lizard," I said, retrieving them from behind the seat. "I don't know if we're doing the right thing, but it's what they want." I smiled at Sean. "I'm ready to head home too."

"We could look at it this way," Harold said. "There'll be a lot more services for them here than in Halfway."

We circled around opposite sides of the truck and met at the back. Harold dropped the tailgate, and Silver Streak and Lizard scurried from the camper shell, the contents of Lizard's jar sloshing about as he climbed down. Once they were out, I leaned inside the camper to gather the two old sleeping bags we were giving them, and Lizard's lingering stench knocked me backwards. "Dear God," escaped my lips before I could censor myself.

"What's that?" Harold said.

"Oh nothing," I answered. "I think I'll leave the rear window open, okay?"

"Sounds healthy to me," Harold said. "All the windows of the shop are open too."

We handed Silver Streak the balance of the cash Harold had collected and the bag of groceries. I held out two postcards and pointing to them, said, "Here's two self-addressed, stamped postcards to mail to us so we'll know how you're doing."

He waved them away. "Just stick around and catch my act, and you'll know I'm on top of the world." He tipped his silver hat to us and waved to Sean. Turning to Lizard, he said, "You ready to see me rock with the big boys, buddy?"

"Uhuh," Lizard said, giggling. He clutched the extra paper bags I'd given him.

We mumbled our good-byes, racked with guilt that we might be doing the wrong thing for these two, and watched the rock star and his side kick hurry toward a neon sign that flashed "Hot Slots." Streak had said this was the location of his gig.

As if reading my mind, Harold said, "It's the right thing to do. Has to be. At least Streak got to Reno. I wonder, though, if they'll even make it through the evening before they get picked up, locked up, or hospitalized." He sighed. "At least they'll get help then."

We couldn't have taken care of them. Two freaked-out, grown men weren't like two stray cats. I couldn't take them to the vet, have them neutered, and keep them around to catch mice. But I kept thinking that we should have taken them to a social services agency instead of just dropping them off. That guilt has never left me. Silent, we climbed back into the pickup and drove home, only stopping to pee and eat.

The next day, Sean's friend Bill, came over to fish the creek that meandered across our property. They collected worms and put new line on their reels. They made sandwiches and packed them, along with cookies, fruit, and pop, into daypacks. Watching their slow progress across the slope, poles in one hand, tackle boxes in the other, it occurred to me that they looked as they would sixty years in the future, two old men on their way to fish, walking with practiced slowness. Their movements carried a dignified solemnity far beyond their years. The epitome of patient hunters, they slipped into their timeless roles as if fishing was all they'd ever done. "You two stay where I can see you from the house," I called after them.

When Sean and Bill came in from fishing, their seriousness had deepened, and they were full of questions. He and Bill had been talking about Lizard Man and Silver Streak and what had happened to them in Vietnam.

"Do soldiers die right away when they're shot, like on TV?" Sean asked.

"Not always, no. Killing is an awful thing."

"Do enemy soldiers have kids?" Bill asked.

"Well sure, they're just like you and me."

"Then how do soldiers know who's the bad guy and who's the good guy?" Sean asked. "I thought bad guys couldn't have kids."

Oh, if only it were that black and white, I thought. "The soldiers on their side wear the same uniforms as they do." I didn't know if I should add the next part but blundered ahead anyway. "Just because one of our soldiers is fighting a soldier from a different country, it doesn't mean that soldier is a bad man."

"Does it hurt when soldiers are shot?" Sean asked.

"Yes, it hurts when they're shot."

"If someone shot me in the stomach, would I die?" Bill asked. "That's what happened to the deer Dad shot last year, and it died."

"A person could die because of that, but no one is going to shoot you."

"Would my guts fall out?" Bill said. "The dear's guts fell out all over the ground."

"Come on you two, enough." I was feeling nauseated.

"It must have been awful for Streak and Lizard when they got hurt," Sean said, looking at me with wide eyes. The possibilities of pain and death had smacked him square in the face.

"Sean, come here." I hugged him to me. "I promise you, Son, you won't ever have to fight in a war."

"Are you sure, Mom?" he murmured into my sweater.

"I promise." Sean rested in my arms, letting me rub his back. Bill lingered a distance away, but it didn't take much urging for him to run into my arms to be hugged along with Sean. Through the tragic experiences of the vets, my son and his friend had confronted life and death and the fine line between them.

Sure, Sean witnessed death each time he saw the quivering gills of a fish cease to flutter. But the damaged Vietnam vets had brought death to the human level. A knock on the door startled me. I'd been a million miles away, worrying. How should I comfort Sean? How much did he understand at his young age?

I swung open the front door. Whitey and Frieda had come to visit. We greeted each other and walked toward the kitchen. "I'll put water on for tea," I said.

Sean and Bill greeted our guests, and then Sean said, "We need to clean our fish."

"Be sure to put a newspaper on the counter," I said. The

newspaper was supposed to catch errant scales, fish guts, and fishy juices.

"Okay," Sean said.

Whitey said, "I'll lend you a hand."

Sean nodded his ascent. Pulling the stringer of fish from his pack, he placed them on the cutting board. He told Whitey, "We made sure they died quick. Then Bill and I told them that we appreciated the food they were giving us. Dad says that's what the Indians do."

Whitey nodded and said, "I do the same thing with my cows. I talk to them and try to make their short time with me as pleasant as possible. They follow me from field to field like pups."

I'd heard him in his fields, calling softly to his cattle. "Here cow, here cow. Come on, nice new green grass just beyond this gate," and then he'd cluck his tongue. Great velvety noses sniffing, his cows trailed after him.

He told Sean, "I think that every person who eats meat should have to at least once kill and dress out his own meat. I think that might cause a few folks to realize that we're sacrificing one animal to feed another and to be more respectful of life in general."

In her raspy voice, ninety year old Frieda added, "One time I flat out asked Whitey if he could only keep a calf or me warm on a wintry night during calving season, whom would he choose? And he said, the calf. He told me that I'd lived a long life and that I'd get a fancy funeral, but his little calves only had a short time to live, and they didn't get a burial at all."

Whitey nodded his agreement and gazed out the window over the kitchen sink. Since our remodeling, he could see his cows from there. He stared absentmindedly at them, a sublime expression on his face.

This strange, suspended moment ended when Harold bustled into the house, his face flushed; I couldn't tell if it was from excitement or alcohol. "Come on out, all of you," he called. 'You have to see this." He grinned. "It's my best one yet."

"Do you want to come, Whitey and Frieda?" I asked while trying to get a sense of how drunk Harold was.

"Of course they do," he assured me. He smooched me, and I smelled beer. "Come on, come on, come on," he urged us. "It's my best one yet."

We followed Harold to the slope of his creations. Old car parts, discarded machinery, scrap metal, stainless steel, and aluminum were welded into Harold's works of art. He called his sculptures "semi-abstract portrayals of humankind's state of disassociation from the natural order of things" or "the fucked up way things are." Harold's sense of the artistic was a matter for debate about town. Locals questioned his taste in art as well as his taste in people, for his out of town admirers were not exactly cowboy types.

As the number of sanctuaries in our woods and the number of sculptures on our hill increased, the number of men who came by Harold's shop for after work beers decreased. Finally, only old Joe came by. He came to hear Harold spin his yarns and as a return favor, kept Harold and me posted as to the town's sentiments regarding the sanctuaries and sculptures and the followers they attracted.

The dwindling crowd of after work cronies had a plus. If Harold didn't stop at a bar, it allowed him to get home sooner. But he still drank the beers he would have drunk with "the boys" as he welded, pounded, cut, and soldered in his home shop. The radio blasted thumping rock-n-roll. Harold welded and drank. Sean wandered in and out, pounding together his own creations.

Harold's eight to twelve foot tall sculptures incorporated such things as toilets for heads and circular saw blades for stomachs. His figures stood in groups and singly. One sat and stared at the sky; another dressed out a slaughtered metal deer that was hanging from the metal branch of a metal tree. A group of five men made of car parts with oil drum beer bellies sat on stainless steel lawn chairs, drinking cans of beer and leering at a passing iron lady in a very short aluminum skirt.

Harold shepherded us to the cause of his excitement, his latest creation. "The Insulated Family," he said and gestured grandly toward it, beaming, proud and excited. "Well, what do you think?" Not waiting for an answer, he added, "It's my best one yet. God, my soul's in this one."

He'd welded together a five-foot by five-foot cage from car axles. Inside was a robotic looking four-foot tall man who, by turning a crank, could manipulate the marionette strings of a tiny family inside the empty housing of a television. Two tiny children watched a tiny TV; a turn of the crank caused their mouths to open and shut. Their mother smiled fanatically as she put four frozen dinners, made of aluminum and steel, in the oven, repeating the act with each turn of the crank. The father hit himself in the head with a frying pan with each crank's turn.

"Wow, Harold," I said as I circled the piece. "How'd you ever manage to make so many parts movable?" I smiled at him. I didn't understand his piece a hundred percent but loved it. "Very impressive. Wonderful as a matter of fact, truly wonderful."

"Why's the father hitting himself with the frying pan?" Sean asked Harold. "What's the matter with him?"

"That's just it, Sean," Harold answered. "He doesn't know what's wrong. He knows something is wrong, but he can't tell what, so he's hitting himself."

"Yeah, Dad, he's hitting himself, so what's the matter with him?" Sean insisted.

"I don't know, Son," Harold answered, speaking slowly. He stared at his art, intense. "I never will know the answer. That's for sure," he murmured, more to himself than to any of us.

Sean looked up to catch the expression on his father's face. "But you made it, Dad."

"Good one, Sean, " Harold said, chuckling, and he reached down to hug Sean. "Because I don't know, I made it."

"I still don't get it," Sean answered. "I need to go clean my fish," he said and walked back to the house. Bill followed him.

"Quite a work of art, Harold," Whitey said. " I have to admit; I don't understand everything about it, but technically, it amazing. All those little people and all those moving parts. Congratulations." He shook Harold's hand.

Frieda spoke for the first time since coming outside. "I think I understand it actually. Pretty much the story of my life, I'm just like that itty bitty wife there."

Harold spun around and faced her. His brown hair was tousled, as usual, and his face, arms, and hands were streaked with the grime of welding metal. "I'm so sorry, Frieda."

"Ah," she said, waving his concern away, "You live, and you die."

Whitey gave his mother a puzzled, sad look. "I think I'll go and help Sean clean those fish," he said.

Harold hugged me. He held onto me as we gazed in silence at his "best work yet." I think for a moment we all realized something personal about ourselves. I didn't know what Frieda and Harold were thinking, but I felt fragile. The thing was, though, I couldn't have explained to anyone why I felt that way.

Chapter 9

The Weird People at the Tea Parties

As the sculpture and weirdo populations on Brown's hill grew, townsfolk began to question Harold and Magdalena's sanity. The fellas quit coming 'round to Harold's garage for after work bull sessions. Talk began circulating.

But none of this didn't in no way affect Harold's business. Folks were practical enough to take their broken down vehicles to an ace mechanic five miles from home instead of driving the hundred miles round trip to Baker City. They did, however, want to distance themselves socially.

Then there was Sylvia and Magdalena and their damn tea parties. When they first started having 'em, Sylvia would flit around town saying, "All you lovely people, do stop by for some tender refreshment of body and mind," and those of us as did go, out a curiosity, as I did, got an eyeful.

In the forest back of the Brown's house, Magdalena and Sylvia had made these hideouts with some of the most bizarre furniture and fandangles in 'em a body's ever gonna see. We reckoned that Harold must a had a hand in building some of the stuff since they were so strange. Hugh, engulfing chairs, as what might swallow a man whole, were painted all colors of the rainbow. The backs on these chairs were three to six feet high, and the cushions were a study in themselves, all embroidered and sequined and patched together every which a way.

One table was painted with a gaping mouth covering the top. The words "give me food" were written real fancy-like under the bottom lip. Another had an entire meal painted on it, complete with a spilled glass of milk. Sylvia thought it was real funny when I tried to wipe up the milk with my handkerchief. "That's perfect," she chirped.

Bells on strings hung from nearly all the branches of most every tree near them sanctuaries. And every weirdo as what came there brought more. After a while, the whole place was a tinkling and ding-a-linging with even the slightest breeze. To add to that craziness, Magdalena, Sylvia, and the weirdoes hung up all these banners and windsocks shaped like animals and monsters.

Sylvia's and Magdalena's poems were everywhere: on tables, on chairs, on pieces of plywood nailed to trees. Us normal folk didn't think them poems made any sense. We decided that was because we hadn't smoked the right stuff, but the weirdoes liked 'em fine. The couple times I was there, I heard 'em saying things like, "It reaches into my soul," and "That poem more than describes nature; it is nature." Hell, say what? That mean you liked it?

Not that all Harold and Magdalena did was party. The tea parties were a weekend thing. A spattering of weirdoes came by during the week to see sculptures or hang out, and Sylvia would show up, always ready to cart food out that she had brought over, but Magdalena and Harold kept working, tea parties, weirdoes, whatever.

On weekends, Sean hung out with the weirdo kids. He seemed to like all the different kinds of folks at the parties. Shit, between the hunks of metal on the front hill and the hideouts, excuse me, sanctuaries, in the back forest, his home wasn't nothing more than a strange kind a playground anyway.

Maybe it was all the weirdness around him that made Sean so much his own person. At the end of Bible Day Camp that August, the youth director had the campers stand in a line, and then asked, "All who have been saved please step forward." Everyone but Sean took a step, pretty brave for a six and a half year old. The others looked back at Sean as the director questioned him, "Why haven't you come forward, son?"

And in front of all those people, he said, "I haven't made up my mind."

The kids waited in suspense for some thunderous response from the director or God, but the director had never had a child not be saved before. He didn't know what to do. Seconds ticked by while he stared at Sean, and Sean stared right back at him. Finally, he broke off his stare and spoke to the saved children. Sean, ignored and unsaved, wandered off to play in the sandbox. That made him a bit of a hero for a time. Kids weren't sure what kind of hero, but they knew he was brave to do what he did.

Sean was home from camp for no more than a day when he had another Bible related encounter. Magdalena told me about it in the store. I'd just finished checking her out, and she was heading out the door. She stopped dead in her tracks and strode back to the checkout counter. Seeming a bit flustered and in need of someone to talk to, she set her bag down and rushed into her story.

"Sean went over to John's house yesterday," she began. "I thought his mother had said she'd bring him home before lunch."

"Hours passed and no Sean. I called their home but got no

answer. I was getting a bit worried when in he wanders, looking dazed and confused. I heard the sound of a vehicle on our drive and figured Mrs. Norton had just dropped Sean off. I thought it a bit odd that she hadn't at least said hello."

I nodded and put in my two bits, so she would know I was listening. "Boy, I bet that was a relief. A lost child is a heart's deepest ache."

Mag nodded in agreement; then she rattled on, waving her arms, her eyebrows raised. "I ran up to him. I thought he must have wrecked his bike or something like that, the way he looked. But no, he told me that he'd been playing with John in their backyard when Mrs. Norton asked them to come in for a snack. She mentioned that she'd heard that he hadn't been saved at Bible camp and commenced to read passages from the Bible to him. At the end of each passage, she asked him if he was saved yet. Each time he said no, she got more upset and insisted that he listen to yet another passage."

I was getting upset myself; I wanted to go check on what those two teenyboppers, Kyle and Jim, were up to in the back of the store, seeing as they were standing in front of all them tiny batteries. I didn't want to seem impolite, but I tried to hurry things along with, "On well, all's well that ends well. Thank the Lord, he made it home." I gave the counter a swipe with the damp bleach rag I'd been using to clean and graced her with my half-nod that was meant to convey "see you later."

Mag agreed with my remark, looking somewhat confused as to what the hell I meant, but went right on talking. "Sean said that he thought he'd never get to leave. He said John went back outside to play. Sean was wrung out, Joe. I thought about giving Mrs. Norton a piece of my mind, scaring me and rattling my boy like that, but I didn't."

Mag shook her head and crossed her arms. Another customer

came up with a cart of groceries. I knew that would shut Mag up, but I still wouldn't be able to go check on Kyle and Jim, who were probably stealing me blind. As predicted, Mag ended her spiel and picked up her bag of groceries. She said, "Sometimes, Joe, I just don't get it."

I grabbed for old lady Barter's goods before she could change her mind; she had a way of doing that, and I started ringing 'em up. By way of closing, I bestowed some last settling remarks on Mag. "Things have a way of evening out, one way or another. Sean's lack of salvation made Mrs. Norton uncomfortable, and folks don't like discomfort. Just keep on being neighborly, Mag, and you'll see things will straighten themselves out."

"Okay, Joe," she said and added over her shoulder as she walked away, "and thanks for listening." She was out the door and gone. I felt a tinge of guilt for wanting her blabbering to end, but I got right to work on packing Barter's groceries. I figured cash in my till would cheer me up.

My wife, Leona, liked Harold's sculptures, and she liked hanging out at the tea parties. She said the folks there really talked about things, really looked at things, and really listened to her, unlike me. She said, sure, the sanctuaries were weird, like some child's daydream come to life, but, hell, why not, she said. When she was there, they seemed natural. And look at Sean, she always said. Wasn't he a decent kind of kid, never stealing or breaking anything at the store?

Leona kept going to them damn tea parties, even after I refused to go anymore. She'd come home cheerful as hell, but after an hour or two with me, she'd calm down and be back to her complaining again. I just didn't get it, and Leona said that was the problem.

Chapter 10

Hoochie-Coochie Dancing While Whitey Watches

Whitey, Sylvia, Harold, and I were in Jolane's on Labor Day evening. Whitey sat at a corner table, nursing one beer the entire evening, watching and listening. Because Harold was drinking, I was sulking. I wanted to go home, relieve the babysitter, and go to bed.

Sylvia was in the process of getting drunk. I'd never seen her like this before. She danced with everyone she could wrangle onto the dance floor, and if no one would join her, she strutted out there in her red wig, green high-heeled go-go boots, and green miniskirt and danced by herself.

The smoke in that bar hung thick as sewer sludge. A wash of nicotine and tar raced into my lungs with each breath. My eyes burned, and my vision blurred as the yellow smog churned and drifted.

I again asked Harold about going home. He was talking cars with his buddies, though, and didn't want to leave. Sylvia called me a party-pooper. We stayed. Being as it was a national holiday, the bar patrons thought it appropriate to get more inebriated than normal, toasting each other with such all time favorites as "to the working man" and "to freedom, shit yes, freedom, that's what it's all about" until late into the night when toasts diminished to more mundane topics. Various body parts were toasted as were various activities involving those parts.

Sylvia had gotten to a level of excitement and intoxication that made her act, and almost look, thirty years younger. She swung her hips and batted her eyelashes unabashedly. Men of all ages flirted with her. Finally, she jumped up on a table and shouted, "Hoochie-coochie!" and wiggled and bumped to the music. Cheers rang out around the room. Mania was in the air.

I snuck over and whispered to her to come on down. "Okay," she said placidly and let me assist with her descent. But as soon as one foot touched the floor, she announced, "Hoochie-coochie street dance, follow me!"

Sylvia swiveled and two-stepped her way out the door, calling, "Come on! Follow me! Hoochie-coochie dance!"

"Goddamn it!" shouted one cowhand wearing jeans, dress western shirt, and Coors baseball cap, and he jumped up and followed her, clapping and bellowing. Pretty soon most all of the bar patrons had emptied onto the street, hooting and banging on anything that would make a noise. As the line of dancers approached Halfway's other bar, curious patrons began popping their heads out the door.

The Home Cooking Cafe's panicked bartender jogged from person to person as they prematurely left the premises. He grabbed glasses as he shouted, "Alcoholic beverages must remain inside the establishment once they are opened! Christ All Mighty! Do you shitheads want me to lose my license? Get your asses back inside if you're holding drinks!" He implored patrons, ordered them, but got limited compliance. "Inside now. Goddamn it! Where's Merle? Tell Merle to get his butt out here and help me round this bunch up! Where're you all coming from?" He asked a reveler.

"Hoochie-coochie street dance from Jolane's. Where's my sweetie, Sylvia? Where's my darlin' dancer?" a cowboy responded with somewhat slurred speech, and he staggered off, swaying and clapping, to join the loose line of dancers weaving their way down Main Street toward Halfway's small residential area. Downtown rung with hooting and hollering.

Since Halfway didn't have very much traffic midday, let alone at midnight, there wasn't a major vehicle backup. The two sheriff's deputies allotted to cover the outlying areas of the county were about a hundred miles away subduing a quarrel that had started when sparks from one rancher's fireworks had landed on another rancher's prize bull. The bull had taken off lickedy-split, tearing through a perfectly good barbed wire fence, and ended up inseminating one of the firework launcher's cows before they could corner him. The fight had started when the launcher refused to pay for the fence or the insemination. Both ranchers had gotten their rifles and were taking pot shots at each other from behind their vehicles, when the deputies arrived.

Consequently, even though several nervous residents called the sheriff's office as the dancers cut through their yards and gardens, and dogs all over town howled and barked, Halfway's rowdy street dance continued for another half-hour until it petered out of its own accord. Watching from Jolane's doorway, I heard soft laughter and turned to find Whitey standing close behind me. He looked at me and shook his head slowly from side to side.

"I should have married that woman forty years ago when I had the chance. Damn." That was the only time I ever heard Whitey swear.

Chapter 11

Deer Hunting and the Son of a Bitch Pig

The second fall after Harold and Mag moved to Halfway, Harold's brother, Mike, a quiet sort and a real straight arrow, joined Sean, Harold, me, and two more fellas for a three-day deer hunt, starting opening day of the season; October twelfth it was. Guzzling beer was a part of the hunt, and Harold liked that part particularly well. Fortunately for all concerned, he waited until after he'd hunted to begin drinking, but I could tell that it kind a bothered Sean, now a first grader, when his dad got drunk that first evening when we were all sitting around the campfire.

I have to admit that we did encourage Harold, with asking for more stories and joking around. Mike and Sean looked on with gloomy faces, but like I said, even though I felt bad that it bothered the kid, I didn't have sense enough to put the brakes on Harold when he'd drunk enough.

Mike tried. He slid mumbled, disparaging remarks in Harold's direction as the flames from the campfire played against Harold's heated face. But despite Mike's obvious displeasure, Harold was three sheets to the wind not long into the evening. Sean sat near his dad chucking rocks at a Doug fir not far off. He looked dog-tired and pissed off. Every time his dad raised his beer to his lips, Sean followed the action. But Harold drank anyway. He must a noticed Sean's unhappiness. He must a noticed that his kid didn't want him to drink, but he didn't pay him no mind.

"I'm going to bed," Sean said.

"Hell, it's not late, Son. Stay up and keep your old dad company," Harold told him. He reached over and tried to hug his son, but being as he was pretty drunk his reach was off, and he tumbled backward onto the soft forest duff. Harold's beer flung into the air, and his legs swung skyward. Everyone but Sean and Mike busted out laughing. Harold, drunk as a skunk, struggled to right himself.

Sean looked pained, I mean like he was in real physical pain, and he said, "There's other people to keep you company, Dad. I'm going in the tent. Good night, everybody." He waved to us and made a beeline for the tent. I felt bad, like I should do something, but I didn't. Instead, I handed Harold another beer.

The hunt that day had been unsuccessful, which seemed to put Harold in a better than ever story telling mood. Every time there was a break in conversation, someone would say, "Tell us another one, Harold." And he would. He told one of my favorites that night, the one about the pig.

He melodramatically waved the air clean of unseen obstacles and began, "When I was a boy, we had a neighbor named Mr. Wilfred P. Janas; he lived alone and raised pigs. He had this one prize boar, named Hannaby's Choice, who did not like being confined at all. Mr. Janas, an ornery old rascal on his best days, built stronger and stronger fences in vain attempts to keep that damned pig in his field."

Harold paused, took a slug of beer, and continued narrating his story. His voice crackled with excitement, and he gestured enthusiastically to us, drawing us in. "A friend of his, actually the only one he had, feeble minded Arlo, suggested that he try an electric fence to hold in that rooting pig. Wilfred trudged down to his local feed and seed co-op, parted with a few of his carefully watched dollars; they were the moldy ones he kept in a coffee can in a hole under the chicken coop, and bought wire, insulators, and switches. He installed the electric fence.

"That night, long about seven-thirty, when old night owl Wilfred went to bed, he turned it on. He slept soundly, dreaming the dreams of the righteous and purposeful, content in knowing that he would wake to still having his prize pig at home."

Harold paused again and took another gulp of his beer. He questioned us jokingly. "What do you reckon happened? Do you suppose that damned pig was still there in the morning?" We conjectured, and Harold nodded, bobbing his head like a pheasant doing a mating dance. He slapped his knee in the throes of his own private hilarity, as if laughing at the absurdity of our guesses even when they were right.

"Yes," he said, "the pig escaped. Long about the break of dawn, Wilfred heard the damnedest squeal and ran to the window soon enough to see Hannaby's Choice, county fair blue ribbon boar, squeezing under that electric fence. He was squealing all the way, but he was going under.

"As he ran to get dressed and track down his pig, he resolved to settle the matter one way or the other that day. Without consulting even Arlo, his one friend, he worked out an idea. Again he went to bed and slept soundly, dreaming his righteous and purposeful dreams. He was secure in the knowledge that his pig would nevermore escape, causing wrack and ruin to his neighbors' gardens. Nevermore, he knew, would that boar cause him to be yelled at and ridiculed by his neighbors.

"Long about dawn that next morning, he was awoke by the damnedest squeal, squeal, squeal. He rose and slowly walked to the window." Harold rose from his seat on an upturned log and imitated Wilfred slowly walking to his window. He mimicked Wilfred slowly parting his curtains, wiping a spot clean, and looking out his window.

Harold slowly gazed around at everybody, a grin on his face. He said, "The squealing had stopped. Wilfred looked out the window and smiled. Slowly, he got dressed and walked to the pig's field."

Harold imitated Wilfred slowly taking off his long johns, leg by leg, walking to the closet to get a pair of jeans hanging there, and slowly walking back to the bed to put them on leg by leg. We were jumping up and down and hollering for Harold to hurry up and get on with it, but Harold kept Wilfred on a grindingly slow course toward full dress as he acted and narrated every minute step of his dressing routine.

Finally, Wilfred put on his padded red flannel hat with earflaps and strolled outside. Harold said, "By the time he got to the place in the fence under which Hannaby's Choice had tried to squeeze, the squealing had stopped indeed."

Harold gestured at Mike. "My brother and I arrived about the same time, for we'd heard that god awful squealing too. And there, in a hole that Hannaby's Choice had dug out under the fence, lay the blue ribbon prize boar himself, deader than a doornail and a little singed where his back had touched the electric fence."

The other fellas and I commenced asking what Wilfred had done wrong since electric fences weren't supposed to kill your stock, just confine 'em. Harold agreed and said, "We asked him what the hell he'd done too, and he grinned real broadly and said, 'I fixed that son of a bitch. I rigged that fence to 220 current. Fried his ass. Made bacon out a him. Now I'm gonna slaughter that son of a bitching boar.' And he walked off chuckling and remarking how that dirty son of a bitch wouldn't be getting out a his field anymore."

We all laughed and swapped stories about various recalcitrant cattle we'd had. Harold lapsed into watching the fire for a bit. I could tell that he was thinking of what story he would tell next break in the chatter, a story to top that one.

Mike didn't laugh though. He leaned over to Harold and as quietly as he could, he whispered, "Lay off the beer. You're about maxed, brother." With his gaze as level as he could make it and his expression a bit strained, he stared at Harold. I got the feeling he wanted to suck his brother inside his own soul and clear out whatever it was that caused him to drink his mind into oblivion.

"Shit, Mike," Harold said jokingly, "I can handle it. You know that. There's no problem." He laughed, put his arm around Mike, and finished off his beer. Then he leaned over to Bob, his arm still around Mike, causing him to lean way to one side and almost knocking him over. "Hey, buddy, see if you can fish around in that cooler and find me another beer, will ya?" Harold asked his pal, and he handed Bob his empty.

"Sure thing, Harold," Bob answered, and he bent down and rummaged around in the cooler. "Hear you go, good buddy." He chuckled and raised his own can to toast Harold.

Mike looked on in dismay. He extricated himself from Harold's arm and rolled his log a distance away from him, watching the fire hunched over, his head resting on his hands and his hands resting on his knees.

Mike had her pegged all right, Harold's problem, his drinking. But Harold wasn't a mean drunk. He never hurt anyone when he was drinking. If anything, he got friendlier and more outgoing. Hell, what could be the harm in that? We enjoyed his stories, what harm done, for Christ's sake?

Mag picked Sean up the next morning. She and Harold thought one day would be enough hunting for Sean at his tender age. It was probably for the best that he missed seeing a shot deer up close and personal, not to mention a night or two more of Harold making a spectacle of himself.

Chapter 12

The Problem with Harold

Harold's brother, Mike, visited us at least once each year, and during our second autumn in Halfway, he came during deer season. He wanted to hunt with his brother.

The first thing Harold did upon Mike's arrival was to take him on a tour of our front slope and his latest metallic creations. Mike listened quietly as Harold excitedly described his artwork to him, but the doubtful, almost embarrassed, look on his face showed he didn't share Harold's enthusiasm for them. The more uncomfortable Mike looked, the harder Harold tried to get him to appreciate what he'd made. Mike laughed with a choppy kind of catching breath and said, "Aw, Harold, I don't know where you get your ideas." But Harold wanted his brother to like his art, and he used his disappointment as another reason to drink.

That evening while Mike and Sean were at the store getting ice cream, I decided to talk to Harold about his drinking. We were outside looking at the sunset. Harold rested his arms against a crossbar of Sean's swing set, a beer in his right hand.

I asked him, "Do you remember the promise you made when we first came to Halfway?"

"Hmmmm?" he said, seeming to pull himself from a deep reverie. "Promise? What promise?"

"You said that once you owned your own business and house, you'd stop drinking."

Harold shrugged his shoulders. "Yeah so?"

"So why are you still drinking?" I asked him. As he stared at me, I saw confusion give way to anger. His head dropped, and he cradled it in his arms. His grip on his beer tightened.

"Why do you always do this?" he asked.

"Do what?"

"We're having a perfectly good time, and you have to go and ruin it." He shook his head.

"I was thinking of what is going to come after, the rest of the evening. You're drinking even more with your brother here."

"Why is that your business?" he said and wiped his mouth with the back of his hand. "Christ," he said, "I'm going to the shop to finish getting the gear ready for hunting tomorrow."

This time he didn't even offer me one of his deals, that he'd drink only so many beers per day or that he'd drink only on week-ends. He had always fudged on his deals, but at least he'd kept offering them. They were some kind of hope. But no deal tonight.

I watched him walk to the shop. He didn't look back. He didn't say he was sorry that he got drunk every night or that he sometimes fell asleep drunk in the shop or on the couch and never made it into bed. I saw him open the door to the shop and heard it bang shut. I wanted to run after him and apologize for ruining the evening as he said I had, but I didn't. I felt the raw hole inside me rip further into my gut and my aching loneliness for Harold grow. I couldn't run after him, but I didn't know how to fix things between us anymore.

I was as unhappy with myself as I was with him. I had spoiled our enjoyment of the sunset. We had been watching a crystalline fall sun slip behind the mountains, and I'd spoiled it. How could I be so angry with someone who had a disease? Harold was not intentionally absent emotionally, not intentionally getting drunk night after night.

But Sean was growing up with Harold's drinking, and I wasn't doing a damn thing about it. I couldn't fix Harold, and I was breaking more each day. I didn't know what to do for Harold, for Sean, or for me. I'd tried everything I could think of, everything I'd read would work, but Harold never participated in these attempts, and he still drank. He said he could handle his drinking himself. He didn't need a group or a therapist.

What else could I do? "Stupid," I muttered as I focused on the closed shop door. "The whole thing is so fucking stupid."

Harold roused Sean and Mike before dawn the next morning. He didn't wake me, but I heard the clatter of their breakfast preparation in the kitchen. I had woken several times during the night, and Harold hadn't been in bed. I swept my hand over his side of the bed. Cold. I wondered if he'd spent the night in the shop, drinking, if he'd gone to sleep at all.

When I sat up in bed, I felt as if I weighed a million pounds. "Oh Harold," I whispered. I swung my feet over the side of the bed and let just my toes touch the cold roughness of the pine floor. Pine, I thought, not much left of the old trailer. I remembered when Harold and I had ripped out the trailer wall and floor, laid this pine flooring, and expanded our room to the outer enveloping wall. No doubt about it, Harold was a fine carpenter. With that thought, my by now familiar remorse slipped over me. Like a fog of soot, it crept upward from my toes, turning all to darkness.

I got out of bed. "Damn it, Harold, why can't you stop drinking?" I demanded of the dark room. I rubbed my face with my fingers and then pulled them through my hair.

I dressed quickly, without turning on a light. When I opened the door and stepped into the hallway, I startled as my eyes adjusted to the blaze of light that met them. I could see Harold, Sean, and Mike hunched around the table, eating and whispering to each other. Harold spotted me.

"Hey, babe," he called as if nothing were wrong. He could get drunk in public, but he was especially sensitive to anyone knowing "our business" as he called it. "We were trying to be quiet so as not to wake you." He waved me forward. "Come and join us, now that you're up."

"Ah," I answered as I walked toward them. "I don't think that my stomach is awake enough yet to eat, but I could go for a cup of coffee."

Harold kissed me lightly on the mouth. His eyes were puffy, the whites spider-webbed with red. "I'll get you a cup," he said. Something about his gaze bothered me; I couldn't read his feelings there. It was closed. His guard was up.

He set a cup of coffee in front of me, at the same time sitting down across the table. Without looking at me, he turned to Mike and said, "You have about five more minutes to finish eating and getting yourself ready, brother. We need to be hightailing it out of here."

"The deer around here must wear those night vision goggles," Mike said. "It's still dark, and there's only a slit of a moon."

"By the time we make it to the spot I have picked out, dawn won't be very far in coming," Harold said and picked up his plate and cup and shoved his chair back with his legs.

"Where are you planning on hunting?" I asked him.

Again, without looking at me, he answered, "Up back of Cornucopia, west of the old slag heaps. Joe and I scouted up there last week and saw three bucks in less than an hour." He looked over at Sean. "Why don't you bring me your plate, partner; we don't want to leave your mom a mess."

"If you need to get going, that's okay."

"Oh, we can squeeze in a clean up," Harold said and flashed me a quick smile.

Mike gathered up the rest of the stuff and cleared the table. With three of them working, they quickly had the dishes washed and the area policed. Then Harold herded Mike and Sean toward the door, but Sean broke ranks and ran over to kiss me good-bye.

I told him, "You be sure and tell your dad if you're getting too cold."

"Okay, Mom," he said and ran out the door.

Harold swung my way and planted a kiss on my forehead, "See you in the morning when you come to get Sean, hopefully with a deer dressed out for this winter's eating. If not, we better have one before our three days are up." He turned to go.

"Harold, I know we can't talk now, but we need to talk when you get home."

He stopped walking and rested his left hand on the doorjamb, his back to me, and rapped the wood with his fingers. "Yeah, talk. I don't know what good it's going to do. Seems like nothing changes anyway."

"The talk itself can't change anything. It's what we do afterwards that makes or breaks it," I said.

Harold breathed out noisily, "You got that right." He spun around, confronting me. "But did you ever notice that after we talk, it's always me who's got to change for anything to work, never you?"

He looked at me accusingly. Is that the way I put things to him? "We'll talk about it," I said. I felt very weary.

Harold laughed. "Yeah, that's the ticket. We'll talk about it."

I listened as Harold started his truck and pulled down the drive.

The wind picked up; it whistled through the trees. I got up and looked out the window. Blackness outside. I became aware of the lingering smell of bacon and eggs. Quietness inside. "We'll talk about it," I told the empty room and returned to rest in the still warm spot in the bed.

On the morning that Mike was going to leave for home, he came with me to water the plants in the greenhouse. For a while, he watched me work, making chatty comments. I think neither of us wanted to hear the words I knew Mike was going to say. Several minutes passed.

"Harold's drinking is getting out of hand, Mag," he said quietly, tracing the smooth metal edge of a planting rack with his index finger.

I reluctantly set down the maidenhair fern I was repotting and looked at him. "I know it is, but I don't know what to do about it. I've tried everything I can think of." My answer was flat. I'd spent my emotions on this already.

Mike waved his hands in frustration. "He thinks it's all some kind of joke, or at least that's how he acts. Oh, I guess he really knows," he said, shaking his head in dismay.

"He knows; he tries, " I said. I wanted to apologize for Harold, to defend him. "But I think he lets everything get to him too much; he doesn't know what to do about his problems, so he drinks."

I pulled dead tendrils off the fern for a while but finally met Mike's sad gaze. "Or that's how it begins," I admitted. "He gets drunk and silly and everyone laughs. That eggs him on. He's the center of attention, loved."

"Will he see a counselor?" Mike asked; I shook my head no. "Would he go through some kind of rehab?" I shook my head no again. "Has he considered joining AA?" Again no. "Is there anything that I can do?" His expression beseeched me to come up with something.

I wished I could say, '"Yeah, just take Harold with you for a couple of weeks, and I'm sure he'll be okay after that." or "If you ask Harold to get help, I know he will." But I knew this wasn't true.

I reached out and held his hand, taking time to compose myself. I was surprised at how truly helpless I felt, how far from Harold.

Mike waited, stroking the hand that held his. I said, "I love Harold. I want him to stop drinking. He needs to stop. He drives drunk. He's falling behind at work. Folks will put up with that only so long. His drinking is destroying our family as well as himself. I've tried what I know, what I've been told might work, what I've read. I'm going to a counselor. I know I do things that make it worse." Tears began their all too familiar journey down my cheeks.

Mike shook his head, squeezed my hands, and released them. The growing fear I saw in his eyes, I knew, must reflect the fear in mine. He stuck his hands in his pockets. "I'm at a loss," he said.

I continued speaking, my voice a low monotone. "Since Harold won't act, it's up to me. What do I want to put up with? How long do I want to live with him drinking, however much I love him?"

"I'll understand whatever you decide to do," Mike said. He shifted uncomfortably.

"I don't know what to do. I have to think of Sean as well as myself. Adultery or something tangible would make the decision easier. But as it is, if I leave Harold or ask him to leave, I'll feel as badly as if I were putting someone on the streets who has cancer and has refused treatment. I'll be abandoning a very sick man, a very sick alcoholic. What kind of a person would I be to do that?" I shuddered; I'd had this thought many times before.

We were both quiet for a while. Finally, Mike said, "I know you're in a very difficult position. But when a person refuses to get help or be helped, and you know they could be helped, I understand whatever decision you make."

We held each other's hands, gathering strength, affirming

ourselves in each other's eyes. "Thank you, Mike," I answered at last.

I had my permission to go my own way, but all I saw was emptiness. "Oh God, Harold," I said and gasped.

Chapter 13

Ramrod Mabel Calls the Sheriff

Harold liked to think he was tough, or at least he wanted other people to think he was tough. But, myself, I always kind a thought that Harold had a raw underbelly open to the weather, a real sensitive body part that he didn't wanna let anyone know was there. To hide it, he drank, and he put on a show. Laugh at my stories, laugh at me, but God help me, don't notice my velvety spot, the one hiding the tenderness of my soul.

That was why he was particularly taken aback when someone called the sheriff on him and his wife. He wasn't ready for it, and it struck him full force in that tender, secret part of him.

I reckoned it was Mabel Harrington who did it. Old ramrod Mabel, corncob up her ass, told everyone as would listen, or not walk away, her opinion on any and all topics. She was sure Harold and Magdalena encouraged every vice known to mankind at them tea parties, even though she'd never actually attended one. She was capable of calling the sheriff strictly on the basis of her suspicions; sure she was right and demanding concrete verification.

I found out about the sheriff's visit from Harold himself. I'd been walking toward Jolane's, about to enter, when Harold's truck came clattering down Main; he was doing sixty easy, right in the middle of town. I stopped, frozen in my tracks, to see what the hell he was going to do, being crazy enough to be racing that fast through town and all.

He swerved a quick right and jabbed the nose of his old Ford into the curb in front of the cafe. Out he jumped, beer in hand, slammed his door shut, and kicked at it with his heel. "Goddamned son of a bitching, wide-assed, pig mother fuckers," he growled and swigged the last of his beer, throwing the can hard at his truck.

I asked him, "Bad day, Harold?"

"Mother fucking bad day!" he exclaimed. "Goddamned cops have been up at my place looking for dope. Mother fuckers!" he yelled as he glared at me.

I'd never seen Harold this angry before; I wasn't sure what he was going to do. So I tried to reassure him. "Just one of those bureaucratic mistakes, I imagine," I said and chuckled.

"They came in response to an anonymous phone call," he said in a tone that sent a chill up my spine. "If I ever find out who the caller was, I'm going to tear him a new asshole, and then I'm going to beat him into unconsciousness and throw his bloodied body to my chickens." He looked at me with the threat of mayhem in his eyes. "Have you ever seen a body after a coop full of hungry chickens get done with it, Joe?"

"Can't say that I have," I confessed.

"Believe me, Joe, I'd do it," he said, but right then, I knew the only violence he might ever commit would be accidental and due to his drinking.

"Let's go have a beer, Harold." I put my arm on his shoulder and guided him toward the door to the bar.

"There were books, papers, cushions, every shitting thing we own, strewn everywhere, Joe," he said. "Mag's crying, saying she couldn't stop them, that they had a warrant. Shit, and what do I do?" he asked, and then answered his own question, "I get mad." I reached to swing open the door. Harold broke away from my guiding hand and pounded the wall with his fists. "Shit! Shit! Shit!" he choked out. I couldn't tell if he was mad at how he'd gotten mad, or if he was mad at the cops. He leaned into his upraised fists on the wall. He was breathing real heavy. His knuckles bled.

"Harold, let's go inside, have a beer, calm down, and then maybe you ought go on home to Mag and help clean up."

Harold followed me inside, not saying anything more until he'd pumped two more beers down himself. Then, inflated with alcohol, he repeated his story about the sheriff's visit and the anonymous phone caller to the crowd at the bar. After he had repeated his threat to said caller, the likelihood of said caller ever stepping forward was none to nil, of course. But the whole topic of sheriffs and their violations of citizen rights was hot enough to start one hell of a lively discussion in motion. Rampant anarchism spread as every alcohol fired cowboy threatened to get his '22 and blow the next police officer as what stepped on his property to hell and back again.

"Shit, man, I dare a cop to try and come on my place," Smithy said. "I'd plug him sooner than I'd open the door to him," and in the spirit of anti-authoritarianism, he spit a mouthful of tobacco laced gunk on the floor.

Mike, the bartender, was on him faster than a fly on rotten meat. "You clean that up pronto, cowboy, or your skinny ass is out a here. And do it again, and I'll show you a plug of my own."

"Shit, crap, and screw, goddamn it," Smithy mumbled as he grabbed a handful of napkins and swabbed up his mess. He flung the ball of gunk overhand into the trashcan about ten feet away behind the bar. It hit with a thud.

"What really gripes me," Harold went on, "is that Mag let them do it. She didn't even resist."

"They did have a search warrant, Harold," I said, as if reason would affect him.

"Warrant, shit. She could have asked to call the judge who issued it. She could have said no and made them arrest her to do it," Harold's face was red, probably a combination of excitement, the heat of the bar, and all them beers he was guzzling as quick as he could.

I was startled when he mentioned Mag and arrest in the same sentence. "Would you really want Mag to get arrested?" I asked.

"You have to draw the line, Joe. That's our place. We were falsely accused. She knew that. She should have resisted. Give me another Coors, Mike." He slid his empty bottle into Mike's waiting hand.

"I don't know, Harold," I said real slow like. "I sure wouldn't want my Leona arrested, no matter what the reason." I pictured my chatty wife in handcuffs, the shocked expression on her face as the sheriff led her to the patrol car.

"Mag knows what I would expect. She could handle it. She should have resisted." Harold gulped his fresh beer down in about four swallows and signaled Mike for another.

"Better keep a handle on them beers, Harold," I cautioned. "You're all riled up. You don't want to do anything stupid."

"And why not?" Harold answered me, grinning. "The cops already think we grow pot." He began swigging his new beer.

I ignored him after that. A drunk Harold could say things so stupid that I wanted to knock his block off. I wondered how Sean would deal with all this at school. His pals at the elementary school didn't know too much about drugs or most any vice for that matter, but they mimicked their parents' suspicions and might tease Sean on the basis of what they heard at home.

Most of the teens in town, on the other hand, knew where drugs and alcohol were to be had, and if the right person had asked 'em, they'd of told 'em that it wasn't at Harold and Magdalena's. But no adult likely to get an honest answer had ever asked 'em so they enjoyed hanging out at them tea parties, acquiring a disreputable reputation. There weren't many ways to rebel in Halfway. Socializing with the hippies and attending Sylvia and Mag's parties were golden opportunities.

So far, Sean had taken the talk in stride. Like I said, he was one to be pulling everything in with them big, moody eyes of his, but his spongy self never let any of it trickle out. No loose talk, no revealing questions. Hard working, goal minded kid, he was. Secrets and dreams were swimming in a sea of experiences in that boy. I wondered when he was gonna reach saturation.

I sat there listening to Harold and the rest of the crew spin their tales of wanton destruction. The Brown's had a reputation; that was certain. Harold's frequent boozing around town didn't help any and them tea parties? Christ! Might as well call the sheriff your own self.

Why just the day before yesterday, I'd overheard three high school boys who were standing outside the front window of my store. The door was propped open for the Frito Lay deliveryman, so I heard 'em fairly clearly. They were talking about their weekend at the Brown's. Short, cylinder-shaped, bullet-headed Jack had the best story. He began, "I saw these brownies with these massive hunks of green, in 'em so I grabbed a handful real fast before the Mag patrol came by."

His buddies interrupted with "righteous brother" and "Watch out for that broad. She'd yank your arm off if she saw you with anything even resembling dope." They all knowingly nodded and real sneaky like, I guess so I wouldn't see, stuffed more chew into their mouths.

"You got that right," Jack responded. He settled his chew into his right lower gum and coughed a couple off times in a way that could a been a gag. He continued, "I stuffed a brownie into my mouth, the whole piece, without tasting it first. I wanted to make sure I got to eat all of it."

"Whoa, score!" exclaimed Brad. He closed his eyes in ecstasy.

"Yeah, man. I wish," Jack said. "I started chewing, thinking, oh man, am I gonna be hi-i-igh, when all of a sudden the taste reached my brain. It wasn't dope; it was seaweed."

"Shit man, for real? Bummer," Phil said.

"I spit it off to one side toward some brush, but a big chunk landed on this hippie dude. Splat, right on his tie-died T-shirt. He had long hair and a beard and about eighteen thousand beads around his neck. He'd been sitting there real quiet up till then. His legs were crossed with his feet up on his thighs. His eyes were closed. When the brownie landed on him, he opened his eyes real slow. He looked at me; he looked at that brownie on his shirt. And I swear to God; he picked up that piece of chewed up seaweed brownie and popped it in his mouth."

"Oh gross! No shit man?" Brad said as disgusted but fascinated expressions passed from boy to boy.

"No lie, I saw it happen," Jack said, nodding in confirmation.

"Whoa, cool. Point out that dude this week-end, and I'll try it," Brad said.

"Righteous," Jack answered.

They'd found their heaven. What more could a Halfway teenage boy want than something that was frowned on, was gross, and was outdoors, so's they could spit chew unnoticed.

Then I saw Whitey come in, and I started thinking about his ma. I figured that Frieda was probably still going to them tea parties. She loved hanging out with the tea party people. She said she had lived all her life in Halfway and found them hippie folks "a welcome relief to sameness." She seemed determined to make up for having missed rebelling when she was younger.

"How you doing, Whitey?" I asked him as he sat down on the bar stool next to me.

"About as good as can be expected," he answered with a smile and nod.

"You hear about all the sheriff ruckus up at the Browns?"

Whitey shook his head and said, "Yeah, my ma saw them pull in, lights a flashing, and called Mag to find out what was what." He signaled to Mike, who brought him over his usual mug of draft; then he resumed talking to me. "Damnedest thing. I wonder who called. Poor Mag was crying when she talked to Frieda." Whitey gazed straight ahead into the woodwork behind the bar, seeing all kinds of things I couldn't, and sipped his beer in silence. "She's over there now." He glanced over at Harold and frowned.

"One time," Whitey began after a bit, "I came to fetch Frieda from a tea party on a Saturday night. I was in need of supper and wanted my ma to make it, like she always did. I told her it was time for her to come home and fix my meal. Actually, it was past time. I'd been waiting an hour already." He took off his worn, brown felt hat; outdoors it sat far back on his head, the brim curled tight on each side. The fluorescent light of the bar reflected a glossy sheen off his weathered skin. He glowed like one of them pictures in a fashion magazine. He shook his head as if he still couldn't believe his ma's response.

"She told me 'Chill out, son, and catch a few of these rays the youngin's are bathing in,' and then she waddled away from me on those bad ankles of hers." Whitey laughed as he recalled their conversation. "I asked her what in hell was I supposed to eat?"

Whitey chuckled softly, remembering. "Frieda answered, 'If you can't figure out what's edible by now, you're one pitiful creature.' She turned to walk away from me again but shouted over her shoulder, 'I'm a liberated woman, Whitey; fix you own damn meal.'

"She hiked up her right elbow so as she could look over her shoulder. She held up her right hand in the peace sign and grinned the broadest, false teeth smile I'd ever seen her manage."

Whitey said that after that, come weekends, he pretty much counted on fixing his own meals. I imagined that if ninety-year old Frieda could have gotten her swollen legs into a pair of them patched up hippie jeans she would have.

Whitey laughed. "I learned something I should have learned long ago, and besides, how could I fault Harold and Magdalena for taking my weekend meal cooker seeing as they helped me when my ma got sick." He was talking about last calving season. As usual, he was counting on his ma, old as she was, to hold up her end of keeping them calves warm.

Calves had the bad fortune of being born from late February through mid March. In Halfway that meant the weather was well below freezing at night and merely not as below during the day. Frieda was supposed to tend to the calves once Whitey brought 'em to the barn. She'd dry 'em off, tag 'em, inoculate 'em, and warm 'em.

In the case of a stillborn calf, she was supposed to skin him and ready the skin to be wrapped around another live newborn who'd lost a mother in birthing. The skin was to confuse the mama cow and make her bond with the new youngin'. It usually worked.

Frieda had got herself a good dose of pneumonia early on that calving season. With all that steam from the warm water, heat from the wood stove, slimy calves, and freezing weather, I'm not a bit surprised. But she and Whitey were. She made herself doubly sick trying to work through it, considering it a mere sniffle. She ended up in the county hospital at Baker City. Ninety-year old stubborn mule.

Harold, Mag, and Sean jumped right in, taking her place. They said it took two of 'em at a time to do her work in the barn. The three of 'em looked exhausted by the time the calf birthing was over.

I asked Mag about it. She said, "I know why Frieda got sick. I don't know why she didn't get sick sooner."

Mag cared for Frieda when she came home from the hospital. She made meals in her own home and carried the steaming food up to her and Whitey. Whitey said that she even washed his clothes. He had always been kind a tender toward Mag, treated her like the daughter he'd never had, but after Frieda's illness, he took his hat off when he talked to her.

So Harold and Mag had one staunch defender in town. Whitey stuck by 'em even after all the hullabaloo with the sheriff.

Chapter 14

Wild Parties in the Poets' Magic Sanctuaries

My knife slid through the tight skinned onion, and translucent circles tipped one after another onto the cutting board. Once the whole onion was sliced, I diced it. I was preparing a stew, heavy with vegetables, light on meat. My wandering attention flicked lightly at the edges of thoughts I didn't care to entertain, searching for a convenient no-brainer on which to settle. I was so self-absorbed that the rapid tapping on the front door startled me. I hadn't noticed anyone coming up the driveway.

I set the knife on the counter, wiped my onion-bleared eyes with the backs of my hands, and grabbed a towel to wipe onion fragments from my fingers. The visitor knocked again. "I'm on my way," I called.

When I opened the door and saw four sheriff's deputies, I was shocked. "Oh my God," I said under my breath, and then more loudly asked, "Is Sean hurt? Is Harold hurt? Oh my God, oh my God." Four deputies: I was terrified.

"No, Mrs. Brown, no one's hurt," Deputy Richardson answered. He handed me a piece of paper. "This is a search warrant. We've received information from a reliable caller who wishes to remain anonymous that you and your husband are cultivating marijuana and supplying said illegal drug to guests on your property." He tapped the back of the piece of paper he'd just handed me. "This warrant gives us permission to look for said marijuana on your property and in your house, shop, and greenhouse. Excuse me, ma'am." He pushed past me. The three other deputies quickly followed.

I stood in the doorway of my own home, my heart beating madly, still not having gotten over the fear that something had happened to Harold or Sean, as the four deputies positioned themselves throughout my living room. Then, systematically, recording each piece of furniture, shelf, and drawer they examined, they probed every item in the room, tossing cushions on the floor, riffling through mail, and emptying shelves and tables. "Wait, please," I begged helplessly. "This is our home. Why are you doing this?" I followed them, in the wake of their chaos, straightening what I could.

They moved methodically from room to room, tossing the contents of drawers and dressers on the floor, clumsily pawing through the contents, feeling no need to apologize. Like a begging child, I followed them, pleading, "Don't do this. Please don't do this." I retrieved clothes from the floor and tried to tidy up.

The deputies completed their search of the house and headed for my greenhouse. "Please don't hurt my plants," I called after them, scurrying to keep up, clothes grasped in both fists. I wanted to call the police and tell them that someone was ransacking my home, but the police were already here.

Row by row, shelf by shelf, they examined every plant. They inadvertently tipped over three pots and broke the tops off two taller plants.

They moved onto Harold's shop and went through that. Last they asked me to show them where the sanctuaries were. I did. They searched them and the surrounding woods.

After what seemed like forever, Deputy Richardson said, "We didn't find anything incriminating, Mrs. Brown. Sorry for the inconvenience, but we have to follow up on reliable citizen tips such as this call." He touched the fingers of his right hand to his hat and nodded in silent leave-taking. The four deputies climbed into their vehicle and sat with the engine idling as they jotted notes and pointed toward the house and shop. Finally, they pulled down the drive. I stood on our hillside, clothes still clenched in my hands, and watched them drive away.

Harold arrived home about a half-hour later; Sean was with him. He'd picked him up from school.

"What the hell!" he shouted the moment he stepped through the door.

I was in the middle of the living room, as I had been for the last half hour, my hands still grasping the same wadded up clothes. "Four sheriff's deputies were here," I said as he spun around, trying to make sense of the mess.

"What?" he asked, his face white, his expression confused.

"Someone called them and said that we were growing dope and handing it out to people. They had a search warrant."

Harold stared at me, incredulous. "Why'd you let the bastards on our property?"

"They had a search warrant," I repeated; now I felt doubly wronged. Why was Harold turning on me? Couldn't he see I hadn't known what to do? That I couldn't have stopped them.

"God damn the shit eating bastards," he hissed.

"We don't have anything to hide," I said; I didn't even know why I was defending myself. "What difference does it make?"

"You never give an inch to a cop," he said, swaying as he stood. He was drunk. He had driven our son home drunk. He pointed a finger at me and waved it in every direction. "Not one thing we do is their business. You got that?" He demanded this more than asked it. He let his head drop to his chest and squinted at me through upturned, red-streaked eyes. Sour, acrid smells of tobacco and beer drifted my way. He'd stopped at the bar and gotten drunk before picking up Sean, and I'd let this happen. I could have predicted he would drive our son home in this condition, but I'd let it happen anyway. This guilt ate at my guts with a far greater sharpness than what the deputies had done or Harold's drunken accusations.

"Go to bed. You're in no condition to discuss anything," I stated flatly.

Harold drew himself up and stared at me; I gazed into his hate darkened eyes and felt only my own complicity. "I'm getting the hell out of this house," he said and turned and walked out the door, slamming it shut.

Forgotten Sean spoke. "Mama, what happened?" he asked, tears on his face. "Why did the policemen do this to our house?"

"Oh, sweetie, don't cry." I scooped him into my arms, dropping my pathetic wads of clothes, and crying now myself. "It was a mistake. The policemen didn't mean to do it. Someone played a trick on them and told them we had bad stuff hidden in our house. They were looking for it." I held his trembling body in my arms. "It's okay, baby, It's okay," I murmured into his ear.

Long into the night I lay awake, with Sean in my arms, wondering what to do about Harold, the sanctuaries, and what the town thought about us. At least the harsh winters kept most outsiders away.

Sylvia loved the forest sanctuaries we had created. She called them her "secret poetic territories surrounded by an unkind land." She had filled them with old furniture she'd bought at yard sales and then decorated. She had even scrounged two tattered mannequins from a defunct store and lettered them with poems. Then there were the "ethereal adornments" that Sylvia and the partygoers added: the bells, windsocks, chimes, mobiles, flowers, dried herbs, and photos. Because visitors wanted to add their own poems to the sanctuaries, Sylvia kept ample supplies of plywood pieces, paint, and brushes. Within a short time, the thoughts of many were nailed to the trees surrounding the sanctuaries. Yes, the sanctuaries could be considered a bit schmaltzy, but in a tender, lovely sort of way.

Frieda really liked the so-called tea parties. "Hell of a lot better than sitting in some damned cafe, slurping coffee," she always said.

Even old Mrs. Hampton enjoyed the parties, in her own way. Her daughter dropped her off and picked her up about four hours later every Saturday during the summer. Eighty-year old Mrs. Hampton followed Frieda around like a shy puppy. Periodically, Frieda turned toward her and rasped, "Back off a little, would you; you're rattling me."

The two basic rules were no drugs, including alcohol and tobacco, and no drunkenness. If a partygoer committed either offense, he or she couldn't come back. That was, except for Harold. His drunkenness was an accepted exception.

The partiers came to kick back. They came to discuss subjects that weren't acceptable to discuss elsewhere for fear of ridicule or lack of a sympathetic ear. They came to reveal their dreams in this safe environment. We got to know the regulars, so many fragile lives.

I kept close watch over the teenagers that showed up. They knew that I'd be on them like a bad stink if they dared drink anything alcoholic or use any drug. Since townsfolk already suspected us of being corrupting influences, I didn't want to give them living, underage examples of our bad ways. If a parent forbad a teen to be on our property, I wouldn't let them be here.

I'd always known that about half of the Halfway folks wondered what I actually grew in my greenhouses. I'd had two open houses, but not many people had come by for either one. The sanctuaries and the presence of outsiders didn't help, and the cops showing up at our door with a search warrant wouldn't help either. Friends had fallen by the wayside until Sylvia, Frieda, Whitey, Leona, and Joe became our only friends. I thought about the long, cold winter ahead and about how much Harold was at the bars, and I grew glum. Harold often didn't get home until after closing, at two in the morning. I knew this couldn't continue. I couldn't keep pretending our life together was normal and okay. I couldn't keep letting Sean grow up in a household where his father acted as he did.

Chapter 15

Just When You Don't Need Them Around, They Show Up

Harold's parents, Dan and Joyce, came for a visit about three weeks after the now locally famous search warrant debacle. Most of the time, I found them easy enough to tolerate. Joyce reminded me of Winnie the Pooh, what with her chubby face and round body and her craving for sugary food. Her favorite expression, "Oh, dear me, dear me," added to the Pooh bear image, but her second most used refrain, "Oh, don't worry about me, I'm nothing. You all get what you want to eat. I'll just get a few standbys to nibble on," was not at all like the lovable bear. No matter how politely or impatiently Mag pressed her, Joyce would not say what she liked to eat, but for sure it wasn't what Mag was buying.

Some days I near as popped a gasket restraining myself from stomping over to her and yelling, "God damn it, woman, tell Mag what you want for supper."

On the other hand, although Dan spoke only when asked a direct question, he at least appeared satisfied with whatever was fed to him. Mag would ask him, "What would you like for supper?"

He'd answer, "Whatever you fix is just dandy by me." Mag, near to exploding, would suggest something like hamburgers, and Dan would say, "Fine, I love burgers, can't wait." He was one of those guys you could a swore had what's called the heebie-jeebies; he was constantly changing position. He slouched; he straightened up; he worked his shoulders up and down; he cocked his head this way and that. His face was a maze of ticks and twitches. I could tell where Harold got all his energy.

But the major difficulties of the visit began when Harold started not showing up at home after work. Of course, that had been his usual pattern these many months, but his folks didn't know it. I wondered how many Haroldless evenings Mag would spend with Dan and Joyce before the shit hit the fan.

Mag hadn't exactly been a fun gal to have around since things had been getting bad with Harold, but now with Harold's folks here and him down at the bar, she was loaded and cocked, just waiting for any excuse to tear a new asshole in the first person fool enough to give her reason. I figured Harold would be fool enough.

On the last night of Dan and Joyce's visit, Halfway High held a pep rally and bonfire to get folks revved up for the homecoming football game. The whole town went; I was there with Leona. I started to worry when on one side of the blaze, I saw Mag, Sean, and Harold's folks, and on the other side, making sure he was out of view, I saw Harold, beer in hand, standing with the bar crowd.

My old eyes had a hell of a time flicking back and forth between the two groups. I was so caught up in anticipating Harold's discovery that I couldn't really enjoy the bonfire or the cheering. About a half hour into things, the wind shifted, and Mag and her group moved to their right a bit to get out a the smoke. That was when Mag saw

Harold.

He was in the middle of spinning one of his outrageous tales for his buddies and didn't even notice her observing him. I was praying Mag wouldn't go over and lay into him right there. She stared at Harold, her anger so intense that I could a swore sparks flew from her eyes. After what seemed like an eternity to me but was probably more like a few seconds, Mag broke off staring at Harold and instead stared into the fire.

The expression on her face was one I wouldn't care to behold again. If a bystander had handed her a gun right then, I believe she could a shot Harold stone cold dead, without hesitation. She was that wrung out, that mad. But no one did, and Mag stared at them flames, boring into their heated depths with her crazed, sparking eyes.

The gathering started to break up. I saw Harold head back to Jolane's with his gang of drunkards. I felt like I should talk to him, tell him to get his ass on home pronto, so I suggested to Leona, "How's about we go to Jolane's for some dessert and coffee?"

Leona was thrilled by my sudden, wonderful consideration and answered, "Yes, dear, that would be lovely. What a nice idea," and she linked arms with me, smiling to beat the band. Shit, a wedge of guilt slid neatly under my rib cage. I'd made my wife happier than peaches in cream when all I'd been thinking about was Harold's ass. Why was Leona so damned happy with little crumbs of attention from me? I figured that I must be one enormous bastard.

Jolane's was packed. A yellow haze hung in the room, and the wood smoke smell from the bonfire, carried in on the clothes of many of the patrons, mixed with the cigarette and stale beer smells. I couldn't see anywhere to sit, then George called out, "Joe, Leona, come sit with us." George and his wife were having lemon cream pie.

"How's the pie?" I asked.

"Can't beat it," George said.

"Leona, I'll go to the counter and order us some pie and coffee. I think we could wait all night to be served sitting here," I said, but what I was thinking was that this would be a nifty way to get a word in with Harold, natural like, without Leona even noticing.

"Why, thank you, dear," Leona said. "You're just full of thoughtfulness tonight." And she beamed her best smile at me. Guilt, guilt, guilt, my own wife needing small kindnesses, and I'm worrying about Harold.

I made my way to the counter, sidling right up next to Harold. I gestured to the bartender, and he said, "What's your pleasure, Joe?"

"I need two cups of coffee and two pieces of lemon pie," I said as if I didn't realize it wasn't his job to get these non-alcoholic items.

"What's a matter, couldn't get a waitress?" he asked, looking mildly peeved.

"Just this once, Bert, I need to have a word with Harold here. There are two free T-bones in it for you. Come by tomorrow and pick 'em up."

Bert eyed me, real suspicious like. He wasn't the regular bartender; he helped out on busy nights like this. He was probably thinking he didn't know all my tricks and that I'd renege on them steaks. "Okay, just this once," he said, sounding cautious as hell. "I'll be by tomorrow for them steaks."

"I'll be expecting you, Bert." I had a couple steaks right near the expiration date that I'd give him. I smiled, then turned and gave the thumbs up to Leona. She grinned and gave them back at me.

"What do you want, Joe?" Harold asked. "Your rig acting up on you?" Harold's eyes glistened; that was the way they got when he was near stewed. I was never sure if it was because they watered more then, or if it was because Harold had entered another realm. He wasn't really with us anymore when he got to that state. He was seeing a whole other world or maybe, I sometimes conjectured, he was seeing his own death.

I cleared my throat before I spoke. "It's not my rig, Harold, that I want to talk to you about," I said slowly. "It's you." There, it was out.

"Me?" Harold said and smiled dreamily. "Not a damn thing to talk about." He smiled again, his mirth radiating up to his eyes but stopping there.

"Mag saw you at the bonfire tonight. She knows you're not working,"

"Mag knows I'm not working without seeing me at the bonfire," Harold drawled.

"Harold, I'll just say it. You're drinking too damned much. I hear you're leaving the bar at closing every night and driving home drunk. Don't you care about what you're doing to yourself?"

"Hmmmm," Harold said and grinned at his glass of beer. "No."

"Don't you care about your family?"

"Mmm, that's a tough one," Harold drawled again. "I know I should say yes. That I'm expected to say yes, but you know, Joe, if you don't give a shit for your own life, it's hard to get beyond that point." He swung his gaze my way, and I looked into them glisteny, other world eyes, and I knew he was right. He was so bound up in his own dance with destruction that all he saw was his own time of endless white blindness.

I was shaken. I didn't know what to say and was relieved when Bert showed up with the pie and coffee on a tray.

"That'll be seven fifty," Bert said.

I handed him ten and said, "Keep the change." I reached for the tray and lifted it from the counter. I couldn't leave without saying something else to Harold so I gave it one last shot. "Harold, you're a good pal and a hell of a mechanic. I'm sure you're a hell of an artist although most of your shit is beyond me. Think about what you're doing, Harold. Think about Mag and Sean."

Harold grinned his slow, dreamy smile; his eyes watering with the white blindness he was seeing, and he said, "Yeah sure, Joe, I'll think about it."

Chapter 16

In Search of Normal

The visit from Harold's parents probably could have come at a worse time, but I'm not sure when that would have been. I was angry with Harold, had been for a long time. Truth was that I was as angry with myself as I was at Harold; how in the hell had our life come to this? When did I start acting like queen of the bitches? And most important, what in hell was I going to do about it?

Into this mess stepped Dan and Joyce. I talked to Harold. "You have to get home from work as soon as you can."

"Yeah, babe, sure thing," Harold assured me with a wink as he ducked out the door extra early in the morning before his folks were up. "I'll be here by six, tops."

The first night, he did get home by six, but after that he closed the bars as usual. I talked to him again. "I can't keep lying to your folks, telling them your working. Come right home from work tonight."

"Yeah, babe, sure thing," he said and kissed me goodbye. But he didn't come home until two in the morning.

I kept pretending Harold was working late; Dan and Joyce kept pretending they believed me. I made dinners that Joyce didn't touch and Dan gobbled down. Sean was used to his dad not being home in the evenings and welcomed having company to play with. Each night Harold didn't show, I spoke less and took longer to clean up in the kitchen.

Except for Joyce's refusal of food and her subsistence on sweets, she and Dan weren't too hard to entertain. Joyce's near constant, "Oh dear me, dear me," was like the mantra of a deranged, whiny toy while Dan was a study in motion. He moved from chair to table to couch in rapid succession, always shuffling the stack of papers he carried. He seemed to be involved in pressing business at all times. I asked him once what he was working on, and he chuckled softly and said, "That's a good one, Magdalena," and he moved from the couch to the dining room table. Harold didn't know or care what his dad was doing. He said his dad had always had a stack of papers with him and that he'd never known why. When I asked Joyce what they were, she said, "Did you ask Dan?"

Finally, after five nights of a no-show Harold, I was tired of hanging around the house pretending that I was waiting for him to come home from work. I said, "Let's go to the Snake River and have a picnic. I have everything packed. All you guys need to do is pile yourselves into the car."

"Oh, dear me, dear me, no. Not without my boy. He got tied up again with work. Such a hard working man, " Joyce said, caressing her words as if she held Harold right there in her arms.

"No, Joyce, he's not working. He's at the bar drinking. I just spoke to him on the phone. Let's go." I stood, grabbed my keys and purse, and walked toward the door.

"Oh, dear me, oh dear me, no," Joyce began again. "We can't

leave without Harold. I'm sure he'll be here shortly. He's just unwinding. Give him a bit more time, Magdalena." Dan moved from the upholstered chair to Harold's recliner. Sean rolled his eyes.

"Joyce, he won't be home until late tonight when the bars close." I was steamed. I didn't care what I said to his parents. I breathed deeply, trying to calm myself, and continued, "We're not waiting for him another night. You deserve to have some fun. Come on; let's have a nice picnic dinner." I smiled and motioned for them to come to the door.

Sean got up and came to stand by me. "Come on, Grandma, it'll be fun."

"Oh, you all just go on without me," she said and waved her hands at us to go. "Don't worry about me. I'm nothing. I'll just sit here and wait for Harold. I'll fix him a little something when he gets home."

That did it; I snapped. "You will not fix him a goddamned little something when he gets home." I was furious, how could she? That's what I'd done for years. What I was now trying to stop doing. I'd fixed it for him. I'd helped him to be the alcoholic he was. "You can stay here if you insist. It's a shame if you do, but that's your choice. But don't you dare fix him anything for dinner. He can get leftovers from the refrigerator." I stopped, caught my breath, and rubbed my forehead with my fingers.

In a quieter voice, I said, "He knows he should be here. He knows he'll miss dinner if he's not. He knows we're all waiting for him. Drinking is more important to him. That may not be how he wants it to be, but it's how it is. We have to face that, and he has to face that. But we can't help him drink." I looked at Joyce pleadingly. "Please, Joyce, come with us."

"No, dear," she responded, her voice shaky this time. "You all go on. Have a good time. You too, Dan. Don't worry about me." She smiled ruefully at me. I knew she would fix Harold as special a dinner as she could wrangle with what was at hand if he came home before we did, but I also knew that he wouldn't come home until long after we were all asleep.

I smiled at Joyce. "Suit yourself. Come on, Dan and Sean. Let's have a picnic." I pledged to keep myself together for this picnic no matter what my insides felt like.

Dan twitched and jerked and looked from Joyce to me and back at Joyce again. Finally, he said, "Let me put my papers up." He glanced briefly at Joyce and scurried to the bedroom with his stack of papers. He appeared in a moment wearing his gray fedora and nappy gray cardigan.

On the last night of Dan and Joyce's visit, we went to the high school's homecoming bonfire. Of course Harold hadn't shown up, and Joyce wanted to wait for him. I was ready to cram the next "dear me" she uttered down her throat and told her, "Get your goddamned ass in the car, lady. You're going to the bonfire, and you're going to have a good time even if I have to set myself on fire to make it happen."

Joyce stared at me, a wet noodle trying to stand up to the bitch from hell. I stared back. I had no doubt who would win. I was prepared to bodily throw her into the back seat of the car. Dan twitched and wiggled but didn't say a word; he looked at Joyce. Sean knew I meant what I said. He broke the stalemate when he said, "Come on, Grandma; it'll be fun."

Joyce's little round chest heaved up and down; her face was candy apple red. She jumped on Sean's out. "For Sean, I'll come." I stood by the door until she had passed through; my eyes focused on her red, angry face.

I couldn't let go of my anger, even at the bonfire. I looked for Harold but at first didn't see him. Then, when we had to move to get out of the smoke, I saw him on the other side of the fire, talking to his bar cronies. My heart broke, and my anger tripled. I could have cut out his heart and eaten it raw. How could he do this? Why was he doing this to me? To Sean? To his parents? I told myself that he had a disease. He couldn't help it. He couldn't help it. He couldn't help it. But as many times as I repeated that thought all I really thought was fuck him, fuck him, fuck him.

About two a.m., I heard the door open and heard Harold enter, chuckling to himself. I got up to encourage him to come quietly to bed; more than anything I didn't want Joyce and Dan up too. Harold saw me and grinned. "How's about giving me a great big hug." He walked unsteadily toward me.

"Yeah, sure thing, Harold," I answered him, my voice iced with disgust. Harold grabbed for me with a misplaced lunge. He stank of beer and smoke. "Harold, God," I said, despite my intent to keep things quiet.

"Not good enough for you, am I?" he said, swaying. He wiped his face with the back of his hand. His shirt was half untucked. He still had on his greasy work clothes. "Shit, woman, you never could have a good time." He pushed past me on his way to our bedroom, bumping into walls as he progressed down the hall. Just before he crossed the threshold into our room, he called over his shoulder, "Bitch," and then slammed our bedroom door.

I heard the muffled sound of slippered feet approaching. "Mag, Mag," Joyce called. "Does Harold need supper? I didn't hear you fix him supper when he came home."

I turned my back to her. I was afraid that I might slap her as likely as look at her. "Joyce," I said, my voice low and hoarse with emotion, "number one, I'm sure he's passed out by now and incapable of eating. Number two, he's your son, but he's my husband. Go to bed."

I heard her bedroom door close behind me. I sat down at the dining room table and held my head in my hands. My shoulders jerked as I caught my sobs soundlessly in my throat. When I'd quieted my panic, I got up, put the teakettle on to boil, and sat down again at the dining room table. I rested my chin on my palms and stared at nothing.

The hissing kettle signaled my boiling water. I poured the water into my favorite mug and absentmindedly stood in front of the stove watching the steam swirl from it. I dipped my tea bag into the water and after a bit, set it aside. I added a generous amount of cream, sat down at the table again, leaned my head on my hands, and thought, but my thoughts dissipated into nothingness, as they swirled, like steam, away from me into the waiting, empty air.

Chapter 17

Drunken Racing in the Dark

The year limped toward its end. When Harold hung out at the bar, he usually carried on about how Mag had told him that he had to quit drinking and start counseling by January first, or else she would make him leave. "Damn bitch," he most always added. I felt sorry for Mag, having her private conversations with Harold aired so freely. Of course, the bar patrons pumped Harold for as much information as they could get out a him. Juice was juice no matter how much pain it was a part of.

But Harold wasn't thinking too clearly, and, as if he were caught in some Twilight Zone loop, he repeated his same tired old stories over and over to those drunk enough to still want to listen. Every few sentences, he gulped his beer like there was no tomorrow, which he rationalized as sort a true. The only thing Mag's threat had accomplished was to increase Harold's alcoholic consumption. He drank himself sick nearly every night, saying, "This is one of the last nights I have left to drink, before that woman who doesn't know how to have a good time makes me quit. I have to drink all I can."

No one, not even the bartender, made a move to stop Harold's drinking. Folks in Halfway seemed to think they were immune to the effects of drunkenness, like we'd not had our share of alcohol related one-car accidents and head-on collisions.

By the end of November, Harold's drinking was affecting his business. His hangovers made it harder and harder for him to get up in the morning. Customers were getting exasperated over not getting their vehicles on the dates Harold said he would have 'em.

They were cornering Mag when she came in for groceries. She told 'em that they would have to speak to Harold, that mechanics was his business, but if they pressed her, she just turned away, muttering, "Fuck off." She had an edge to her.

Hell, Harold's boozing wasn't her fault. She could no more control that man's drinking than they could, but her angry mood and Harold's revelations of every foul thing they did to each other soon made her a target of contempt as well as Harold. The sanctuaries and strange hillside sculptures were hardly issues anymore.

The ugly moods of some of his customers brought out the ugliness in Harold, which was none too far from the surface with all his drinking. He got pissed off real easy. Shit, he wasn't even funny no more. He knew he'd lost control, but he couldn't figure a way of saving himself. And he wasn't one to ask for help. He was one proud alcoholic, Mr. Self-sufficiency.

With the Christmas season coming, the town was done up in colored lights and them plywood decorations that I think had been around since World War II. Celebrating was in the air. Every church group and club in town held some kind a festival or bazaar during the last two weeks of December. Lots a groups held dinners at the cafes.

Some followed 'em up with dancing. Harold joined every merry making group as would have him, ready to party with the best and the worst of 'em. At this point, he'd do anything rather than go home and face the music.

Two days before the Halfway Utility Company held their Christmas party at Jolane's, we had another heavy snowfall. The day before the party, it warmed enough to allow traffic to reduce the snow left on the road after plowing to slush. Then the night before the big shindig, the temperature dropped to a frigid ten degrees above zero, and the roads here about were coated with a thick layer of ice. The gravel the highway department put down helped some but not much.

But road conditions didn't keep the utility company crowd from their Christmas party. Construction and maintenance workers from the dam on the Snake River, who lived in company housing near the dam, drove the eighteen miles to town in their four wheelers, ready to party. They were a rowdy bunch, and Harold slid right in with 'em, slinging down beers as fast as he could.

Along about midnight, Harold and another guy got the idea that they would see how fast they could drive the perimeter of the downtown area in Harold's pickup while seeing how many beers they could down each circle, a circle being six blocks.

A crowd gathered in the doorway of Jolane's, timing 'em and keeping track of how many beers Harold and the other guy, Johnny, drank each round. This already outrageous situation soon got totally out a hand.

Harold was the driver. He held a beer in his left hand, his arm resting on the open window of his truck. With each lap, he drove faster over that icy road. His truck swerved and fishtailed as he gunned it on the straightaway, the two-block section in front of the town's businesses.

Along about the fifth or sixth lap, Harold's driving was getting pretty uneven. I don't know how many beers he'd had by then. He started using the cars parked along the road like padded walls meant to be bounced off of. The drunken crowd at the doorways of both bars cheered him on. Some even trotted down the street trying to keep up with him, sliding every which a way in their sneakers and cowboy boots and falling on their asses. Harold got even more reckless.

The bartender at Jolane's had been trying to calm his patrons down or at least bring them indoors so they wouldn't be encouraging Harold. But none of 'em listened to him. I heard him call the sheriff.

Harold circled, and the drunks cheered. I wondered if any of 'em realized that it might be their cars and trucks that Harold was so glibly bouncing his pickup off of. I doubted it.

Finally, Harold didn't reappear. The onlookers waited. No Harold. They got cold standing in the doorways with nothing to occupy 'em and went indoors.

Along about three in the morning, after the bars had closed, the deputy sheriff showed up. Jolane's bartender told him what had happened and took him outside to look at the cars that were left.

"Well, where's Harold?" the deputy asked.

"Don't know. I've been tied up here. I haven't had a chance to check," the bartender answered.

The officer retraced Harold's route looking for his truck. He found it nosed into a big snow bank, where the snow had been gathered and shoved off the road a number of times, but Harold and his buddy weren't inside. The truck was mighty banged up but drivable.

From deep inside a sound sleep, Mag told me, she heard a knock and then the doorbell. She said she woke up terrified, hearing someone at the door that time of the night, someone other than Harold anyway. Sean had heard the doorbell and came to stand at her side.

The deputy sheriff told her the news. She said the worst part was that he said that there might be injuries, that he was still investigating. He asked her, "Is Harold here?"

Mag said that she told him, yes, he was, but that he was asleep. "I need to talk to him," he said. Mag said she didn't figure that she could wake Harold, drunk as he was, but she would try. She said her mind reeled with the possibilities of the wrack and ruin Harold had caused.

After shaking Harold and hollering in his ear, Mag told the deputy that she couldn't wake him. He heaved a tired, exasperated sigh, she said, and told her, "Tell him to come see me first thing after he wakes up tomorrow. I don't care how sick he feels. Good night, ma'am," and he left Mag to her own private horrors.

Harold's joyride was the talk to the town for the whole Christmas season. Having the side of a vehicle bashed in gave the owner a bit of fame and a story to tell. A small town relished an incident like this. The possibilities for gossip were endless.

Mag no longer walked like a zombie; she walked more like a tired old lady. Sean slid in and out of his days, the quietest and smoothest he'd ever been. Harold didn't show himself at the bar no more. He was buying beer and drinking it at his shop, like he used to.

The court asked each person who'd had a vehicle damaged to provide estimates of repair costs. Harold got copies of these and sent each person a down payment and a plan of repayment, as the court decision said he must. Somehow, he got to keep his license. I never figured that one out, something to do with his business and the repayment decision. As soon as he could, Harold sold a couple vehicles he'd repaired and fixed up and paid off his debt.

On January second, I saw Harold's loaded, battered pickup pass my store window, headed out a town. He'd finished up all the jobs he'd scheduled; I knew that. I hadn't known for sure that he was gonna leave. Dumbbell, wake up! I shouted at him in my mind.

Goddamn it, Harold, get it together! But he didn't hear my thoughts and just kept driving on out a town, a vague, lifeless expression on his face.

Mag and Sean came in to shop later that day. Mrs. Norton was in line to check out when they came in. "Mighty chipper for a woman whose husband just took off. Wouldn't you agree, Joe?" she whispered to me after Mag had passed by.

"A person's got a eat," I answered her. I didn't want to get into no religious come-up-ins with Mrs. Norton.

"Well, when you stray too far from the ways of the Lord, He finds ways to cut you down to size. He got to Harold, but it doesn't seem as He's yet reached Magdalena. She seems to have treated this whole thing as so much water under the bridge."

I packed Norton's groceries as quick as I could, hoping to speed her on her way. I couldn't piss her off too bad, what with her having all them kids and having to buy lots of groceries to feed 'em, but I couldn't stomach much of her retribution talk.

She said, "I wonder what it's going to take?"

Foolishly, I asked, "What's what gonna take?" I'd been trying not to pay any attention to her. I don't know why I asked her a question. I could a kicked myself.

"I wonder what terrible thing is going to have to happen to Magdalena to wake her up to the presence to the Lord," she stated matter of fact.

I was stunned, and I must a been staring at her for a while 'cause she asked, "Joe, your jaw's dragging. What's the problem? You got my total figured up?"

"Yeah, thirty-five dollars and fifty cents, please." I knew in my gut I should ream her out good, but I didn't. God help me; I didn't, and I regret my cowardly love of a dollar still. But a guy's got a make a living, don't he?

Mrs. Norton placed her money in the palm of my hand, and my

palm began sweating with the touch of it. "Bye, Joe, I'll be seeing you tomorrow. You know how all them youngsters eat." She wheeled her cart out the door. An incoming customer held it open for her. "Thank you; the Lord thanks you," I heard her say as she went out.

Rumors about the state of the Brown's marriage and about Harold and Magdalena flourished. Someone said that they heard from someone else that Mag was supplying teenagers with herbs that caused abortions. When Mrs. Norton repeated the rumor to me, I asked her, "Have you checked it out? Have you asked Mag if she's really doing that?"

"Are you kidding? What would you expect her to say? Of course she'd deny it." Mrs. Norton laughed at my ignorance. "This may be the thing that does it." She pressed her lips together in a determined frown.

"What thing?" Dummy me, I'll never learn to stop asking questions.

"The terrible thing that brings her down, Joe. The retribution of the Lord."

"I don't think so, Mrs. Norton. I don't think Mag'd be so stupid as to give abortion herbs to teenagers." I wanted to add, "or that the Lord would engineer the event," but I didn't.

The abortion rumor made the rounds, causing various responses. Some didn't believe it; some did. I heard versions of the same damn rumor six or seven times from customers. Finally, as I was checking out Mag's groceries one day, her usual: plain low fat yogurt, Muenster cheese, and old fashioned oatmeal, shit like that, I asked her, "Mag, have you heard the rumor about you giving teenagers herbs that would cause an abortion?"

She looked at me real surprised like and said, "That's silly, I don't even grow herbs that could do that, but anyone can gather them on most any of the higher slopes in the spring." She grimaced. "Who would have thought of a thing like that, Joe?"

"Beats me."

"Me too. Bye, Joe." Mag seemed a bit preoccupied that day. But then she never did put much stock in the public's opinion of her. Maybe she should a. I don't know. Maybe it would a helped squelch the rumors floating about town.

Speculation about the Browns was interrupted by talk about the surprise new couple, Whitey and Sylvia. Accompanying Whitey all over town, Sylvia clearly wanted everybody to know about the romance. She preened and pranced and wiggled her hips, stuck on Whitey like mucilage on paper. She acted like a flirtatious teenager around him, and he seemed to like it. Whitey stood with his arm hooked in hers, his battered hat on his head, grinning like a love-starved puppy and basking in his incredible good fortune.

Whitey pulled chairs out for Sylvia and carried her groceries. He worked around her place, repairing things that had set broken for years. They went out for dinners in town and as far away as in Boise. Whitey remarked, "Boise has grown a bit since I was last there in '56."

Sylvia told me, "Whitey and I are preparing furniture and decorations for our own magic sanctuary up at Mag's. I'm writing special love poems for it." She grinned real demure like. "It's colors are going to be rose and purple." I thought I might mosey up to Mag's place come summer just to see that sanctuary and to see Whitey hanging out in it. I figured I'd a seen about near everything I had a mind to see if I saw that.

I asked Frieda what she thought of Whitey's new flame. She chuckled and answered, "I thought I'd die before I saw my boy married or at least shacked up with someone. Maybe now I'll see one or the other." She picked up her sack of groceries, chuckling still. "Do you suppose it's too late for grandchildren, Joe?" She cracked up, laughing so hard I feared she'd split a gut.

Chapter 18

Harold's Face Sucked in the Sunlight

As soon as we had waved good-bye to his folks, I asked Harold to come into our bedroom. "I have something important to talk over with you."

Sullen and hung over, Harold swung the bedroom door shut. He stood with his hands resting on his hips, his fingers splayed out across the front of his worn jeans. He scowled at me. Bright sunlight streaked through the east window and across his face and shoulders. His milky white, hung over face sucked it in. His lips were parted, and he looked as if he might throw up at any moment.

I launched into what I wanted to say, my voice a little too loud and a little too strident. "I've come to a decision," I said and paused. I struggled to catch my breath. "For the sake of our relationship and for Sean, you have until the end of the year to stop drinking and to get counseling. If you don't, I want you to leave our home."

I stopped speaking, tense, waiting. I expected Harold to protest. After all, this was his home too. He had as much right to ask me to leave. He could drink in peace then. But he didn't ask me to leave. He didn't say anything. He just nodded and stood there, staring at me. I could see a tinge of sadness deep in his eyes and around the corners of his mouth, but mostly I saw wild, beyond reason anger.

My uncertainty was already building reasons for a retreat. If Harold objected, I would make deals. "I know I need to make changes too," I said. "Do you want to talk about this?" I asked.

"Why?" He shifted his gaze to the floor. "You've made up your mind." He raised his head and stared at me. "Suit yourself."

Harold's expression changed from sneer to consternation; his face was so pale, so very sad. Inside my head, I pleaded with him to be the old Harold, to reach out and tenderly hug me, hold me or at least beg, cajole, make a new promise, one that he would fulfill. He didn't.

He turned and opened the door. "Cunt," he said and walked from the room. I remained sitting on the bed, hunched over, my elbows resting on my knees. I ran my fingers up and down a piece of pink ribbon I held. I focused on the ribbon. I heard his last words over and over as I curled and slid the ribbon through my fingers.

I stared at the ribbon, crying. "Harold, you didn't mean that. You couldn't mean that." I had wanted rescue, a miracle, but now knew neither would come. I cried myself out. By then, the ribbon was limp, its ends in tatters. I stood and tossed it on the bed. I went into the bathroom to wash my face of tears.

I walked down the hall to the kitchen. The clock's hands showed noon. Sean was at school, and I knew Harold wouldn't be home until at least midnight. I put the teakettle on for hot water, and as I waited for it to heat, I thanked Harold for not protesting. I was firm again in my decision. He would either have to stop drinking or leave.

Harold descended even further into the dark recesses of alcoholism those last months of the year. When he came home at night, he was so full of alcohol I worried that his condition approached alcohol poisoning. He staggered to his shop, falling, and cursing each time he fell.

Each night I walked to the shop after I figured that he had passed out. Using a flashlight to guide me, I made sure he had gotten inside and that he hadn't started the shop on fire in a drunken attempt to light a fire in the woodstove.

I'd find him sprawled on the floor in front of the woodstove, maybe a jacket under his head for a pillow, maybe his head on the cold cement floor. I wanted to cover him, but I didn't because then he'd know that I had checked on him. I banked the fire and adjusted the damper and air intake so that the fire would last the night.

Sometimes I looked at him in the flicks of firelight. His only sign of life was an occasional belch and his light breathing. The air in the shop warmed, and the stench of stale alcohol filtered throughout it as Harold exhaled his poison into the room.

I made myself turn and leave, making sure the door was shut firmly against the freezing cold. I went back to my still warm bed and breathed in its clean smell. I lay thinking over my future, wondering. As reluctant as I was to admit it, I was relieved not to have Harold passed out next to me, not to have to contend with him belching or farting alcohol fouled emissions, not to have to contend with the stifling odors of exhaled alcohol and the other errant smells that clung to his often unwashed body and greasy clothes.

Up until I saw Harold drive off in his loaded pickup on January second, I hoped that he would relent and that I would get my old Harold back. He chose to leave town completely. He could have stayed in Halfway, but he didn't. He didn't say goodbye. He left while Sean was at school. I watched him through the living room window of our house.

He stood beside his loaded truck for a few minutes and looked toward the house. He put his hand on the door latch of his truck to open it, but he didn't. He lowered his head and looked at the ground. Again, he stood without moving for several minutes. He shifted his weight from side to side, and then he straightened until he looked rigid. He stared at me through that big window. Then he opened his pickup door, jumped in, and started the engine. He backed up, got headed down the driveway, and drove away. And that was it; he was gone.

Was that it? That couldn't be it, I told myself. But he was gone. This was what I'd wanted, wasn't it? No, what I had wanted was for Harold to stop drinking. Or leave, my mind inserted every chance it got. Or leave. He chose "or leave."

The phone rang. With tenderness, Sylvia spoke into my ear. "Harold's been sighted driving out of town in his loaded pickup. Do you want to talk about it?" Bad news traveled fast in a small town.

"It would be nice if you could come over, and we could chat about poems and writing and have chocolate chip cookies," I answered, "but I don't think I can talk about Harold leaving yet."

"I'll be right over," she said. "Bye, Mag, and hang in there, okay?'

"Okay, Sylvia," I whispered, my voice fading. I felt as if I clung to my soul by a thread. "Bye."

I hung up the phone and launched into preparations for baking a batch of chocolate chip cookies with pecans. I turned the oven dial to 350 degrees. I measured two and a fourth cups of flour into my favorite green ceramic, mixing bowl. But the phone's ringing interrupted me.

"Hello," I said as I spooned baking soda into the bowl.

"Hi, Mag, this is Evelyn. I saw Harold driving west out of town, all loaded up," she said. There was a pause. I could hear her draw deeply on her cigarette. "What I want to know is, did he finish my

Buick before he left? 'Cause I figure he's not coming back, right?"

I wanted to bang the phone down hard, hurt her ear. "Drive by the shop and check it out yourself, that's about all I can suggest." I hung up.

I lifted another bowl from the cabinet. Into it, I measured the brown and refined sugars. I added eggs and vanilla. I walked over to the refrigerator, opened it, hesitated briefly between margarine and butter, and brought the butter over to my bowl, chunking a cup's worth into small pieces and tossing them into the bowl with the eggs and sugars. With my electric beater on low, I creamed the mixture. I worked methodically.

I added the creamed mixture to the flour mixture. I thought only about the cookies I was making, nothing else. I stirred. I added chocolate chips and nuts and worked them into the dough with my fingers. Then I ladled heaping spoonfuls onto a cookie sheet.

I glanced at the time so that I would know roughly when the cookies might be ready. I picked up the teakettle and carried it to the sink. I filled it but didn't immediately take it back to the stove. Instead, I rested it on the lip of the sink.

I stared out the window at our snowy, frozen slope and at the lofty Wallowa Mountains beyond. Wind was blowing snow on the topmost peaks, and giant swirls sparkled in the sun that beamed down coldly on everything.

The phone rang again. I returned the teakettle to the stove and turned the burner on medium. Morbid curiosity drove me to answer the ring.

"Hello."

"Hello, Mag, I'm so sorry. I just heard about Harold leaving. Are you going to be all right?"

"Who is this?" I didn't recognize the voice.

"Oh, silly me, it's Marge, down at the co-op. I just heard. I was out back when Harold drove by, and Ed told me what was going on.

What happened, Mag?"

I'd only spoken to Marge as she'd rung up my purchases. She had never called me before, never been particularly friendly before. "Not now," I said and hung up.

I checked the cookies. The first batch had just a hint of browning, the way I liked them. One by one, I lifted them from the cookie sheet and set them on the wire rack to cool. I heard a knock on the door, and Sylvia let herself in.

She walked over to me on her spiked heels, her rabbit fur coat flapping in her self-made breeze. She reached for me with her thin, long fingers and rosy colored nails. We hugged. I shut my eyes.

"Okay, Mag, I smell chocolate chip cookies. Let's eat up a storm. And look what I brought." From her worn canvas bag, she withdrew a half-gallon of rocky road ice cream. "We're going to pig out. It always works for me."

"Yeah," I said. My soul seemed to ease back into me as I gained strength in Sylvia's presence. "Let's pig out."

"And, say, can we make a pot of coffee? I brought a little something to help wash all this down our gullets." She pulled out a fifth of Jack Daniel's.

My fear of alcohol surfaced, but my internal voice told me, "You're not Harold," and I said, "Yeah, sure, I'll make coffee. I think I have some half and half too."

Sylvia and I gabbed about our writing. She read me her latest poems. We ate cookies and drank our Irish coffees. Sylvia imitated Whitey in a friendly, funny way, and we laughed giddily. I didn't realize how much time had passed until Sean opened the front door and quietly walked in. I could see that he knew his dad was gone.

He headed down the hall toward his room. I called to him, "Sean, could you come here for a minute, please?"

He stopped. He must have been considering whether he wanted to obey because he stood motionless for many seconds. At last, he turned and came toward me. I put my hands on his shoulders.

"Yeah, Mom." He looked at me with those huge, soul-piercing eyes of his.

"I'm sorry, Sean. I had to do it. I . . ."

"I know." He held his gaze on me.

"Your dad didn't say goodbye because he's not thinking straight right now."

"I know."

"This just might be the thing that makes him think, causes him to get help, makes him stop drinking."

"Uhuh." I believed his wondrous eyes saw my clinging, wounded soul peeking at him from behind my back.

"He'll be back."

"You sure of that, Mom?" he asked; his shaggy, honey brown hair partially fell over one eye, but still he stared.

"No, I'm not." I pushed my fears into the center of my chest, and they made my chest ache. "I hope that's what happens."

Sylvia looked from one to the other of us as we spoke.

"Do you believe in miracles?" Sean said, still staring.

What did this little boy of mine know? "Yes, I do, Son."

He smiled sadly. "I love Dad. I hope he comes back and doesn't drink too."

He hugged me. I wanted to hang onto him forever, keep him close and safe and near. "Your dad loves you, Son." Afraid I would cry, I wanted to lighten the mood and said, "Have some cookies. They're chocolate chip."

"Okay," he said mechanically. He took a cookie, bit off a small chunk, and stood, eating it, without expression.

"Well, for Christ's sake, sit yourself down, Sean," Sylvia commanded him. "How about I get you a glass of milk to go with the cookie?"

"Okay," Sean answered, gazing at the table, I'm sure fearing for his father's well being.

When I went into town, people I barely knew stopped me. They told me how sorry they were about everything, and then they pumped me for information about Harold. We were the talk of the town, and folks wanted details. I didn't know anything about Harold's whereabouts or condition so I couldn't give them accurate information even if I'd wanted to. And I didn't want to.

So I made up stuff. I told one person that Harold had enlisted in the Navy. I told another questioner that he'd jumped ship after enlisting in the Navy. I told a third person that he'd gotten permission from the Navy to stay in Borneo, the locale where he'd gone AWOL, because he was doing such fine work teaching the natives the auto mechanics business.

The recipients of my lies listened and hesitantly asked a few questions. I elaborated. Then I looked at my watch and said, "Oh gees! Got to run, I'm late." And I dashed off.

Sylvia told me to quit messing with people. She said, "They believe you."

I hoped they did. I didn't care what they thought. I was pulling for Harold to quit drinking and for me to make it on my own. I didn't want what I considered false concern.

I often thought about why we had come to Halfway. We had come so that Harold could have his own shop and once he had his shop, stop drinking. Yes on shop. Nope on drinking. Since Harold would stop drinking in Halfway, we would have peace of mind. Nope, didn't happen. We'd be a happy family in our own home. Yes on the own home thing. I had wanted my own greenhouse and the closeness of mountains. Yes, I got both of these wishes. I was comfortable in Halfway. I didn't have all the things I'd hoped for, but I had plenty. Enough. The big hole was Harold.

But I couldn't hide in a small town. I could hide from the rest of the world, but I couldn't hide myself. A small town accentuated all aspects of me. Sometimes that worked to my benefit, sometimes not. And a small town couldn't bring me peace of mind. I had to bring myself peace of mind. I was still working on that one. I figured that it was a long way off.

I threw myself into working with my plants in the greenhouse and once the snow melted, outside the greenhouse. I trimmed mulched, and fertilized my roses. Spreading manure, I readied the garden and the flowerbeds for spring. I pruned fruit trees and cut back grapes and raspberries. I reset my strawberries, filling a trough beneath them with manure. In the greenhouse, I started basil, oregano, and aloe. The feel of the moist dirt and the frailty of the young plants soothed my stress and eased me back into the natural rhythms of the living world all around me.

Then Whitey and Sylvia became a couple. I chuckled each time I saw them. The sight of those two lovers made me believe in romance all over again. Whitey beamed. His ruddy cheeks were rosy with happiness. He cooed to Sylvia as much as she flounced and cooed to him. He sent her flowers and sappy cards. She wrote him love poems and designed a sanctuary dedicated to their love. They acted as if they were nineteen instead of in their sixties.

Even Frieda was affected. She waded through the snow, wearing her black rubber snow boots, telling everybody about her son's romance. She'd never been a gossip, but she wanted everyone to know about her son's great love. She was radiant.

And Frieda loved having Sylvia around. The two of them visited while preparing meals. They visited over cleaning up. I enjoyed their chatter and hearing their reminiscences. Their utter joy of living always leaped, galloping and dancing, from their mouths, present in every syllable. But Frieda wasn't as strong as she had been before her pneumonia, and Sylvia took her place, at Whitey's side, during calving season. Frieda approved of her replacement.

I was making it through my days. I worried about Harold. I felt guilty and angry, but I was making it. Then my parents called to tell me that they were coming for a visit. I hadn't told them that Harold was gone and that I didn't know where he was. Since I preferred they didn't know until I felt stronger, I didn't want them to come. But my mother said, "Our flight arrives April thirtieth, into Portland this time. We'll do a little sight seeing along the way to your place."

"The weather could still be a little cold the further east you get from Portland," I warned them.

"We're used to that. Remember, we're from Iowa. We know cold," my father assured me.

I couldn't dissuade them from coming, and they arrived in the evening on May first. Sean was already asleep when they got here. I hurried out to meet them. As we hugged, they began asking questions.

"Harold's shop looked like it had been closed up for some time," my dad said. He looked around. I knew that someone in town had told them he was gone. It was too late for Harold to have been at his shop. My dad reached into the car and pulled out a sack of groceries. Yup, someone had told them, probably overjoyed that they'd gotten to be the one to tell.

I decided to get the inevitable over with. "Harold's gone. I told him to quit drinking or leave. He left." I lifted my hands up in a "that's it" gesture, then let them drop against my sides.

My mother looked at my father with an "I could have told you that this would happen" expression on her face; she said, "Hon, it was just a matter of time." She looked at me with a tight-lipped smile.

"You betcha, doom and gloom were destined to come from day one of our marriage. What can I say, Mom, but then we're not going to get into it." My parents had been against my marriage, but not because of Harold's drinking. That hadn't been apparent as a problem when we were first married. They had been against it because he was a mechanic. They had hoped for a doctor or a lawyer as a son-in-law. I had eloped with Harold.

I grabbed a suitcase and trudged toward the house. My feet, clad only in my fuzzy slippers, were beginning to get cold. "Come on in," I said. "It's May, but it's cold out here." I heard them murmuring behind me. Conspirators, my paranoid mind told me, and I tried to ignore their whispers. "I'll get the rest of your bags. Watch your step. It could be slippery on the doorstep. It rained quite a bit today."

I set the suitcase in the spare bedroom and rushed back outside to get the others, but my parents had beaten me to them. My dad carried their two large, black suitcases; behind him, my mother toted her small red suitcase and the grocery bag I had seen earlier. I took the groceries from my mother and set them on the counter. She looked around the room. "We made a lot of changes since you last saw the place," I said. I lifted one of the suitcases from my father's hand and headed down the hall with it.

Once we were all in the living room again, I called them over to the dining room table where I had spread out pictures of Sean and me. I planned to use these as a diversion, to avoid talking about Harold.

"Come gather around. I made a cake, and I'm brewing some decaf. It'll be ready soon. Let me tell you all about the cross country skiing Sean and I did this winter."

My parents were a bit ruffled and uncertain. They listened quietly and ate cake while I talked about the pictures of brilliant, sunny days, full of whiteness and two smiling people dressed for cold. They didn't express much in the way of a response, but then they were probably having difficulty processing all this new information. I knew they cared. They liked Harold despite their initial opposition, and of course they had hoped that I'd have a happy marriage.

They went to their room without further comment about Harold; they needed time to process. I imagined them, like two generals, planning their moves once they got more information, after they figured out what would be the best outcome, to them.

As a countermeasure, I planned too. I arranged for constant company for the duration of their visit. I knew they wouldn't talk to me about Harold if other people were around. I arranged for people to be around almost all the time. I knew I was silly to do this, but I felt too weak to talk to my parents about Harold, especially since I didn't know what to say.

The first day, we spent with Frieda, Whitey, and Sylvia. While Whitey excused himself at various times to tend to his cows, Sylvia and Frieda more than filled the gap of his absence. They chatted enthusiastically with my parents all through our lunch with them. Frieda asked my parents so many questions that they were kept busy responding to her, and Sylvia flashed her engagement ring and enthused about her upcoming June wedding. Everything was going so well that they asked us to stay for dinner.

When we returned home that night, my mom said, "We need to talk."

I begged off, saying that I was really tired. "How about tomorrow?"

"Now is better," my mother answered. She headed toward the kitchen and began preparations for coffee.

"I'm sorry. I can't. I worked hard in the greenhouse so that I could have this time free to spend with you, and I'm really tired." Since guilt worked for them, I thought I'd try it.

"You could sleep in," my mother said.

"No, I can't," I responded. "Sean has to be up for school, and we're going to the Episcopalian Spring Fling Second Hand Sale. You have to get there early to get the good stuff. Then there's the luncheon. Then there's the fashion show that the Home Ec class at the high school's presenting, and there's a tea after that. And we're scheduled for dinner and a movie tomorrow night with Whitey and Sylvia." I said all this rapidly, in one breath.

My mother looked over at my father. They were onto me, but they didn't know how to handle this. A frontal assault, they could handle, but this stumped them. And maybe I was misjudging them, maybe they would be gentle mentors, but foolishly I guessed, I was determined not to find out. Their visit shoved that stubborn, independent streak in me to the forefront. This characteristic of mine could be a major obstacle; I knew that. But knowing this didn't stop me from acting like an idiot loner screaming, "I am a rock; I am an island." This made me realize that I needed to go back to counseling.

The visit whizzed by; my parents looked tired. I was tired. We visited people and attended social functions nonstop for five days. As we loaded their car for their departure, my mother made one last effort to discuss Harold, mentioning my "dismal future in this small town alone" and "a possible return to Iowa."

"No, Mom, this is my home. I'm staying in Halfway." I leaned into the car and kissed them good-bye. I told them, "Don't worry. We'll talk more next time. It's just too soon." I heard the phone ringing.

"I'd better get that. I'm expecting a buyer to be calling. That might be her. You two be careful now. Be sure and stop for the night as soon as you get tired. I love you. Bye," I called over my shoulder as I dashed for the phone, leaving my parents hanging and feeling guilty that I had. I hadn't been fair to them; they felt badly. I hadn't comforted them. "Add that to the list of my failings," I whispered as I gave them one last wave and swung into the house.

"Hello," I huffed into the receiver.

"Mag, it's me," Harold said. He was crying. "It's me, Mag." He sobbed openly.

"Where are you, Harold?" I asked. I didn't know what was coming. My breath grew shallow.

"I'm in Phoenix, Mag. I want to come home. Please, Mag." He

sobbed deeply. My heart ripped.

"Have you stopped drinking, Harold?" I asked. I breathed in and out, in and out. What would I do if he said he had stopped? I didn't know.

"Mag, I can't do it alone. I want to come home, Mag. Please."

"Harold, you couldn't stop drinking when you were with me."

"It'll be different now. I swear. Please, please, Mag. I'm begging you." He pleaded, sobbing.

"Harold, I would love to say, yes, come home, but I can't. I can't ask you to come home until you've stopped drinking. Until you've proven your determination to continue to not drink." I winced with each word. I knew that I had to say those words; with Harold sobbing and begging, I had to say no.

"Doesn't our love mean anything to you, Mag?"

Low blow, Harold, I thought. "It means everything to me. And I won't have it dragged through the slime of booze any longer," I said and paused, readying myself for my next words. "I'd rather not have you at all than have you drinking."

I heard Harold sobbing.

"Why don't you give me your address so that Sean and I can write you? Your phone number would be good too."

Harold rattled off a phone number and an address and apartment number. "Are you working?" I asked.

"Yeah, I got a mechanics job in a shop here," he answered through sniffles. "I'm starting to get a handle on my finances."

"That's good." I was glad he was able to work.

"I'll send you some money as soon as I can."

"That's not what I'm worried about just now," I assured him, but actually, I was worried about money. Things were tight. "I'm worried about you."

"The guys in the shop go out for beers after work each night," he said.

"Yeah?"

"I go with. Except they go home at six, and I stay until closing."

"Did you go out last night?" I asked. It was a Tuesday morning.

"Yes," he answered. He sobbed loudly into the phone. "I'm weak, Mag. I need you to keep me on the straight and narrow."

"I can't do that. I wasn't doing it. Was I, Harold?"

"No, I guess not. Gees, Mag, I don't know what I'm going to do."

"You have to decide that for yourself, Harold. I can't do it for you."

"I have to get to work, Mag."

"Okay, Harold. Call when Sean's home from school. He misses you."

"Okay, I miss him too. I miss you. I love you, Mag."

"I love you too."

"Bye."

"Bye."

The phone clicked. Harold had hung up. I was so afraid, so guilt filled, so unsure.

Chapter 19

Whitey's and Sylvia's Wedding

Shit! Give Christ a horse and send him on a Crusade! How was I supposed to know that her parents didn't know that Harold was gone?

Mag's parents came into the store, saying they'd just pulled into town for a visit, and her dad asked how Harold's car repair business was going. All I said was, "Mighty generous of Harold to be teaching them Borneo fellas how to fix cars." I was only trying to shed a positive light on the matter. I didn't realize they didn't even know that he'd left Halfway, let alone the country.

As soon as Mag's dad got that shocked expression on his face, and her mother's mouth fell open, I knew I'd messed up. I tried to backtrack by saying, "So's I hear anyway. Ain't necessarily so. Half of what you hear is way out a the ballpark. You might check Harold's shop on the way up to Mag's. See if you see him." I told 'em where they could find the buffered aspirin, the reason they'd come in. I was sweating like a pig on a barbeque spit. I turned to check out old lady Stewart and giving 'em a nod, said, "Have a nice visit now." I saw them get their aspirin, and then they got a cart. They spent considerable time wandering up and down the aisles, tossing stuff in their basket, heads together, whispering to beat the band.

Mag never asked me how her folks found out about Harold, and I sure wasn't gonna mention it to her. She was so busy planting, weeding, and making deliveries that she was always in a rush when she came into my store. She'd fly through the aisles tossing stuff into her cart, then wait, nervous as a cat in a violin factory, as I totaled her bill, and no sooner had I handed her the receipt as she'd tear out a here like she was on fire. We barely got in a few words of chatting, hardly enough to determine the weather or the time of day.

On the fifth of June, my wife and I got an invitation to Whitey's and Sylvia's wedding. The whole town was invited to the reception, but only a limited number of us were asked into the church, the wedding part. I didn't consider this to be none too great a privilege but the misses sure did. She announced to me that we were going to Baker City to shop for new clothes for the wedding.

"Jesus Christ, Leona, what the hell do we need new clothes for? We're not getting married." I never could understand that woman.

"We're invited to the wedding. Everybody's gonna be coming to us when we arrive at the reception and asking us what the wedding was like. We have to look decent. People will be looking up to us." She nodded my nod, she'd kind a adopted it over the years, pissed me off.

She had her mind set, and there was no turning her back. We went to Baker City and got them clothes. New clothes are God awful uncomfortable. Leona bought some fluffy blue thing, had this damned stiff, blue netting bouncing out in circles all the way down the skirt. She made me buy a new suit, hard to imagine, ain't it, a new suit just to attend a wedding. But she said my thirty year old suit wasn't good enough no more, 'sides the fact that it didn't really fit no longer.

The fifteenth of June rolled around, the day of the wedding. I planned on working in the store until just before it started. Concentrating on work was pretty hard to do though, what with Leona calling every ten minutes asking me when I was coming home to get ready. Every time, I told her, "Soon enough, don't sweat it," and hung up.

The last time she called, I hollered, "When I damned well feel like it," but as soon as I hung up the phone, I told Dolores to take over and headed out the door to go home and get ready to attend the damned wedding.

We got to the church early, no wonder, considering how Leona was carrying on. A little girl named Darlene, Sylvia's high school aged granddaughter, asked us which side, bride's or groom's. We said either side was fine. She said, "Cool," and led us into the church.

The Episcopalian Church was a drafty, old, wood frame building. The windows were just regular windows, aluminum frames, yellow curtains. The floor was dark lacquered pine, pitted and slivered. The pews were pine too, but they were clear stained so that they looked kind a yellowish.

I'm not sure what the altar was made of. Could a been a folding table for all I knew. It was hidden behind a fancy religious cloth that had gold braid all over it and a big gold color cross in the center with a gold color circle around it. Normally three candles burned on the altar, and, in the center, a Bible was propped open with a golden metal cross behind it.

For Whitey and Sylvia's wedding, the place was filled with flowers. Bouquets of pink roses stood on the altar where the candles and Bible usually stood. At the end of every pew row, up against the wall or window, was a tall, spidery metal stand topped with a huge vase full of all colors of flowers. Pale pink, baby blue, and ivory colored ribbon draped from window to window. Each window had a huge bow placed above it. All across the front of the church, more black and white metal stands held vases of roses and carnations and a mix of every color of flower. The stink of all them different kind a flowers drifted together and hung heavy in the air.

Leona drew in her breath and put her blue-gloved hands to her cheeks as we walked to our seats. She was beside herself with wonder. A person'd thought she'd seen the great pyramids or something. "Look at this, Joe. Ain't it something. Oh Lord!"

"Put your hands down and close your mouth, for Christ's sake," I muttered. "You're bordering on embarrassing me." She shot me a peeved look and lowered her blue gloves. Then she noticed the display at the front of the church and began again with patting her cheeks and exclaiming on the beauty of it all.

Matters weren't helped none when Nancy and Bob sat down next to her. Nancy leaned over Bob, and the two of them went on and on about the particulars of the flowers. Bob stared straight ahead. I tried to catch his eye to show how disgusted I was with this female carrying on, but he never wavered his focus from the spot at the front of the church where the candles normally would a stood on the altar.

In no time at all the church began to fill with guests. Leona and Nancy acted like they were the official greeters, waving and nodding and acknowledging folks as they came in.

Old Mrs. Hampton creaked over to the piano that was off to the left side up front. She settled herself on the bench, which was no easy matter for her. I wanted to go shove her old body down 'cause she hung suspended like, slowly lowering herself for what seemed like hours. Finally, with a tiny plop, her scrawny butt hit the bench. Everyone in the church hushed.

Slowly, she raised her long, skinny fingers, with the big knots for knuckles. She held her hands poised over the keys for at least two minutes as she sat there with her eyes closed. I was afraid that she'd fallen asleep.

Then she turned her leathery, scrawny neck, opened her eyes, and looked toward the back of the church. Someone, I think it was Charles, Sylvia's only child, who lived in New York City, nodded at her. She nodded back.

Her fingers came crashing down on the piano. Strains of the wedding march boomed out a that piano louder than all get out. Old Mrs. Hampton added trills and crescendos. Her hands were dancing over them keys. I looked at her face. Her eyes were shut.

The wedding party made their way down the aisle. Frieda and Whitey's lifetime friend, Andy, were first. Frieda smiled peacefully and leaned on him for support. Then came Sylvia's daughter-in-law, Becky, on the arm of her grandson, Charles Junior.

Magdalena and Sean followed. My wife told me that the long, pale pink satin number Mag was wearing was a bride's maid's dress. With her long, dark hair and ruddy tan from being outside all the time, she was pretty enough. Sean looked like a little grown up in the light gray tux he was wearing. He had the handsome looks of his dad. The youngest of Charles's kids, a cute little dark haired girl named Sue, carried the rings on a pink satin pillow.

Then came Sylvia on her son Charles' arm. I'd been waiting for this. I couldn't believe my eyes. She was rigged out in the whole shebang. Her wedding gown was white, stark raving white satin. Every square inch of it was covered with lace. Lace down her arms and stretched between her fingers. Lace over her chest and a lace veil over her face and her red bouffant wig. Lace over the full, billowing skirt that dragged on the floor and had a train a mile long. A train that the same high school aged granddaughter who had seated us carried the end of.

Sylvia carried a bouquet of tiny pink and white roses. It was the size of a dinner plate. Pale pink, baby blue, and ivory ribbons that matched the ribbons on the walls trailed from it.

She was beaming. Her rosy lips were pulled so far back from those big white teeth of hers that I thought they might pop right out a her mouth even if they weren't false. Her cheeks were rosy as a monkey's bottom. Her eyes sparkled diamonds. She looked around at each and every one of us. God, she looked happy.

Charles, on the other hand, looked nervous and uncomfortable. I figured that he was no longer used to the goings on of the town he was raised in.

Whitey had entered the church from a side door. He was dressed in a gray tux too. His silvery white hair and leathery tanned skin above that gray tux made him look like a movie star.

He looked only at Sylvia. And the look he gave her was one of pure joy, like he'd died and gone to heaven. Happy three times over! Rosy cheeks to match Sylvia's, eyes big as saucers staring at his dressed in white bride. He came to stand next to George, in his own gray tux.

I had to admit, Leona was right. This was gonna be one day to remember. I think even most of the men were caught up in Sylvia and Whitey's romantic second chance. Old Mrs. Hampton boomed on, pounding that Acrosonic a good lick till that giant train of Sylvia's was arranged and everyone was in place. I swear, she knew when to stop at the very right time even though her eyes were closed tight.

Sylvia and Whitey had written their own vows. Gees! They lost me on this. Sa-a-a-ppy! The women oohed and aahed all over the place. A few, including my wife, started to cry. I could hear blubbering and rustling hankies all over that tiny church.

Finally they said their I do's, exchanged rings, and kissed. I didn't know old Whitey had such passionate kissing ability. And everybody cheered. I saw a few men wipe their eyes.

Old Mrs. Hampton started playing a different song; I didn't recognize it. Leona said it was a rock n' roll tune, "You're So Beautiful to Me", or some such fool nonsense. Sylvia and Whitey streamed out, Sylvia holding her train over one arm, exploding with good cheer, love, and sex, yes sex.

When we got up to Sylvia and Whitey in the receiving line, I could see what all them pink papers were that I'd seen the women in front of us holding. They were copies of the wedding vows. Leona twittered, "Yes, Sylvia, I do want a copy." She hugged Sylvia and Whitey, congratulating 'em over and over.

I wanted to shake hands, but Sylvia grabbed me and hugged me, plastering my cheek with a big wet kiss. Whitey shook my hand. He was grinning a silly ass grin. "Congratulations, Whitey," I told him.

"Yah, yah," he answered and grinned even wider.

Then came the reception at the town park. We drove over from the church. The park was only a block square. It was busting at the seams with people. Newly shined cars and pickups were jammed into every available space in a two-block radius around that park.

I dropped off Leona and was pulling away to find a spot to park when she called in the window, "Don't forget to get the fruit salad from the trunk."

Leona had mixed up about ten gallons of that fruit salad with the tiny marshmallows and sour cream. That was our contribution to the reception potluck in the park. My part of it was to carry it from the trunk of our car to the picnic table. It near broke my back carrying it all the way to the park. If I'd a known that there was so much salad I'd a dropped it off with Leona.

I found Leona and told her that I'd delivered her salad and that I'd probably be crippled for the rest of my life 'cause of it. I don't think she was listening 'cause she said, "That's nice, Joe." Then she got all excited and pointing with both hands, shouted, "Here comes the bride and groom. Hooray! Here they come!" She was jumping up and down. I thought she'd gone nuts.

Then I saw the whole rest of the mob at the park moving toward the entrance as one jumping, clapping mass. They jammed the gates. Whitey and Sylvia had been driven over from the church in a gray limo. Whitey got out; he grinned and waved. People cheered and clapped.

When Sylvia stuck a white, high-heeled shoe out the door of that limo, the crowd began cheering crazily. Whitey reached his hand inside the limo to assist his bride. As Sylvia slowly slid her entire body out a the car, the crowd erupted with wild shouting, clapping, and jumping, trying to get a look at her. You'd a thought she was the Queen of Sheba.

Once all of her was out a the car, the cheering compounded itself. Whispers of "Ain't she lovely." "She's wearing white, can you believe it, but why not, ain't she be-e-e-autiful!" and "They look so-o-o-o-o happy!" tittered and bounced from person to person.

Then Sylvia, linked to Whitey, started working the crowd. Sylvia's lips were likely plum wore off by that evening; she laid so many kisses on so many cheeks, bearded and unbearded. Whitey kept raising his hand to his head to tip the hat that wasn't there.

Folks asked Leona and I about the wedding just like Leona said they would. She gave me an "I told you so" look. I almost felt important in my new suit, white shirt, and maroon tie. For an afternoon, I was one of the in-crowd; I'd been at the wedding of the century in Halfway.

Food was piled along five or six picnic tables, and grills were smoking up the atmosphere, frying hot dogs and hamburgers. Sylvia and Whitey had sprung for kegs of beer and bottles of every color of wine known to mankind. Tubs of pop cooling in ice were setting all over the park. The day was sunny with a tinge of a cool breeze.

A live band, brought in from Baker City, assembled and started playing tunes from the forties and fifties. All the old codgers and their wives commenced swaying and making their way to the cement slab dance floor. Leona got that fuzzy look in her eyes. I knew what was coming next.

She said, "Joe, we haven't danced in ages. Come on, Joe, let's dance." And she tugged at my arm, yanking me in the direction of the dance floor.

"Leona, you know how I hate to dance. Lay off, for Christ's sake."

"Joe, even Ed's dancing."

"Good for Ed. Unhand me, Leona." I pried her gripping fingers from my arm.

"Joe, you promised."

"I never did no such thing!"

"Yes, you did. Last Christmas when we discussed your not dancing at Bob and Nancy's Christmas party."

"I just wanted you to stop crying, is all."

"But you promised, Joe. Everyone else is dancing."

She stared at me with that fuzzy eyed look of hers. I knew pretty soon her eyes'd squeeze shut, and the tears would start. I weighed in my mind the chore of dancing versus the pain in the ass of Leona crying. That woman's tears knotted my gut up fierce.

I said, "I'll dance one dance; that's all."

Leona cheered, "Oooh-eey! Just you wait, you'll be having such a good time that you'll want to keep dancing all night!" She pranced up to the cement slab with her stiff blue netting jutting this way and that with each wiggle of her hips.

"Christ All Mighty, what have I got myself in for?" I said.

Leona finagled two more dances out a me, but that was all. God, I hated dancing, but she did get a thrill from it.

Along about six o' clock, the limo pulled up to the park entrance again. The crowd hushed. The band silenced except for the drummer, and he began a loud drum roll. Sylvia and Whitey said their last good-byes and waved to everyone. Sylvia hugged Charles, his wife, their three kids, Magdalena, Sean, and Frieda. Whitey followed close behind doing the same.

Everyone called, "Good-bye! Good-bye! Have a good trip!" And Sylvia and Whitey dove into the limo and were driven off.

Whitey, who had just recently renewed contact with the outside world, was on his way to Europe for a one-month honeymoon. Andy was gonna look after his cows and pastures. Mag was gonna check on Frieda. The fairytale wedding moved on to the fairytale honeymoon. How was life in Halfway ever gonna measure up for the happy couple after this?

Sean didn't go see his dad until he'd quit drinking for a time. That was along about August, eight months after Harold had left. His mother drove him to Boise and put him on a plane to Phoenix.

The first time I saw Mag in the store after I'd heard this, I muddled over how to ask her how long Harold had not been drinking. She must a read my mind 'cause she said, "Yeah, Joe, Harold says he's stopped drinking now for two months, and he wanted Sean to come down. " She took a twenty from her wallet to pay for the groceries. "Harold's going to stay in Phoenix for a while longer to make sure he can hold it together. He says he doesn't think he should see me until he's more firm in his sobriety. I agree."

"Seems things are looking up," I said.

She nodded. "Yeah," she answered. She fumbled with putting the change in her purse. She looked up at me; her eyes were sad. "But you know, Joe. This waiting is hard." She looked longingly out the window.

"Oh, things will work out soon, Mag," I said. That was all I could think to say.

"I hope so, Joe, because I just about have no more waiting in me." She picked up her bag of groceries, tossed a "Bye" my way and thumped out the door in her work boots.

"Gees," I thought, "Poor Mag." Wasn't that just the way life was. Like a bucket a worms, all wiggly and slimy and forever slipping out a your grasp. Life held out the chance of catching something great with them worms, just enough to egg a person on so's he couldn't help but to keep grabbing for them slimy bastards.

I thought about Leona and me. I knew I cut her to the bone sometimes. I regretted it later. But at the time I did it I didn't care; I was mad or tired or fed up. Or all three. And she ripped at me from time to time too. Same reasons, I was sure.

I was getting near teared up thinking about it. I figured I'd better go home and dance one more dance with Leona before she had no more waiting in her.

Chapter 20

The Slide Show

According to Halfway custom, when anyone took a vacation outside Baker County, that person shared the trip with the rest of the town by hosting a lecture and slide show at the Grange Hall shortly after returning. Those interested in learning about their neighbor's vacation brought a dessert and arrived at least twenty to thirty minutes early to socialize and eat. Folks were eager to learn about Whitey and Sylvia's honeymoon, but three weeks after their return, the lovebirds hadn't scheduled a date. These folks were getting antsy.

One day, Joe asked me, "When are Whitey and Sylvia gonna have their slide show, Mag?"

"Soon, Joe, soon," I answered. "You know how newlyweds are." Those two were acting like twenty year olds.

"Folks are asking me every day when they're gonna do it. I need to know so's I can keep folks informed." He placed my granola and yogurt in my bag extra carefully. "The freshness is gonna be plum wore off if they don't do it pretty soon, Mag." He didn't bother to hide his impatience.

"Okay," I said, "I'll get a date out of them. How about next Friday, Joe?"

"Friday's the men's softball game against Baker City. It could run late into the evening. They better pick another night." He waited for me to suggest another possibility. He hadn't given me my total yet.

"How's Saturday evening? Do you suppose that date would fit into everyone's social calendar?" I was getting impatient too. It wasn't as though I didn't have enough on my mind without worrying about scheduling Whitey and Sylvia's events.

"Naw, that wouldn't be no good. That's when them Chautauqua musicians put on their performance. Those culture club people are most likely interested in the trip and would be pissed off if they had to choose." He waited again.

"Well, how about Sunday?" I asked. I wondered why seeing the honeymoon slides right away was so important if the town's social calendar was already so packed.

"Sunday evening about eight o' clock would be great," Joe said and smiled. "That'll be eight fifty-two, Mag." He shoved the grocery bag toward me and nodded, Joe's signal that he'd concluded business.

I handed him a ten. He asked, "You got two cents?"

"Yeah, here you go."

He handed me one-fifty in change. "Thanks, Mag, Now you have a good day. I'll look forward to seeing you at the slide show. You get those two to agree to Sunday now, okay?"

"I'll do my best, Joe." I turned to go.

"Oh, the slide show's finally gonna happen," said old Mrs. Hampton, who was waiting to check out next, "'Bout time. When,

Mag?"

"Maybe Sunday at eight at the Grange Hall, Mrs. Hampton. Bye," I called and waved to Joe and her.

As I stepped outside the store's entrance, Sally Weaver flipped her arm out sideways and grabbed my arm. She said, "They can't keep us waiting forever, Mag. When're they gonna do it?"

"Maybe Sunday at eight at the Grange Hall."

Her grip loosened. She asked, "Usual refreshments?" Sally was tiny, but she was strong.

"Uhuh. You bring sweets, and I'll bring the coffee." I rubbed the spot where she had latched onto my arm.

"Usually the slide person brings the half and half and the sugar too," she reminded me. She dug in her purse until she located what she was looking for, her shopping list.

"Okay, I'll do that." I turned to go.

"Ain't nothing pornographic in them slides, is there?" Sally was grabbing for my arm again.

I moved out of her reach. "I wouldn't know, Sally. Whitey and Sylvia are awfully lovey-dovey, might be some indecent exposure, you never know," I told her, grinned, and headed toward my truck again.

"Could you ask them to sort through their pictures and eliminate the risqué ones?"

"No, I couldn't, but if you're concerned about it, why don't you ask them that question, Sally?" I called.

"Ah, Sylvia scares me a might. I don't think I could."

"Then I guess you'll see whatever they bring. I haven't even cleared that date with them, by the way. Joe pressured a possible date from me." I slid behind the steering wheel.

"Well, those two have been holed up together at Whitey's since they got back so's no one has gotten a chance to ask them."

I glanced at my watch. "I have to run, Sally. Bye."

"Could you bring some of that powdered coffee creamer? Some folks prefer that you know."

"Will do, Sally."

She smiled, satisfied. "See you Sunday, Magdalena."

"See you, Sally," I answered and began humming "Ride Sally Ride;" it happened every time I saw her.

On Sunday night, I arrived at the Grange Hall at six-thirty so that I could help Whitey and Sylvia set up; I felt a guilty obligation since I was the one who had committed them to do this. Old Mrs. Hampton was already sitting on a folding chair outside the door; a shiny, red plastic purse rested in her lap, and her long knobby fingers perched on top of it. She looked like an aged condor about to take flight.

"Hi, Mrs. Hampton," I said. "You have a bit of a wait. The slides don't start until eight."

"No matter, I don't have nothing better to do," she answered dryly. "You gonna start the coffee early?"

"I could."

"You best do that. And did you remember to bring any of the powdered creamer?" She looked at me with her obsidian black eyes. "Sally said she reminded you."

"Huh? Oh, the creamer. Yes, I brought the creamer." I fiddled with getting the key I'd picked up at the fire station to fit into the old galvanized padlock. As I opened the door, a rush of sweaty, stale air escaped into the outdoors. Square dancing practice had been held in this room earlier in the afternoon.

"Come on in, Mrs. Hampton. As soon as I bring in the supplies, I'll start coffee." I offered her my hand to assist her rising. She arced up slowly, barely leaning on me, and just as slowly, she teetered toward the door. I headed to my truck to get the slide projector.

After I set down the projector, I unfolded a chair for Mrs. Hampton, who'd just then made it into the room, and I began setting up curved rows of chairs facing the screen that pulled from the ceiling at the far end of the long, rectangular room. I opened all of the old wood frame windows that would open, about half were permanently stuck shut.

Sean, who'd been outside playing on the monkey bars, came in to help. "Hi, Mrs. Hampton," he said. She nodded at him.

I ran water into the Grange Hall's large coffee maker, filling the receptacle with the amount of coffee Sylvia had told me would suffice, set it on a table where its cord could reach a plug, and turned it on to brew.

"It will be a while until that's ready," I called over to Mrs. Hampton, who was eying the coffee making progress. She nodded.

The librarian at the county library in Baker City had gathered together books that featured places Whitey and Sylvia had been. I'd picked them up Friday after my dental appointment. They were coffee table type books, large with big glossy pictures. I placed them, opened to no particular pages, on a table next to the coffee and dessert table.

Bob arrived about seven to set up the slide projector. First, he resituated the little wooden table it was on numerous times, searching for "the perfect place" that would yield a clear picture that everybody could see. Then, he began what seemed like an endless process of minuscule focusing adjustments, using the slides he'd brought in for this purpose. Sean sat down to watch Bob's show.

About seven-fifteen, Sylvia burst through the door. She was dressed in a red and orange puffy sleeved, full-skirted Spanish dress. "Olla," she called. "Buenes noches." She walked over to Mrs. Hampton and kissed her on the crown of her white hair.

Whitey arrived with Frieda on his arm shortly after Sylvia's grand entrance. He carried two huge boxes filled with books and mementos of their honeymoon adventure. He tipped his hat to Mrs. Hampton, Bob, Sean, and myself.

Frieda whispered, "Hide me," to Whitey when she saw Mrs. Hampton notice her and began her slow ascent. She waved and called out, "Hello there, Betsy, just stay where you are. I'll talk to you in a while. I have to help Magdalena get ready."

Frieda hurried over to me as best she could on her bad ankles. She turned her back on the slowly approaching Betsy Hampton and whispered to me, "Quick, what can I do?"

"You could set out cups for coffee while I finish setting up chairs."

"Thanks," Frieda said. "Betsy's a dear, but she bugs the hell out a me."

"Bring those boxes over here, mi esposo," Sylvia sang out merrily to Whitey. She and Whitey arranged their remembrances on the table with the books from the library. Then Whitey carried the books he had brought to the table with the slide projector and set them down.

Guests began arriving, bearing their sweets. Sylvia greeted them and helped them arrange their contributions on the table.

She remarked over each dessert, "Oh how lovely! Looks almost too pretty to eat." Periodically, I checked on Bob, who was still clicking and adjusting the slide projector. About fifty or sixty people milled about, chatting and having coffee and dessert. A few scrutinized the souvenirs or leafed through the travel books and brochures.

At eight o'clock, Sylvia clapped her hands over her head while swaying through the crowd saying, "Time to sit. Show time."

Frieda inched away from Mrs. Hampton, saying, " I need to fill my plate and coffee cup. Wouldn't want to run dry during the show." She returned with a full plate and brimming cup and sat next to me. Betsy reappeared from somewhere and slowly lowered herself onto the chair next to Frieda. "Damn," Frieda muttered.

Whitey and Sylvia walked to the front of the room, to where a little wooden podium stood. Whitey had gotten his books and the remote clicker for the slide projector. His imagination, simmering for sixty years as he wandered his fields, had been ignited by his honeymoon trip in Europe. He had returned frantic with excitement, eager to learn more.

Sylvia and Whitey ran their lecture like a duo of sports announcers. Sylvia served as the "color" person, adding details of style, fragments of conversations, or a person's occupation while Whitey assumed the factual narration role. His spirited monologue contained so many historical facts and anecdotes that I kept checking to see where he kept his notes, but he had none.

He referred to his books occasionally, not to read excerpts or anything like that. He knew the information by heart, but to show us where we might, in fact should, look for more information ourselves.

He elevated a thick History of Italy volume in his right hand and said, "You need to realize what's out there, because if it's in this world, it's also embedded somewhere inside each and every one of us. Our past is here." He paused, pointing to his chest with his free hand, the heavy book in his other hand still raised above his head. He could have been a preacher proclaiming the righteousness of his upraised holy book.

He gazed solemnly around the darkened room. The hairs along my spine rose in anticipation. I stared at Whitey as if some great revelation would come with his next words. His thrill was contagious.

He continued, "We are all part of the whole world, the ugly and the glorious." His gaze landed on Sylvia. "It took me sixty years and my own resplendent explorer, Sylvia, to realize the full enormity of this."

He surveyed the crowd again. Softly, he said, "My fields, my cows, and the towering Wallowas have now expanded in my thoughts as I observe all aspects of their existence. They are part of me. I am part of them. And we are all part of everything that has ever been and will ever be." He shook the upraised book. "We need to know that. Our children need to know that."

The room had gotten utterly still. No one even whispered. I heard the coffee maker sputter and raindrops drip from the eaves of the roof and splatter into puddles below. Whitey spoke of vastness, of forever. I felt awed; I think most of us did. After a few moments of this startling oration, Whitey lowered his book and cleared his throat. He glanced over at Sylvia and grinned. "Okay folks," he said, "time for intermission."

Whitey and Sylvia had taken so many slides that they'd had to edit considerably to reduce their show to a three-hour length, so the intermission was a welcome relief. People spoke in hushed tones, as if they were in church. Andy, with as many winters of feeding cows and enduring hardships behind him as Whitey, walked up to his pal and held out his hand to shake. Whitey nodded and reached out his hand. The two long time friends solemnly shook hands.

Andy said, "We always knew these things, but we never took in the full power of it all." He placed his left hand on top of their shaking hands. "It's like a quarter inch of wet snow on top of a whole mountain of frozen snow. It doesn't seem like much until it comes thundering down on you in an avalanche."

He looked at Whitey in that intense way people accustomed to looking long distances view objects close at hand. "And if that crystalline quarter inch is so all dang powerful, just think what's hidden inside the mountain."

"Yah, yah," Whitey answered him. "There's no end to the learning."

Sean went to see his dad in August. The visit went well; Sean said that his dad wasn't drinking and that they had fun. We eased into fall. Sean began second grade. The weather cooled, the nighttime frosts started, and finally the depths of winter cold were upon us.

In February on the 15th, Frieda died. Her death was both expected and startling. No one knew her exact age, even her, but she was somewhere in her 90's, yet so vigorous as to disguise her true age. She passed away peacefully during the night. Sylvia called me as soon as they found her.

Frieda's wish was to be buried in Halfway Cemetery next to her husband, parents, and grandparents. She wanted only a graveside service.

We gathered at the cemetery on the afternoon of the eighteenth. Huge, wet snowflakes began falling just as the ceremony at the gravesite began. The snow captured all sound; the minister's measured syllables were muted.

Whitey looked as if, at any moment, he might jump into Frieda's grave and yank her from her coffin. His grief and the wet flakes of snow seemed to pull him toward the cold, exposed earth. Sylvia wore black, and she didn't wear her red wig. She leaned heavily on Whitey, sobbing, her own white hair blending seamlessly with the falling snow. Sean and I stood next to them; my right arm linked with Sylvia's, my left around Sean's back. My face was soaked from snow and tears. Sean clung tightly to me; Frieda was as much a grandmother to him as were his actual grandmothers.

Frieda's many friends huddled around her grave. The heavy, huge flakes covered their heads and shoulders. They whispered to each other, and the cascading flakes muffled their words.

The minister concluded his comments. I knew this not by what he said because I couldn't hear him, but because I saw him step forward and uncover the mound of loose dirt. He scooped a handful from the top and tossed it on top of Frieda's casket, which rested at the bottom of her grave. Then, in turn, we each tossed a handful of dirt onto Frieda's casket, as was her wish. As my handful showered her coffin, the volley of hollow thuds bounced dully against my brain. My only thought, "Oh my God, Frieda, I will miss you terribly."

When the funeral was over, Sean and I sat with Whitey and Sylvia for a few hours; then we went home. We settled into the overstuffed easy chair that was big enough to accommodate both of us and our blankets, books, popcorn, and hot chocolate. Even though he was getting too old for it, I read to him until he fell asleep in my arms. We stayed in the chair all night. As Sean slept, I listened to the crackle of the burning logs in the woodstove, feeling the warmth and life of my son.

Harold was staying sober; he said he was working his way through AA's steps, his home group being mostly artists, and he was determined to make a better life for himself and his family. I told myself not to count on him, but I knew I was. I waited for him to return, uncertain what I would do when he did.

Chapter 21

Frieda's Death

Frieda passed away during the night of February 15th. We knew she was around ninety, but no one knew her exact age. I'm not sure she knew it. Born at home, she claiimed she never had a birth certificate.

Frieda's ceremony was held graveside. A large group assembled at the ramshackle, little cemetery just outside town. Fresh, black dirt was heaped beside her grave. An awning sheltered the casket and hole. A small pile of loose dirt right next to the grave had a blue cloth covering it. I reckoned the gravediggers had had a hard time digging in the frozen ground. I wondered if they'd had to use pick axes to break through the crust.

Large flakes of snow began tumbling straight down just before the Episcopalian minister said his first words. The flakes were the kind that stuck to you, heaping you in white. The air was still. The raw, newly dug dirt not sheltered by the awning was covering quickly.

The minister said his spiel. He kept it short, considering the cold and the inches of new snow accumulating right before our eyes. That was a relief anyway. When the casket was lowered into the ground, Sylvia, Whitey, Andy, Sean, and Mag hugged each other into one tear streaked huddle of bodies. Sylvia's son, Charles, had planned on being here, but the weather had put a stop to that. He'd been grounded in New York. The coffin touched ground with a tiny thump, and the pallbearers slipped the ropes from under it.

The minister said a few more snow muffled words as he lifted the blue cloth from the little mound of dirt by the hole. He chucked in a small handful. Then Whitey, Sylvia, Andy, Mag, and Sean did the same. We listened to the minister say another prayer for Frieda's soul and for all our souls; at least that's what I think he was saying. I couldn't rightly hear him through the flakes of snow falling between him and me. Some folks walked up and tossed dirt on the casket. A few prayed over it. Then, gradually we filtered out a the cemetery toward our now white cars, mounded up with snow.

At the rough-hewn, two by four gate, I stopped and turned back toward Frieda's grave. Leona asked, "What is it, Joe?"

I didn't know how to explain it to Leona, but I said the words I felt I had to say, "Bye, Frieda. Thank you for living through all the hard and soft of life. Thank you for hanging in there so long." And, by God, I don't know why, but I saluted her.

Leona had been watching me and listening to what I was saying, and she straightened up and saluted her too. We stood there with folks slipping past us in the tumbling snow, saluting Frieda's grave. Whitey, with his group in tow, came up to us. He paused just long enough to tip his hat and say, "Thank yah."

Sean visited his dad a second time over spring break. Mag drove him to Boise to catch his plane and picked him up at the end of the week. He came in the store on their way home from the airport, and I asked him how it went.

He said, "Dad was kind a jumpy, kind a like Grandpa, but he still isn't drinking. He's meeting with some other people who used to drink. I can't remember the name they call themselves."

"A.A.?" I asked.

"Like that, but it was A.A.A."

"That's an auto club, son."

"No, it stood for Artists in Alcoholics Anonymous," he said triumphantly, proud that he had remembered the whole name.

"Not just Alcoholics Anonymous?" I asked.

Sean shook his head.

Christ, I thought, leave it to Harold to find some fool off the wall alcohol support group.

"They light candles and chant, you know, the usual stuff," Sean said and shrugged his shoulders.

"Yeah, the usual," I agreed. I just hoped Harold's group was true to AA in everything but the chanting and candles. Shit, poor kid had a cross to bear, loony coming at him every which a way but Sunday. "Do you really think he's quit drinking?" I asked.

"Yeah, he's different. He cries, then gets all happy, and then he gets silly, and does stuff with me, and there aren't empty cans or bottles of beer all over."

"So you're okay with how the visit went?"

He looked up, startled like. He seemed surprised that I asked him this. "Yeah, I'm okay or mostly okay." He paused and did that fiddling thing with his fingers just like Mag did. "But sometimes I wish it was over one way or the other. You know what I mean?"

"Like your dad was home?"

"Yeah, that would be part of it. But more than that, I wish I knew for sure how things were going to end. Is Dad going to go back to drinking or is he coming home and not drinking?" He squinted his eyes at me.

"Yeah, I understand. Not much you can count on these days; is there? And each thing you can put in your corner, to count on, helps. Nice talking to you, Sean." Mag came up to the checkout counter and started sliding her groceries my way.

"Yeah, you too, Joe," Sean said, and he started lifted groceries out of their cart.

Chapter 22

Hot for Harold?

"I don't want to be foolish," I whispered to Sylvia. "What should I do?"

"The only fool is the one who hides her emotions," she said. "Be open and see what happens."

I sensed Harold's presence behind me in the dark theater. He sat two rows back; we'd said hello to each other in the lobby, but that was it. He hadn't tried to initiate further conversation. But simply because I'd seen him, I yearned to be by his side. He'd only been in Halfway a week, and my injured psyche told me to hang tough, not yet. So I sat with Sylvia and Whitey in the ancient movie theater, tiny lights blinking randomly above me in the night blue ceiling.

Sixteen months had passed since Harold had left town. This was my third May in Halfway. Until a week ago, I hadn't seen my husband for sixteen months. I hadn't looked into his eyes or touched him for sixteen months. I wasn't sure how I should behave. He'd dropped Sean off every day this week, and our exchanges had been pleasant but constrained. The self-assurance with which I had been bolstering myself was dissipating. An involuntary "ah" escaped my lips.

"What's that?" Sylvia asked.

"Nothing," I answered. "I didn't say anything."

When the movie ended, my stomach knotted. I remained slouched in my seat, engrossed in watching the credits roll by. Sylvia and Whitey got up and stood in the aisle talking about the movie. At length, Sylvia leaned over to me and said, "Hon, are you going to get out of that seat some time this year?"

"Hey, I like to know who worked behind the scenes. So sue me." I got up and scooted over to the aisle.

"He'll probably be waiting for you in the lobby no matter how long you take," Sylvia said.

"Yeah, I expect he is."

"Do you want me to check?" Whitey asked. "Or I could tell him to leave so that you could come out." The corners of his lips curled in the hint of a grin. That old man had sure gotten an active sense of humor since he had a sweetie.

""Ugh! Okay already, I'm ready to leave; see," I said and demonstrated by running in place. "How hard can it be? I say hello to him and be on my way. Come on."

Grinning, Sylvia linked arms with me, and we walked up the aisle. When we pushed through the doors into the lobby, there was Harold, as Sylvia had predicted, leaning against the ticket counter, waiting. Sylvia's grip on my arm tightened as she shoved me in his direction.

"Sylvia, cut it out."

"Calm down, honey; it's for your own good. You have to get over your jitters sooner or later, and you'll just be worrying until you do. So you might as well work on it now as some other time." As we neared Harold, she called out, "Why Harold, how're you doing?"

"Sylvia," Harold responded, "and Whitey, you two have younged twenty years since I last saw you. Marriage must agree with you."

Whitey raised his right hand to hat brim height to tip his hat before he remembered that it wasn't there. The gesture made him appear to be giving Harold an abbreviated salute. "I'm pleased to see you back in town, Harold. Sylvia and I hope you plan on staying in Halfway, and . . ." he paused and stared Harold straight in the eyes, "we hope you're done with alcohol."

"Whitey!" Sylvia acted as if she were shocked. "You're so direct."

Harold's gaze briefly locked with Whitey's and then shot over to me. "No problem, Whitey," he said. "I like a person who speaks to the point."

He held out his right hand as if to shake mine. "Hello, Magdalena," he said. I extended my hand; he gently slid his rough mechanic's hand around it. His fingers touched my palm and the back of my hand. He brought his left hand forward and cupped my hand in both of his. The nerves in my hand tingled, and my arm felt on fire.

"Hello, Harold," I said, my voice ragged. It's nice to see you this evening." I smiled. My chest tightened, and I could hardly breathe. I felt Harold's hands shake. His nervousness surprised me. Tears came to his eyes. He'd cried on the phone, but I hadn't seen him cry before.

"And it's nice to see you out and about," he whispered. He lowered his head a moment to compose himself, then lifted it just enough to look me in the eyes. "I've been wanting to speak with you all week. I want you to know that I mean to make good the hurt I caused you and Sean." He dropped his head again and lifted one hand off mine to wipe his eyes. When he looked up, he was grinning, but I could see tears in his eyes. "I'll let you all get on your way. I'll be by tomorrow to take Sean for the day if it's still okay." I nodded, and he squeezed my hand.

"Goodbye, Harold." That was not what I wanted to say. He lifted my hand, again clasped within his two hands, to his lips and kissed it ever so lightly.

"See you at nine." he murmured and tenderly released my hand. He faced Whitely. "Whitey," was all he said, and he shook his hand. Whitey smiled. To Sylvia, he said. "You're always different, and you never change. Quite a lady." Sylvia laughed heartily and thanked him. They shook hands and hugged.

"Hold on to your grand thoughts, Harold," Sylvia said and chuckled.

The following day, Sunday, a soft knocking on the door wakened me. Sean was still at his friend's house, due home at eight. My alarm clock read six-thirty. I called, "I'll be there in a minute. Hang on."

I found my robe and slogged to the door. When I swung it open, I saw Harold, dressed in a new sport coat and jeans, a red carnation in his lapel and a bouquet of red carnations in his hands.

"Please accept these, Magdalena," he said. His eyes showed his trepidation, but he grinned his broad, toothy smile. "I can't erase what has been; I can only try to make it up to you, and whether or not you ever have me back, I hope to make both our lives better here on out."

"We'll take it one step at a time," I said. Shadows of longing rose up in me, but my brain screamed caution; I didn't want to get hurt again. I had stopped seeing a counselor a while back but thought I might begin seeing one again to get a better understanding of my emotions.

"You don't have to accept the flowers or the breakfast I brought, but I hope you do. I made it myself."

He must have seen my confusion, or sensed my hesitation because he said, "It's okay if you say you'd rather not have the breakfast." He grinned. "Really."

My fortitude wavered the slightest bit while my painful memories redistributed themselves around me like a fortress. "No, it's okay, I mean, it's very thoughtful of you." I hunted for the right words. "Sean's not back yet. He spent the night at a friend's house." I was sure he already knew this. "That's why I was able to go to the movies."

"Yeah, he told me he was going to be at a friend's house. I'll have the food in and on your table in no time," he said and turned to get the breakfast from his truck.

Barefooted, I padded to the table, sat down, and waited. I thought that I should get up and go wash my face at least, but I didn't move. Harold soon returned with a huge cardboard box. He set it on the floor on the opposite side of the table from me, and then he bowed.

"Magdalena, I know that I did and said a lot of things for which you should hate me for a lifetime, but I intend to make amends." He stared into my eyes; I knew where Sean got that soul-searching look of his. "I intend to do whatever it takes to win you back, and whether or not I ever accomplish it, I swear I will always treat you with love and kindness from here on out." He grinned again.

"Harold, I don't know . . ."

"Don't worry, Magdalena. I don't expect any promises or even nods in my direction, ah, yet," he said softly. "But hopefully, with time, you may forgive me. Hopefully, in time, you may love me as you once did." He smiled. I was having a hard time maintaining a facade of neutrality, seeing the sadness in his eyes.

"As you may recall, I never made a nice breakfast for you in all the years we were together. My sobriety has caused me to recollect that painful fact, among many others. To demonstrate my capability and my intentions of fixing you future breakfasts, I have prepared a lovely meal for you this morning."

He squatted down behind the table. I heard a rustling noise and cardboard being pushed aside. He rose, displaying two covered dishes, one in each hand. "There's more, hang on," he said, and he dove behind the table again. I saw only his hands the second time as he placed a large covered casserole dish on the table. With the third round of dishes, the whole of Harold reappeared.

"Are you sure we can eat all this?" I asked. Harold seemed to have brought enough food for quite a few people. He must have installed a stove in his shop.

"Oh, this isn't for me. It's all yours," he said. "I thought it would be inappropriate of me to assume that you would want me to stay. I'll get you started, and then I'll leave. You need time to consider your options, to consider your risks." He shrugged. "Not something a person can do on the spot."

He spooned chili rellenos onto my plate, and wafts of jack cheese, chili pepper, egg, and cumin teased my taste buds. He opened a small container of salsa. A square dish with a plastic lid contained cornbread and an oblong covered dish was full of chopped fruit. The thermos of coffee already had half and half in it. The last item he revealed was a basket lined with a white towel and covered with a red towel. Cinnamon and sugar coated donuts were mounded inside.

"Harold, I didn't know you could cook like this." I was dumbfounded.

"I couldn't, but I learned." He was pleased with himself. "I better go now." He stepped toward the door. "Mag, I love you with all my soul. Goodbye for now and enjoy. You deserve this and much, much more. I'll be back at nine for Sean."

"Harold, you're welcome to join me." I craved his company and feared his acceptance of my offer.

"No, not yet, that'd be pushing it, even for me. Enjoy your food. You'll be seeing more of me. Bye." He flashed me a quick smile.

"Thank you, Harold, for this wonderful meal."

He nodded, turned away, and strode purposefully to the door. I heard him close it quietly behind himself.

Harold sent me poems and love letters every day after that. In them, he listed in detail his feelings for Sean and me. He chronicled events that had happened in our lives. He apologized. He had searched his soul, he said, and had discovered emotions and memories that surprised and thrilled him. He was amazed.

I honestly couldn't say whether Harold wrote good or bad poems and letters; the rawness and utter self-revelation of his words grabbed me too instantly and too strongly for me to judge his writing in any way. Cautiously, I considered the possibility that Harold had changed.

He left presents on our doorstep: his artwork, food that he had made, plants, and flowers. He showed up one day and cut the grass and did repairs around the house. I came back from deliveries in Portland and found our old VW bug tuned up and looking sharp.

A few days later, as I was working in my lavender garden, I heard the sound of gears groaning as Harold's old pickup pulled up the grade to our home. Then I saw Harold; he grinned and waved at me. And I saw why his pickup was straining so. In its bed was what looked like every blooming plant imaginable. He parked by the house and loped down the slope toward me. His new sport coat flapped in the breeze, and the pink ribbons on the package he carried fluttered in every direction.

"How're you doing, Mag?" he called.

"Fine, Harold. What's happening here?"

"I'm continuing my courtship, Mag." To him it was simply a matter of fact.

"Harold, I don't know if . . ."

"I wish I had a choice, Mag, but I don't. I have to try my damnedest to win you back. I love you too much." He gazed at me with that mournful look he had of late. Assuming a theatrical pose, he said, "Dear Mag, I have brought you a bounty of living things, all vital and determined to thrive, but they are not half as full of purpose as I. I love you, Mag."

"Harold, I still need time," I said, floundering in my search for firm emotional ground.

"I'm not expecting you to know what you want just yet," he assured me, "but I'm going to be galloping in a circle until you decide." He smiled. "And I'm aiming to be gracing you with gifts and affection." He offered his pink-ribboned box to me. "I know you enjoy the taste of white chocolate so I located this in Boise when I picked up the plants."

I tentatively reached for the candy; white chocolate was my favorite. As my hands touched it, Harold slid his hands over mine and gently squeezed. "I am sorry for the years of pain I caused you," he said. "Please know that."

"You don't have to keep being sorry," I whispered, having lost my voice along with my fortitude. "I played my part in our troubles. I can see the pain you feel."

"Oh, I think I should continue to be damned regretful for a while yet," he said, "but on a lighter side, are you able to take a break for lunch? Can I help you finish anything so that you can break?"

"I could stop now, I guess," I said, looking over the lavender I'd been cultivating.

"Can I help you with anything first?"

"No, I'm getting it finished. Anyway, don't you have a shop to get back to?" I asked, remembering that it was a weekday.

"I came in at four-thirty this morning and got all the jobs I'd scheduled for today finished by eleven. Sean doesn't leave school until two-thirty, and folks won't be showing up to get their vehicles for another couple hours yet. So, I'm okay."

"Oh, good," I said. God, I'm lame, I thought. "I didn't want you messing up your work because of me."

"I have it under control, honest," he said, still looking at me with that soul grabbing gaze of his.

"I didn't mean to be nosy or anything."

"Hey, no problem, fair question. Lunch now?"

"Yeah, sure, why not." That sounded noncommittal enough.

Simultaneous with my last words, Whitey's pickup rounded the curve downhill from his place. Sylvia waved from the passenger window as Whitey turned into our drive and stopped next to Harold's truck. They got out, waved to us, and approached the blooming truck bed. I could barely hear Sylvia's animated remarks. "Oh my, how lovely." Whitey took off his hat and scratched his head. Then the two of them began picking their way down the soggy slope. Sylvia's high heels sunk into the spongy earth with each step, causing her to hang onto Whitey's arm for balance.

"Wait there," I called. "We'll come up." I turned to Harold. "I can't deny that I have strong feelings for you, Harold, but they're all messed up. I love you, but I'm afraid of you. I'm afraid things could become as they were before. I'm afraid I'll act as badly as I did before, not just what you'll do." I wanted a guarantee that I knew he couldn't offer.

"I know," he said. "I'll do what I can to ease your worry, but you know and I know that eternal sobriety isn't guaranteed. All I can do is promise you I won't drink again and do what's necessary to insure it. I can't guarantee it."

"I know. I know," I said. "How do I know that I can trust you to keep trying?"

"Time," he said, "and your gut feelings."

I wondered if that would be enough. "I guess that will have to do," I said. "Time and guts." We trudged uphill to Whitey and Sylvia.

"Harold," Sylvia said, "where on earth did you get all those plants? I know they don't have a selection like this in Baker City."

"You're right, Sylvia," Harold said. "They don't, but they do in

Boise. I drove there yesterday evening, picked up the plants, and got back to Halfway about three this morning."

"That means you haven't slept," I said.

"I meant to, but I was juiced," Harold said. He must have seen me wince because he added, "Not with alcohol, with love, Mag, love." He flicked his fingers at Whitey in a quick sort of wave. "Hello, Whitey, you still keeping an eye on me?"

"Howdy, Harold," Whitey said and shook his hand. "Good morning, Mag." He tipped his hat to me. "You bet I am, Harold, but what I mostly want to know at this particular moment is whether this load of goods comes with a labor package. Are you going to dig all the holes necessary to plant these lovelies, Harold?"

"Astute observation, Whitey. Yes, I do intend to dig the holes to plant the plants. But for this very moment, since you're both here, would you like to join Magdalena and I in the magnificent palette pleaser I've brought for lunch? There's plenty."

"We wouldn't want to intrude," Sylvia said, fluttering her fingers. She clearly wanted to stay. The drama of the event fascinated her. I wondered if someone in town had called her and told her that Harold was headed my way with a truckload of plants. That was probably why she and Whitey happened to be driving by.

"Mag, is it all right with you if Sylvia and Whitey join us?" Harold asked me. "I should have asked you before saying anything."

"Of course."

"How lovely," Sylvia said. "What's in the box, Mag?"

"White chocolate. Harold did a lot of shopping in Boise."

"This is going to be an intriguing meal," said Sylvia. Whitey smiled at her; he liked her excessive statements.

"Well, we best be skedaddling to the dining room. I have a lot of planting to do today and tomorrow too, probably. Right this way, folks," Harold said and waved us grandly toward the house.

Chapter 23

Harold's Giant Metal Mag

When I saw Harold's battered truck putt-putting east past my window, it took me a while to register the significance of it. At first, I just casually noticed the truck and him and thought, there's Harold. Then my brain woke up and screamed at me; there's Harold! Harold's back in town.

I glanced around to see if anyone I might relay this important news to was around. Bob and Nancy were in the rear of the store by the vegetables. As usual, they were picking 'em over, like two old hens, searching for the best tidbits. With all their jostling and selecting, every produce item I'd set out was getting bruised. Their probing fingers did as much damage as a flock of frenzied hens scurrying through the bins would a. But since they were the only ones in the store, I hustled on back there and tapped Bob on the elbow. "Bob, guess who's back?"

"Martin Ogelby? Is Martin out a jail already?" he questioned me, surprised as hell. "I didn't think that old bugger'd have the nerve to come back."

"No," I corrected him, disappointed he'd stolen my thunder with his incorrect guess, "it's not Martin; it's Harold. I just now saw Harold drive by in his same old Ford pickup he's always had."

"Shit, is that so? Maybe now I can get my rig fixed decently again," he said. Then he turned to me and with a wink, whispered, "and maybe we better look into purchasing some stock in Jolane's." His wife frowned disapprovingly when we chuckled so he straightened up, took on his somber, vegetable-picking look, and went back to the business of scratching through my produce.

"I reckon he's planning on claiming his family back," I added.

"I bet he damn sure is, Joe. I hope he plans on staying. Like I said, there ain't nobody around here can fix my pickup worth a tinker's damn. How much you wanna bet he wins Mag back?"

"I ain't taking that bet," I answered, " 'cause I'm thinking he will too. Harold has the goll-dangedest stick-to-it-ness when he really wants something."

Harold appeared to be living in his shop. He parked his truck out front of it when he first drove into town and then continued to park there every day, kind a like he was advertising his return. And I never saw Mag's car linger in the vicinity of his shop. I was aching to know if anything was happening between 'em, but when Mag came shopping at the store, damn if I couldn't figure how to bring the subject of Harold into the conversation. She shopped quietly and then stood with her eyes staring at the linoleum while I rang up her groceries, not saying a word, not even her usual line of aimless chatter that I ignored. She was kind a folded into herself, not even looking for chitchat.

Finally, I thought of a way to mention Harold. I asked her, "Will you be going to see that new movie at the theater with Harold?"

Her head shot up. Her eyes looked real startled like. "With Harold? Why No, I'm going with Sylvia and Whitey." She rummaged in her purse and pulled out her billfold. "How much do I owe you, Joe?" She gazed at me, her eyes glazed over, her mind a million miles away.

She's one confused lady, I thought, on overload, most likely. I bet Sean's happy to have his dad around again, and I can imagine how Harold's working at her, itching to get her back and to get back in his own home.

Mag paid her total and thanked me. Thinking I should cheer her up a bit, I told her, "I'm the one as should be thanking you." She nodded vaguely and left the store, her eyes scanning the pavement.

Harold came by for groceries a few times, but other folks were in the store all them times, and I never got a chance to talk to him. Saturday, Leona and I went to see the new movie, like we always did, first night it showed in town. By chance, we sat two rows behind Harold near the rear of the theater. I called up to Harold, "Hey, Harold!" He turned around and saw me.

"Yo, Joe. Hello, Leona," he said. He stood and reached over the intervening row with his outstretched hand. "Long time, no see, Leona," he said and shook Leona's hand and then mine. "I've seen Joe several times already this week."

"Yeah, a man's got a eat," I said, shaking his hand. I was hoping to get information about the possible length of Harold's stay.

"Yup," he said and withdrew his hand. "Well, I better be sitting down, I'm most likely inconveniencing these folks." He smiled his broad, charming smile to the couple sitting in the seats between us.

He was wearing a new looking, green shirt. He was tanned and lean and looked handsome enough. The most noticeable thing about him though was that he was stone cold sober.

Harold set about cleaning up and repairing his shop, and the Monday after the movie, he reopened it. Folks hurried in with repair jobs, as much to scope out the situation as because they were glad to have their crack mechanic back. His business was flourishing by the end of the first day he opened it.

He worked like the dickens each day, and after taking Sean home, he worked into the nights, and, whenever he could, he campaigned to regain Mag. He courted her with all the fixings and trimmings of romance. Hell, we'd just gotten used to the billing and cooing of Sylvia and Whitey when sober Harold had to turn romantic. And this was sure to be no easy courtship either. Mag would most likely resist Harold's advances with all her womanly strength, and she was a strong woman, what with all that gardening and hiking.

But Harold's first moves on Mag weren't no sissy bouquet of flowers, like most guys would a tried. No, this one time Harold brought Magdalena a whole truckload of blooming idiots. His truck was so loaded down when he chugged past my store, I wasn't sure he would make the grade out a town in the direction of his house.

Happy as a nose picker with a schnoz full of snot, Harold rolled down Main Street, his elbow hanging out the window, wearing his new sport coat. He had a flower in his lapel, and his just combed hair was glistening, it was so clean. His eyes glittered with intent. He was one focused man. He neither acknowledged nor noticed the waves and salutations directed at him as he rattled down Main Street.

His truck wasn't nearly out a sight when fingers began pointing in the direction of his departing vehicle. Heads were shaking, and jaws were flapping. A few folks actually discussed the possibility of driving up to the Brown's place, parking down the road, and walking up through the forest. Spying! They said that if they got caught they could say they were lost.

A few hours after his sputtering departure, Harold zoomed back down the grade into town. He was grinning like a fool on fire. He swerved hard into his parking space in front of his shop and leaped out a his truck. He'd changed into work clothes while he was at his place, mostly likely to plant all them blooming idiots that had been in his truck, I figured. He swung around, his truck door still hanging open, and stopped cold. He stared at this old pile of scrap metal he had stored next to his shop. I could tell he was concentrating by the way he was turning his head from side to side real slow like.

Then he raised his head and appeared to be looking at the clouds, or maybe he was looking at Cornucopia Peak; I couldn't for sure tell from my store. As he stood gazing into the distance, I was positive that fifty sets of eyes up and down Main were watching him to see what his next move would be.

I was about to turn away and ring up old Mrs. Hampton's groceries since she was yammering at me to get a move on, when Harold slapped his thighs with his hands and did a double spin while flapping his bent arms up and down like a lame chicken attempting to fly. He no sooner stopped spinning then he rushed over to his scrap metal pile and began pawing through it, slinging rusty iron out a his way. He selected about ten thin round steal rods, half inch diameter, each twelve feet long. Cradling these in his arms, he loped behind his shop; the six feet of rod on either side of his body bowing in rhythm with his stride.

"Joe," pleaded Mrs. Hampton, and she tugged on my sleeve, "get your tush on over here right now. I'd like to make it home with these groceries before my dinner hour is long past, and it's time for bed." She tottered back over to the register and stood there frowning at me. I put her off just a half minute longer to make sure Harold wasn't coming back out front.

I decided that I wouldn't be seeing any more of Harold for a while and a dollar's a dollar, so I said, "Sorry for keeping you waiting, Mrs. Hampton. We'll get you on out a here in a jiffy." I rung her up and as quick as I could, and hours later, after finishing my closing up chores,

I slipped over to Harold's to see what the old boy was doing.

He had four pieces of that metal he'd hauled out back welded together by the time I got behind his shop. He had sectioned two of the rods into smaller pieces, four sets of each length. He was bent over, facing away from me, picking up a six-inch piece of rod. I noticed an open can of Pepsi within arm's reach.

"Howdy, Harold," I said. "You're working mighty late. Got a big job to turn out by tomorrow?"

He twisted his body in my direction. His welding hood was down; he lifted it with his gloved hand. "Hi, Joe!" he answered enthusiastic as hell. "This isn't a paying job, Joe. I'm creating a semblance of my one true love, my Magdalena." He grinned. "You'll have to pardon me. I have t'get back to work on this." He winked, grinned, and took a slug of his pop.

He flipped the hood down again, sparked his arc, and using metal tongs, he held a short piece of rod in position against a piece already welded in place. He heated the juncture of the two pieces until they glowed red. He worked the arc all the way around the joint. He set his welder aside, and as soon as the weld had cooled he gently tapped the protecting slag from it. He inspected the results; then reached for his welder and repeated the process. Tedious work. I stood twenty minutes watching him fuss over that one weld.

When he stopped to replace his welding rod, I said, "Well, I reckon I'll be taking off now, Harold." I puzzled over what else to say, then added. "Good luck with Magdalena."

He raised his welding hood. "Thanks, Joe," he said. Then he looked serious. "I know I screwed up major. I'm aiming to make amends for that." He grinned, sudden like. "I'm going to win the affections of my lady again, no matter what it takes." He quit grinning just as sudden and said, "And I'm not going to mess things up again between us, ever." He looked as if he might tear up. I couldn't tell for sure; the shadow of that welding hood obscured his eyes.

I wanted to comfort him, I guess, so I said, "You two are meant for each other. Things'll work out. Bye, Harold." I wanted to get out a there fast, too deep of an emotional territory for me.

"Bye, Joe. And thanks again," he said. He lowered the hood, sparked his welder, and was at work on a new weld before I left.

Conjecture about Harold's prospects for success commenced. Would this do the trick for Harold? Would Magdalena take him back? Would he fall off the wagon? How soon would he fall off the wagon? Was Harold out a his gourd?

Ed had his own special interpretation of events. He said, "Harold joined one of them cults while he was down in Arizona."

"What makes you figure that, Ed?" I asked him.

He grimaced his face into a snarl and said, "He's telling you that's a sculpture of Magdalena he's building when it's as plain as the nose on your face that he's constructing a monument to Satin." He nodded, affirming his suspicions.

"I don't know, Ed. It do look a mite like Mag."

"You're blinded by your friendship to Harold and Magdalena." He seesawed his hands at me. "Wake up, man; it's Satin, and we have a cult member right here in Halfway."

I stared at him, befuddled. He waved his right hand at me in a dismissive gesture. "Ah, same old story. Folks is always too blind to notice." He walked away, forgetting to pick up his change, shaking his head in disgust.

Each dawn, Harold was in his shop, tearing into motors, getting his mechanicing business out a the way so's he could weld on his metal Magdalena. Long about mid-afternoon he was done with his work-a-day work and into his art.

All that us nosy folks got for standing around, probably ruining our eyes by accidentally looking at the welding arc, were short, mostly incoherent answers. Harold was absorbed in his creation. Periodically, he paused in his work just long enough to flip up his hood and gulp down more Pepsi. The pop cans accumulated as fast as his beer cans used to, but he didn't get drunk. The amount of sugar he was getting from that pop kept him fired up. He welded until Sean showed up, and then again after he took him home until who knows when. We'd all left and gone to bed.

The Saturday after Harold began his welding, Mag came into the store. About ten folks were in it, and all ten heads sprung up. Twenty eyes stared at Mag for a second or two, and then sought each other for suggestions of a next move.

Sally didn't hesitate. She didn't look to anyone but God for approval. She walked right up to Mag and said, "Hi, Mag, you just get back from Portland?"

Mag looked weary, like she'd been driving a long stretch without a break. "Yeah, Sally, I just now got back," she responded. She raised her shoulders and rotated 'em. "What's up?"

Sally stomped right into the opening Mag had given her. "Harold, that's what's up," she said. "He's building a huge monstrosity behind his shop that he says is you, but Christian folks think it's the devil." She braced for battle.

Magdalena gazed at her; she seemed distracted. She sighed long and heavy. "I don't have the time nor patience for your bullshit right now, Sally," she answered her. She headed toward the pop. "But you keep your Christian eyes on Harold, okay?" She selected her pop and brought it up to the register. I rung it up and gave her change for the dollar she'd dropped on the counter. I wanted to tell her, "Way to go! All right!" but I didn't.

She pocketed the coins I gave her and pulled the metal ring on the can. "Thanks, Joe," she said. "I'll talk more later. I'm tired."

I nodded and said, "Better get home and take a nap. You look like you're drove out."

She nodded and scuffed her sneakers wearily toward the door. She turned to face those twenty eyes again and said, "You all better keep your eyes on Harold. No telling what he's building. Maybe, like Frankenstein, it will come to life and terrorize the town." She broke up with laughter as soon as she stopped talking. She was guffawing as she walked out and even as she passed in front of my window.

Two weeks later, I was sweeping the sidewalk in front of my store when I saw Harold drive his truck from out behind his shop. A fifteen or so foot spidery metal sculpture towered above the bed, swaying from side to side with every bump and dip the tires rolled over. The ropes that tied it to the truck groaned and popped with each sway. Regardless of what Sally and Ed said, it looked the spitting image of Mag to me.

Harold crept along Main in the direction of his house. All the shops emptied; sixty some people lined the walks. What an event! This was better than a cattle drive through town, and there wasn't gonna be no shit on the sidewalk when it was over.

Grace and Sally huddled in front of the post office, pointing and whispering into their hands. Bob waved and yelled, "Hello, Harold," and broke into clapping and whistling. Wanda came running out a the utility office to see what was the matter with Bob. He grinned at her and kept right on clapping. A scruffy group of Forest Service seasonal employees, probably from a fire crew, took Bob's cue and commenced hooting and hollering "Go, dude!" and "Far out!" The rest of the folks just looked on quietly. A giant metal sculpture moving down Main Street was something to see, an event to remember. They'd form opinions later, depending on what their friends thought.

Sylvia and Whitey came cruising into town as Harold approached the electrical wires strung across the road. The wires were lower than his sculpture. Sylvia leapt out a the truck, waving her arms for him to stop. "Wires! Wires!" she yelled. I think he'd already noticed 'em, but immediately after her yelling, Harold, wearing his new brown sport coat again, climbed from his truck and sauntered on over to the other side to join Sylvia and Whitey who were already standing there, staring up. The three of 'em stood in the middle of Main Street trying to figure out a problem that none of 'em could figure out and even if they did, they couldn't do anything about it.

Someone must have alerted George at the utility office of the impending disaster for he came jogging over to stand by Harold. From his gestures and the words I could hear, I guessed he was none too happy. Harold just stood there placidly listening to his irate lecture. I don't know if he was unreasonably confident that all would be worked out or if all his overworking and the steady stream of pop had induced a sublime state of calmness.

Sylvia intervened. I couldn't hear her, but I could see her pointing first one way and then the other. She put her hand on George's shoulder and drew him close. He was no longer shouting or saying anything. His arms were crossed over his chest; I think he knew his arguments were losing ground. Then I saw him nodding yes, and he walked off. He had a kind a dazed look on his face.

Folks milled around. Bob and several of the Forest Service bunch strolled out to join Harold, Whitey, and Sylvia. I saw Whitey tip his hat to 'em. One car in each direction was backed up by now, a real traffic jam for Halfway. These folks climbed out a their vehicles and joined the other bystanders.

I reckon ten minutes passed before George pulled his utility rig onto Main. He leaned out his window and signaled to the backed up cars heading east to get out a his way. The owners ambled over to their vehicles, three of 'em by then, and waving to their friends, got in and backed up enough to allow George to pull his truck in next to Harold.

George maneuvered around and got the boom of the mechanized bucket under the wires. Then he climbed out a his cab and into the bucket. He raised it until his head and shoulders were above the wires. He set the wires into the clamps of a hydraulic arm that was attached to the bucket and extended the arm until the part gripping the wires was directly in front of the highest point of the sculpture. He waved to everybody to step back in case the wires snapped; it wasn't until later that I found out he'd turned off the power. Then he raised the mechanical arm and the wires over the sculpture. He signaled a come-ahead to Harold.

Harold jumped back in his pickup, started his engine, and crept forward with infinitesimal slowness. George waved him on, inch by inch. The sculpture passed under the wires with only inches to spare.

I broke out cheering and most of the rest of the spectators did too. George hollered at everybody to stay back. He lowered the wires and brought the mechanical arm back to him. "Keep clear!" he yelled again 'cause a few folks were headed toward Harold's idling truck. George lowered the bucket back onto the bed of the truck and climbed out. Folks cheered for him. He climbed down a ladder on the side of the utility bed. He shouted. "All clear!" and folks dashed onto the road, clambering onto his truck and hanging all over Harold's.

Sylvia hugged Whitey. I could see Whitey blushing with pleasure even from the distance of my store half a block away. Harold chugged out a sight, and the crowd dispersed, returning to their shopping and bill paying. I went into my store to get back to work. As an eyewitness, I was sure to be asked all kinds a questions about Harold and his creation. What a day!

Chapter 24

Heavy Metal Courtship

The phone rang. "Hon, I had to call and tell you about the stupendously wonderful event that just happened downtown," Sylvia blurted out smack on the heels of my hello, "and I wanted to give you notice before the rest of the town began calling you with news of your husband's latest caper."

She sounded cheerful, but my throat constricted. "What do you mean, Sylvia?"

She laughed merrily. "I can't wait until you see it, Mag. It's a blast."

"What's a blast? What are you talking about?"

She forced herself to stop laughing and said, "All right, all right, let me get myself together." After taking in a noisy breath, she continued. "Harold's on the way to your house with a giant sculpture of you perched on the bed of his truck." She cracked up again. "He made it out of steel rod, but, amazingly enough, it looks just like you, Mag. And the best part is," Sylvia paused to giggle again, "that there was a big to-do and traffic jam on Main while everyone waited for George to get his rig and raise those sagging lines that stretch from Jolane's to the pole in front of Hampton's place."

"I take it Harold managed to get under."

"Yes, he did, but your colossal image was close to cutting off Hampton's power. Folks cheered and clapped. People came out of houses and stores to watch. Sally and her gang pointed and shook their fists."

"Sally already told me about Satan's likeness one day when I was in Joe's store."

"Satan? Oh well, that's Sally for you. Personally, I like the sculpture, Mag. I think it's a real tribute."

"I'm sure I'll like it too."

"Well, I have to get going, but I wanted to get to you before the gossip mill did," she said. "Whitey and I saw the whole thing. It was so exciting. Well, bye now; we'll be over to see you shortly. You can count on that."

"Bye, Sylvia. See you later."

Sylvia was right. I had no sooner replaced the receiver when the phone rang again. Sally was on the line.

"Mag," she said, "what do you intend to do about the monstrosity approaching your place of residence?"

"What do you think I should do, Sally?"

"Do you honestly want my opinion?" she asked.

"Yes, I do," I answered. "I may not take your advice, but at least I'll know what you think."

Sally hesitated. I guessed that she was rummaging through her mind to determine whether my remark was an insult.

"Okay, Mag, here's what I think you should do." She caught her breath. "You should refuse Satan's messenger entrance to your property. Then you should come to my house and let me banish the evil stench of Satan from your presence."

"I'll keep that in mind, Sally."

"If you value your soul, Magdalena Brown, you will heed my advice."

"I'll consider myself warned. Goodbye, Sally."

I hung up. Sally's notion of Satan seemed so preposterous that I didn't see how she could actually believe it. The phone rang again. This time I let it ring and went outside so that I wouldn't have to listen to it. I halfheartedly pulled weeds from around my fruit trees. I'd been working for a while when I saw Whitey's rig round the uphill curve from town and turn into my drive.

As soon as the truck had rolled to a stop, Sylvia swung open her door. "Mag," she called, "wait until you see it!" She slid her arm under Whitey's and strutted over to me. Her giddy excitement had reached Whitey, and he beamed at Sylvia and me like the Cheshire cat.

"Harold loves a show. I bet it's a doozy." The whole town was involved, as usual.

"It was the damnedest spectacle," Sylvia said.

"The crowd?"

"Well, them too. But, you see, George was going to make Harold back up and go around the long way to get to here. That would've added over eight miles to the trip. Harold's traveling about two miles an hour, I imagine, just creeping along, you know. With the additional miles tagged on, he would have had to camp out overnight." Sylvia glanced at Whitey, whose gleeful expression set her off on another round of snorting and giggling. They both broke into riotous laughter.

Whitey took up the narration. "Sylvia single handedly talked George into getting the utility rig and raising the lines." He glanced at Sylvia conspiratorially and winked. "I think she used blackmail of some kind. They were standing mighty close, and she had a grip on his arm."

"No one will ever know what I know, especially his wife," Sylvia said and meekly patted her red bouffant wig.

"Oooohwee! I knew it!" Whitey said. "This here's one clever lady, who has happened to be in all the wrong places at all the right times."

Sylvia brushed off his comical flattery with a wave of her hand and batted her mascara-laden lashes. "I'm much more than a pretty face."

"Whitey, Sylvia, hi," Sean called as he ran from the trees behind the house; he'd been playing in the sanctuaries. He hugged first Sylvia and then Whitey.

"Sean, your dad's on his way here with a surprise," I told him.

"Is it that big sculpture of you he's been working on?" he asked.

"Yes, that's it. We're going to sit on the porch and wait for him. Do you want to hang out with us?"

"Sure," he said, "but first I want to get some of my cars and trucks to play with," and he dashed back up the hill and into the dimly lit trees.

I brought out the pitcher of tea that had been cooling in the refrigerator, and we sat down on the porch to await Harold and his sculpture. Time seemed to have stopped. I was sure Harold had broken down. Finally, we walked down the slope and around the curve toward town. Sean rolled his cars down the road as we walked. Harold was not in view; we walked back uphill.

"Do you suppose something's happened?" I asked Sylvia.

She dismissed my worry. "Hon, figure it out. You're over four miles from town. At two miles an hour, the least time he'll take to get here is two hours."

I had wanted to wait lunch until Harold got here, but I finally warmed soup leftover from yesterday's supper. We sat and ate, our legs dangling over the edge of the porch, enjoying the warm sunshine. Sean poured his soup into the beds of his toy pickups and into the bucket of his crane. He hadn't liked the soup last night on the first go around; I wasn't in the mood to stop him.

"I'll make more for us to eat when Harold gets here." I told everyone.

"I wouldn't get ahead of yourself. If Harold's true to his new form, he'll bring a nine course meal," Sylvia offered. "What you should worry about is having enough room to eat Harold's food."

"Is Dad bringing supper?" Sean asked. "I hope it's pizza."

I was about to respond when we heard the sound of Harold's engine as his overburdened truck struggled to make the final grade. I set my bowl aside, making an effort to seem casual. Then Harold's truck rounded the corner, and I saw the sculpture for the first time. "Wow!" I gasped despite my vow to be reserved, and I ran down the gravel drive, stones flying from the souls of my sneakers.

Sean wasn't far behind me. "Daddy, daddy!" he called.

We reached the juncture of road and drive at the same time Harold did. He'd been grinning and waving at us since he first saw us. By the time our paths met, he was whooping with joy and laughing so hard he was crying.

"Magdalena! Sean! Yie-yie-yie-yie-yie-yie!" he hollered, shouting his words out in uneven jerks. "Magdalena, my dear Mag! Lookee, it's you! Yie-yie-yie-yie-yie!" His waving hand flew from windshield to rear cab window as he pointed backward to his sculpture.

He rolled his truck to a stop in front of us, jumped out, and with mock pride, swaggered over. He wore his new sport coat; from the number of times he'd been wearing it, I suspected that he knew how handsome he looked in it.

Every part of him danced in opposite directions. He kicked his legs, flapped his arms, and twirled in an impromptu dance of exuberance. Then with deliberate effort, he stood perfectly still, his arms hanging loose at his sides. Onlookers' cars began accumulating on the road in front of our place.

Harold said, "Magdalena, I love you. I promise on my soul to be the good husband you deserve, and Sean," he said, turning to his son, "I love you, and I promise to be the good father you deserve." Then spreading his arms to encompass us both, he said, "Please let me have a second chance."

My heart pounded in my chest. I wanted to run into his arms; I was hungry for this Harold of old, the man with whom I had fallen in love.

"I won't hurt you again," he said as if reading my thoughts. "I swear, I won't ever hurt either of you again."

He stretched his fingers to embrace us as he stepped forward. My eyes flashed from the towering image of me to Harold himself, beseeching me. I still wasn't sure if I should believe this man. "Harold," was all I was able to utter, and I was crying. All the accumulated pain and anger that I'd held inside spilled out.

He kissed my lips and face. My hurt and pleasure mixed, and my wounds scabbed, in the first stage of healing. I clung to Harold. Longing and loneliness needled me, edging their way along my spine, and I pressed closer to him. Sean hugged us both.

Harold clung to me and cried too. He chanted, "I love you, Mag. I love you. I love you. I love you, Sean. I love you. I love you." My ear was against Harold's chest, and I heard his strong heartbeat. His head rested on top of mine. His warm tears dropped onto my face. I heard cheering from the road.

"Are you two going to stand there all day boo-hooing?" I heard Sylvia say as if from a distance, even though she stood less than three feet from us.

Harold stroked my head as he answered, "We might, Sylvia; we just might. And by the way, would you mind unloading that hunk of metal from my truck? It's sort blocking Mag's drive." I felt the vibration of his vocal chords and heard the rattle of his laugh.

I lifted my head and looked at Harold. I reasoned that unloading the sculpture postponed my final commitment. "Do you think the four of us can unload it?" I asked him.

"Why sure we can, no problem," he answered. "I built it on wheels. Come and see."

When we'd all gathered around the truck, he pointed to the sturdy frame and wheels he'd welded underneath his masterpiece. "I can lower it the same way I got it into the truck. With the winch." He pointed to that piece of equipment, which was bolted to the front of the truck bed, but then he got a puzzled expression on his face. "Only trouble is, although I know that I can't travel on the slope with the sculpture in my truck, I don't know how far I can tow the sculpture once it's on the ground, without it toppling, that is." He craned his neck to look at the apex of his work.

"We might as well get started." Whitey said.

"I'll help," Bob called as he walked toward us.

"Me too," called someone I didn't know; he was a young longhair, and he wore a forest service shirt.

Harold told them, "As George would say, be careful and watch up. I wouldn't want anyone getting cold-cocked by my art." He kissed Sean and me once more before pulling himself away. Then he swung the tailgate down and from under the sculpture's dolly, slid out two sets of metal rails over which the sculpture would roll. He positioned one behind each rear wheel. He checked the two guidelines that stretched from metal Mag's eye sockets to the front bumper of the truck. He'd rigged pulleys with ratchets so that they would maintain tension while feeding out line as the winch lowered the sculpture. He waved to Whitey and Sylvia, who were safely positioned to give advice. Whitey gave him the thumbs up.

Steel Mag groaned and creaked as the winch let her slowly roll down the inclined plane to the gravel. Once she rested on the ground, Harold positioned his truck in front of her. He and Whitey attached the towline, and Harold began inching his truck forward. He left the gravel drive at the spot where the slope met it fairly on the level, and he headed uphill to an area about twelve feet from the drive. All of Harold's other creations on the hillside seemed to wait in suspense for this new addition to come to rest so that their rust-a-day life would be peaceful once again.

Harold continued to inch forward. When the sculpture swayed, he stopped and waited for it to stabilize. Bob and the unknown forest service worker moved the rails forward as Harold reached the end of the other set. I walked even with the truck, fifteen feet away, watching for signs of trouble, but none appeared, and in less than twenty minutes, Harold reached the spot he had selected.

The fifteen-foot metal Magdalena had arrived at her new home. I heard clapping and whistling from the road and then the sputtering starts of engines. Harold shook hands with Bob and the forest service guy, and they returned to their vehicles.

Harold inspected the sculpture and explained to us how he would later remove the wheels and stabilize her. Then Harold asked Sean, Sylvia, Whitey, and I to find a comfortable location while he returned to his truck for a picnic basket and blanket. "I brought red grapes, crackers, cheese, and pop. We can sit here on the slope and admire the sculpture."

"Well, I guess I was wrong when I said you would bring dinner," Sylvia offered, "but this will do nicely."

"What was that?" Harold asked her. "Did I miss something?"

"Yeah, hon, I thought you'd bring dinner," Sylvia answered and brushed her hand across his cheek, "but I'm sure you'll come up with something. Go get your food."

"I did bring dinner. It's in the truck," he said. "But it's not dinnertime yet." He checked his watch. "Oh, I guess it is. I forgot how slow I'd be getting here."

"We'll eat dinner later," I said. "Let's have that picnic."

Later that day, I told Harold how much I loved him and told him that he could come home. I knew we would both had work to do if we wanted to rebuild our marriage. In the past, we'd scripted our rolls destructively; if we were to succeed this time, we would need to rewrite our parts.

Chapter 25

Lovey Dovey Harold's Ruining It for the Rest of Us

That sculpture did the trick. Harold moved back in with Magdalena, and folks began spotting 'em together around town, shopping and riding in the truck together. I considered putting up a chart to enter H and M sightings on; they were such a hot topic.

But Harold didn't let his conquest of Magdalena's heart go to his head. He continued to pursue her love with the vigor of an eighteen year old.

After he closed his shop each night, he walked over to my store. "Mind if I use your phone for a sec, Joe?" he asked tonight as he did every evening.

I always wondered why he didn't call from his own place before he came over to mine, but I never asked. Maybe he thought he'd forget what he was supposed to buy. "As long as it's not for a call to Jamaica," I answered, as I did every evening.

He chuckled and punched in his home phone number. "Magdalena," he spoke softly into the receiver, then paused for her response, "I love you, babe. Do we need anything at the store? Just thought I'd check." Pause. "Uh huh. Let me fix dinner tonight." Another pause. "Uh huh, yeah, okay. Yeah, sure, I can fix that. I'll get the mushrooms." Pause again. "Okay, love you. Be home soon. Bye." He gently replaced the receiver and gazed at it briefly as if Mag was staring back at him over the phone lines. He sighed, turned, and smiled at me. He was clearly a man who could not believe his good fortune. "Thanks, Joe," he said.

Each night, he bought the groceries that they had discussed. Some nights Mag told him that they didn't need anything. Either way, Harold always purchased something, like ice cream, fancy marmalade, or expensive cookies that I stocked for the tourists.

I'd never seen Harold act this way before. He had turned into one of them "sensitive" guys. All the women loved it. My wife started bringing him up as an example of what my behavior should be. At times, the new Harold really riled me.

Leona and I ran into Harold and Magdalena at the Fourth of July celebration at the park. We saw 'em coming from a distance. Harold was holding onto Magdalena's hand. Every now and then, he slipped her hand into his farther away hand and embracing her with the close one, gave her two or three playful pecks on the cheek. Then he released her and gently switched hands again. They grinned at each other like two pups in love. Both of 'em seemed near to jumping out a their skins with joy.

Their carryings on made me sick to my stomach. It reminded me of Whitey and Sylvia. Harold and Whitey were sure making it tough for the rest of us guys. The women in Halfway glommed onto that sort a crap like fleas to a cattle dog.

Leona leaned over to me, grabbed my shirtsleeve, and

whispered, "Joe, look. There's Harold and Magdalena. Ain't that sweet. They're so in love." She hung onto my sleeve, giggling and covering her mouth the way she does.

"Christ All Mighty," I answered her. "You'd think they were fifteen. Why can't they act like grown folks?"

"Oh, Joe," she murmured and lightly slapped my arm, "It's romantic." She scowled and looked at me real stern. "And there's nothing wrong with a little romance, you old fart. You should try it some time."

We were abreast of Harold and Mag by then, and Leona rushed forward to meet 'em. "Hello, hello, hello," she cooed to 'em. "I'm so happy to see you two together and everything working out again." She reached forward and lifted their two clasped hands into hers. She cradled 'em in her two hands like they were a lost baby newly found. "I'm so happy for you both."

Harold and Mag acted as dingy as Leona. They grinned at her, loving every minute of her attention. "Thank you, Leona," Mag said. She placed her free hand on top of Leona's hand. Then Harold put his free hand up there too.

I was staring at this big ball of holding hands and three people grinning at each other like mindless morons. Shit, I thought; I'll have hell to pay tonight from Leona. Her thinking that we could be like these two. I wanted to beat the living vinegar out a Harold. Out loud, I said, "Howdy, Harold," and I nodded at him. Then I looked at his wife and said, "Mag," and nodded at her. "How's business, Harold?"

He broke off his gleaming stare at Leona and looked over at me. His blissful feelings were still shining in his eyes. "It's fine, Joe. Better than ever. In fact, life is better than ever." He lifted one hand off the ball of hands and clapped me on the arm. "You and Leona'll have to come up and visit some time. Maybe come by for coffee or sodas in the evening. Any evening."

"We will, we will," affirmed Leona enthusiastically, and by her tone of voice, I knew we would.

All of a sudden, them three dropped their hands and hugged each other right there in front of a park full of town's people. In front of God and country! On the Fourth of July! I was feeling near nauseous.

They stood there patting each other's backs and grinning, happy as cows in clover. I looked around to see who might be watching. George and Ed were over by the roped in outdoor bar, staring, pointing, and laughing. "Christ," I muttered.

Leona got all teared up. She was wiping her eyes as they all backed out a the hug, patting each other on the back as they released one another.

"Leona, don't we need to be getting over to see your friend Judy's crochet booth? Ain't she expecting us already?" Anything to get out a the public love fest.

Leona turned to me, a surprised expression on her face. "You said wild bulls couldn't drag you to look at her frilly doilies, Joe." She looked disoriented for a moment; then she burst into an ear-to-ear grin. "Oh Joe," she said. "Ain't you wonderful!" She beamed over at Harold and Mag. "Your loving ways are rubbing off. I knew they would." She hooked her arm under mine. "We'll be by this week, Harold and Magdalena. You two have a great Fourth of July. Bye, bye now." They all waved to each other and called several more byes. I nodded my nod and dragged Leona away.

She was jabbering about Judy's crocheting and steering me toward her booth. "Hold it now," I said and stopped her. "You don't really think I want to go see Judy's junk, do ya?" Her face fell so far it nearly touched the ground. Her eyes got all watery. "I'm going to have a beer with George and Ed." Tears actually started streaming down her cheeks. She looked numb. I turned away, determined to make it over to the bar area and have a beer with my buddies, but all I could see in my mind's eye was Leona standing there still as death, crying.

"Shit," I said to myself and hurried back to her. She was still standing there. Her head was bent down. She was fishing for a hanky in her purse. She looked so small, shrunken like, and old. I felt rotten.

I came up to her and stood in front of her. She was still pawing through stuff in her purse. A lipstick fell to the ground. She kept rummaging for a hanky, sobbing quietly. I reached down and picked up the lipstick. I held it out for her. She didn't seem to notice. She just kept digging around in that damned purse. I pulled my hanky out a my back pocket. It was clean so I offered it to her. "Here, use this."

Her shaky hand reached out for it. "Thank you, Joe," she said quietly. "Go have your beer." She wiped her eyes, her head still bowed low.

I looked at her. I felt real bad. Mad at myself for making Leona cry. Mad at Harold for starting this whole romantic thing. Mad at Leona for thinking I would be romantic, for assuming I was doing a nice thing when I said we needed to go see Judy's stuff. Didn't she know me by now? Why didn't she know what I really meant? Couldn't she read between my lines?

What could I do but reach out and wrap my arms around my weeping wife. I held her close to me and patted her back. "Oh, Joe." She sobbed into my chest.

She stretched her arms around me and drew me in even closer. Then her left hand reached up and braced the side of my head, gently tilting it downward. She raised her tear-streaked face to mine and kissed me on the mouth; right there in the park, she kissed me on the mouth. And to show how feeble and old I was getting, I kissed her back. What was I do? Two old fogies, kissing mouth to mouth in the middle of the Fourth of July celebration.

And then, to make matters worse, I started to feel aroused. I knew this could get even more embarrassing in a few moments if I didn't do something real quick.

I cupped my hands around her face and delicate like pulled her away from me. "I'm sorry I was mean, Leona," I said. "I'll go see your friend's crocheting with you and then we can both go have a beer. Okay?"

"That would be wonderful, Joe," she said, beaming; her face was streaked with tears. I took the hanky from her and wiped them.

"And don't get too tired today. We're gonna have to finish this body contact stuff away from the public eye later tonight."

"Oh Joe, don't you worry. I won't be too tired. I'll be anticipating." She clamped her arm onto mine again. I let her do it. We walked on over to see Judy's crochet work.

Without alcohol to slow him down or hang him over, Harold's artistic production nearly doubled. Seems about nearly every weekend, Harold was recruiting someone to help haul a new sculpture out a his shop and onto the hillside in front of his house. The hill bristled with metallic shapes, flashing in the sunshine and rusting in the rain.

Sylvia's tea parties took on new vigor and attracted new enthusiasts. Folks as far away as Portland showed up at the store, looking for Harold and Mag's place. They rented motel rooms in town. They spent money for groceries and gas and for meals at Jolane's and Home Cooking. Locals welcomed their money, smiling at 'em while cultivating their resentments of 'em. It was one of them classic love-hate relationships.

George at the utility company and Ed at the feed and seed were the two most vocal in their opposition to this influx of strangers. I figured that was because they weren't gaining anything from the visitors. Ed was developing a true hostility toward 'em. He caught me as I was locking the front door of the store one evening and told me about it.

"They come into the co-op, picking everything up, laughing and whispering to each other," he said angrily. "They never buy anything. A few stop and chat with me about what a quaint little store the co-op is. Quaint! Is molasses and bran quaint? Is antibiotics for gestating cows quaint?" He spat disgustedly into the road. "I tell you, Joe, Harold and Mag are a bane upon this town."

I didn't wanna cause Ed to take his beer purchasing to Baker City, which he would if I made him mad, 'cause it netted me a fair sum each month. But I thought how strange the co-op must appear to an outsider, the dusty, rambling shelves, the merchandise that sat on the shelves for as long as it took to sell it. I swear; some items had been there since my childhood. I pictured all them baseball caps and that winter gear tacked all over the walls, Ed's thirty-year old marketing strategy. Quaint, I thought. Ed's lucky they didn't break out in wild peals of laughter right in his face.

To Ed, I said, "I'm sure they mean no harm. They're just city folk. They're used to all them big, slick stores like you see on TV."

"Then why don't they stay in the city and go to them stores," he grumbled.

"We go to Boise sometimes, and some folks even go to Portland sometimes. I reckon they have the right to come here."

"But there ain't as many of us as there is of them," he said, "and they wouldn't be coming here if it weren't for Harold and Mag." His hackles were up, I could tell. "They're a bane on Halfway; I tell you," he said again.

I tried a different approach. "The women all like the new and improved Harold."

"Yeah, that's another thing I have against him."

Ed always irritated me anyway so I decided I'd had enough of him for one day. "I got a be heading home, Ed," I said. "Bye." I nodded my nod; he spat on the sidewalk and nodded back at me. I didn't dare tell him why I had to rush. Leona had called Harold and Mag and asked if we could come by and visit tonight.

Chapter 26
What Michelle Says

As my nursery sales grew, I found myself constantly struggling to keep up. Harold pitched in when he could, and Sean contributed his little boy share, but I needed more help. In October, I hired the only person who responded to an ad I'd placed in the local paper, a sixteen-year old girl named Michelle. She worked after school from three-thirty to six.

Michelle worked hard, and I was pleasantly surprised by how much of a difference her help made. We became friends, mine being the motherly role, of course, but with our growing closeness, I began to notice certain things about her that startled me. She peppered our conversations with sexual innuendoes, and Harold mentioned that Michelle's sexual remarks sometimes made him uncomfortable. But neither of us knew what to do about it or if we needed to do anything about it.

In early December, we decided to invite Michelle to dinner, still without any clear plan of what to do. We'd eaten and were visiting in the living room, but still Harold and I hemmed and hawed, unsure what to say next. Finally, we excused ourselves, saying we had to wash the dishes. Michelle volunteered to help, but I suggested, "Maybe you'd like to go with Sean to look at the stray mama cat and her four new kittens who've made a home under the chicken coop."

"Kittens? Cool. Maybe I'll take one when they're ready. Show me, Sean," she said, and she hurried him out the back door.

"What do you think?" I asked Harold after they were gone. "How about, we have dessert, talk a little bit, and then after Sean's gone to bed, we tell Michelle how much we appreciate how hard she works, but we have to ask her to watch her language."

Harold frowned and shook his head. He smudged his hand over his hair and then slowly across his face. "There's something about Michelle that's off. It's more than the sexual words she uses. It's the way she acts that's telling us something." His whole face sagged with worry. "I'm beginning to suspect that she's been abused."

"I wondered about that; she seems to know too much, even for a sixteen-year old. But what should we do?" I asked again.

"I have no idea. I'd say we're sort of out of our area here," Harold answered. "Maybe we should lay her off until January, give us time to check things out, like you suggested yesterday. I don't know what else to do."

We had dessert on the table and were drinking coffee when Sean and Michelle came in. Sean was looking down and seemed subdued.

"Hey, you two, dessert's ready. Pumpkin pie with whipped cream. I know it's one of Sean favorites. I hope you like it too, Michelle."

Michelle hurried over, but Sean remained by the door. "I think I'll go to my room," he said. "I'm full, and I don't feel good." As he turned to go, I could tell something else was wrong. "I'll be right in to check on you," I said. I wanted to rush after him but knew I had to speak to Michelle first.

"I love pumpkin pie," Michelle said, grinning. She plopped down on the chair next to me.

I served her pie and milk. "Michelle, I have bad news," I began and paused. She stopped eating and looked at me. "I won't have any work for you after this week, that is, until January. I'm sorry."

"That's fine," she said and resumed eating, not seeming at all upset, the reaction I'd been worried about. "Actually, it's good. My homework is piling up, and my mom's been after me to keep up so no sweat," she popped another chunk of pie and whipped cream into her mouth. "That'll work out fine." She grinned at me.

"What a relief," I said and smiled at her and Harold. "I was worried that you'd be hurt."

"Naw," she said and even patted my hand. "Come on, we're friends. We have to be honest with each other, right?"

"Right, Michelle," Harold answered and smiled at her. "On that note, we have something else we need to talk about."

"In a few minutes," I said. "I have to make sure Sean's all right." Michelle flashed me a weird look. I smiled at her. "Don't worry, it's nothing bad. We would just like to talk to you about something. I'll be back in a few minutes." I rushed down the hall to my son. His eyes wide open, he was lying on his back on his bed. "What's up, Son?" I asked as I sat on his bed.

Sean sat up and hugged his knees. He said, "I don't know. Michelle and I were looking at the kittens, holding them and watching them play, you know. Then she winked at me and asked if my dad ever visited me in bed at night." Sean shook his head. "You should have seen her face, all funny looking, when she said that. I don't know what she meant, but it gave me the creeps."

Sean's face tightened with the intensity of his words. He went on, "The way she looked at me was weird. I told her that you guys sometimes stopped by to say good night or something like that." Sean squirmed, remembering.

He continued, "Michelle stared at me, then she giggled and said, 'You know what I mean. Visit you, like when you're punished.' " Sean gazed at me, awareness of something discomforting apparent in his expression. "When I didn't answer, she looked at me like she was mad and said, 'Nothing, dummy, forget it.' She didn't talk to me again."

"I'm sorry she made you feel bad, Sean," I told him. "I'll talk to her about what she said."

"No, don't. I think that'll make her mad."

"She won't be mad, and she won't be coming around after Friday. I just told her, okay?"

"That's good."

"She'll be leaving soon tonight, okay? Her mom is picking her up at seven."

Sean nodded and looked down.

"Do you want me to bring you a piece of pie?"

"No, I don't feel like any."

I kissed his forehead and hugged him. "I'll be back with your Dad as soon as Michelle leaves. We need to talk about this. You call me if you need me before then." I shut his door, hoping that would make him feel more secure.

Michelle was at the door putting on her coat when I came in.

"My mom's here early," she said. "We'll have to talk tomorrow when I get here."

"Michelle, I don't want you to worry, but we need to talk about some things. Okay?"

She frowned and shrugged her shoulders. "Did I do something wrong in the greenhouse?"

"No," I said. "Your work is great. It's other stuff." Her mother honked. "We'll talk tomorrow."

"Okay," she said. She waved goodbye and hurried out the door.

Harold and I were as honest with Sean about what Michelle said as we thought we could be for his age and understanding. He was really troubled by this new information and what it meant about his conversation with her. The next afternoon as Michelle helped me pot new cuttings, I fished for a way to ask her about her conversation with Sean, but she opened the topic for me.

"Look," she blurted out, "I know Sean must have told you about me asking about what you guys did when he was punished, but he didn't have to make a big deal out of it. I was just checking you guys out, okay?"

"Checking us out for what?" I asked.

"God!" she shrieked, the first time she had raised her voice with me. "You're just like my father, suspicious. Can't a person say anything? Can we drop it already?" She scowled at me, hands on her hips.

"Michelle," I answered, a little shaken myself. "I wasn't interrogating you, but we can't drop this. You need to be honest with me about what you said to Sean." Michelle stared at me as if I were a stranger, but I kept talking. "If there's anything you want to talk about, I hope you know that you can trust me to keep what you say between us."

She maintained her tense posture but exhaled noisily. Then, smiling coyly, she said in a soft, simpering voice, "Whatever you say, Mrs. Brown. Would you like me to pot the rest of these lavender starts now?" Her fixed, tight smile sat oddly on a face empty of emotion. Her cold eyes showed no emotion.

With growing uneasiness, I said, "Yes, Michelle, that sounds like a good idea. I'll give you time to think about what I just said, but we need to finish this conversation before you leave at six. Harold and I have both noticed your sexual references and are uneasy with some of the things you say. We need to talk, Michelle." We worked the rest of the afternoon in silence.

At six sharp, Michelle said, "Quitting time," and walked out the door.

I ran after her and caught up to her as she was opening her car door; she had driven herself over. "If you don't talk to me, this is it. I won't be able to hire you back in January. You can get your last paycheck in the morning before school."

Michelle fixed me with a vacant stare and said, "Stay out of my life." She turned her car around and drove down our drive.

Michelle came the next morning at seven to get her check. Harold and I thanked her for her hard work and told her we hoped she would change her mind about talking to us. I wanted to keep the door open for her to come back to work. "I would like you to work for me again, but I need you to be honest with me, especially when it comes to my son," I said and handed her check to her.

She turned to leave, not having said a word since entering our home, but at the door, she turned back to us and said, "My parents' car hasn't been running very well. I might need a push to get it started."

Harold said, "Give me a second to put on a jacket, and I'll take a look at it."

"I need to make Sean's lunch," I said. "Call me if you need help pushing." I turned again to Michelle. "Once more, goodbye and thanks for all your hard work." She nodded halfheartedly, and I felt that I should reassure her. "I hope to have you back here in January." I touched her shoulder, intending to hug her, but she flinched, and I withdrew my hand.

"Well, let's get your car started so that you can get to school," Harold said and headed for the door.

He kissed me as he passed by, and out of the corner of my eye, I caught Michelle's sneer. "Goodbye, Michelle," I repeated. "I'll miss having you around."

"Yeah, well," she began, "that's the way it goes." She looked at Harold. "I'm ready, Mr. Brown." She walked out the door. Harold and I exchanged worried looks; then he followed her outside.

I didn't notice how much time had passed as I made Sean's breakfast and bag lunch. He came out of his room dressed for school. We had thought it better that he not be in the room when Michelle came by.

I heard the front door open softly behind me but didn't turn around. "Well Harold, did you solve Michelle's car problem?" I called, confident that he had.

Harold crossed the living room but didn't respond. He walked toward the kitchen sink to wash the grease from his hands but instead slouched onto the counter and leaned his face on his hands. I glanced at him. His face was ashen, and his eyes showed confusion and a tinge of fear.

"My God, Harold, what happened? Are you all right? Is Michelle all right?"

Harold whispered so Sean wouldn't hear. "Babe, something's terribly wrong with that girl. I think our suspicions are correct. I have to tell you what happened. I don't think I should be alone with her anymore. Hell, none of us should. I don't know what that kind of behavior from a little twerp like her means for sure, but I have a pretty good idea." Harold spoke quickly. He rubbed the backs of his greasy hands over his forehead.

I whispered back. "What happened, Harold? I still don't know what happened." My gut twisted into its favorite knot.

He dropped his face into his hands again, oblivious of the grime. "Christ," he spoke into his palms. He lifted his face and stared at me straight on; his cheeks were streaked with grit. "Here's what happened. I went out with her to her car. I asked her to get in and try to start it. She did. It didn't start; it was cranking, but the engine wasn't turning over.

"I signaled for her to stop. I got my truck and pulled up behind her. I told her that I was going to open the shop door and push her in so that I could see better and be warm.

"I worked on her car, rewired some loose connections, cleaned her plugs, got the car running for now, and told her I would order the parts she needed. She thanked me and then the crappy stuff happened."

Harold paused. He looked over at Sean who was concentrating on his breakfast, pretending he wasn't trying to hear what we were saying. Harold's cheeks flushed. His words spilled out gruffly, "She asked me if this was where we were going to do it. Red warning lights flashed in my brain. I said, 'Excuse me?'

"She walked over to me, swinging her hips. She had a frightened look on her face, even as she murmured real sexy like, 'Yeah, your payment. We're out here alone. You fixed my car. You expect payment, right?'

"I told her it was on the house, not to worry, and scrambled over to open the door. I called for her to pull her car on out. She stood there for a few seconds, looking surprised, then said, 'I don't get it.'

" 'What's to get?' I shouted from the door. 'Come on, Michelle, pull that puppy out so I can shut the door before it's freezing in here.'

"She shrugged her shoulders and said, 'I just don't get you people.' She got into her car and pulled out. I walked over to her window and told her to have her folks drop the car off in a few days when the parts came in. I'd fix it on the house for all the hard work she did for you."

Harold drew away from the counter and pulled himself slowly upright. He let out such a long breath it seemed as if he'd been holding it for the duration of his speech. He squirted dish detergent into his palms, turned on the water, and began washing his hands.

As he dried them, he said, "Now, I may have read her all wrong, Mag, but I sure as hell thought she was coming on to me. And it didn't seem as if she was doing it because she was a wild kid or had a crush on me, or anything like that. I could see her fear even while she was swivel-hipping and talking sexy. I got the feeling that she was acting that way because she felt she had to come on to me, that I would expect it."

He grabbed the teapot from its place on the stove and slogged over to the sink to fill it with water. I stood as I had throughout his monologue, a sandwich bag in my left hand and my right hand gripping a sandwich. "What should we do?" I said.

"I was thinking maybe we should call children's services and see what they have to say," he answered. He set the teapot on a large burner and turned its control knob to high. "I don't know if this is enough to get them to investigate, but we sure as hell need to tell them."

"Yes, we do."

"They might have some advice anyway," Harold went on. "At least I hope they do." He sighed.

"I hope so because I keep worrying that we're handling this all wrong," I said.

We called children's services as soon as Sean left for school. They said what we told them was not enough to warrant an investigation. They warned us not to "lead" Michelle by suggesting abuse to her, and they warned us to watch our own behavior around her, saying, "If she's that kind of girl, carrying on like that, you don't want to get caught in a compromising situation."

After we got off the phone, we sat in silence. I told Harold, "I need to take a bath. For some reason, I feel filthy."

He nodded his head and said, "I know what you mean. Normally, I might ask to join you, but right now that idea doesn't feel right."

Later that week, I talked to Joe about Michelle since I knew he saw and heard most everything that went on in town. He pretty much indicated that he'd had similar suspicions, but like me, he had nothing real to base them on. His advice was to keep our thoughts to ourselves. I imagined dreaded, awful things happening to Michelle, with no one there to protect her. I cogitated over how to help her but could hit on no solution.

Two weeks later, long after Harold and I had ended our evening and gone to bed, loud knocking at the front door awakened us. The sudden noise sent us into instant alertness, and we rushed to see who was there. Harold flipped on the outdoor light and opened the door. Michelle stood in front of us, sobbing. A car that I didn't recognize idled in the drive. Michelle waved for them to leave.

The driver stepped out of the car; she was a friend of hers I'd once met. "Are you sure you're okay?" she called.

"Yeah, I'm fine now," Michelle answered. "You can leave."

"All right, see you tomorrow," she said and got into the car and pulled away.

We brought Michelle in, and because she was shaking uncontrollably, I wrapped her in blankets. "She's not freezing to death," Harold said. "She's upset. We don't want to swelter her." He removed one of the blankets.

"I told my dad that he couldn't do it anymore," Michelle said between sobs as we eased her into the oversized armchair.

"Do what?" Harold asked.

"What's going on?" a groggy Sean interrupted.

"Nothing for you to worry about, Son," I said. "Michelle came by. Come on, you need to get back to bed." I escorted sleepy Sean to his room and tucked him in.

When I returned, Harold and Michelle sat in silence. I sat down next to Harold on the couch. Michelle stared from one to the other of us. "I got to know," she whispered. "My daddy says that all parents do it, that it's the way of the Lord. He says that I would be One Fallen From Grace, a fallen angel, if I refuse him." She stopped speaking; her eyes darted back and forth between Harold and me. "He says that I'm not supposed to speak of this to anyone, that I will bring disgrace to myself and my family in the eyes of the Lord if I do, but I have to know."

"What do you want to know?" I wanted to be clear what her question to us was. I didn't want to be accused of leading her.

"I got to know if what my daddy says is true."

"What does he say?" I asked. A chill ran through my body; I feared what I anticipated her saying.

"Daddy says that all fathers lie with their daughters. He says that his sanctifying sperm keep me from being evil and falling into the ways of Satan as Eve did."

"Are you telling us that your father has sex with you?" Harold rasped; anger seethed through his words. He fisted his hands.

"Harold, be careful, no suggestions, remember." I felt imbecilic for saying those words, but the uncomfortable feeling I'd gotten after talking to the children's services counselor revisited me.

Michelle threw off the remaining blankets and approached us, shouting a stream of words. "Yeah, Mr. Brown, Daddy has sex with me. He had sex with me tonight. But I want to know since you don't have a daughter, do you lie with your son, or do you use other men's daughters? You didn't want me. I thought I must be too ugly."

"Hold it, Michelle," Harold cut in. His face blotched red, and the veins on his neck pulsed. "Hold it right there. He gripped her arms just below her shoulders; she wriggled to get free. "Fathers don't lie with their daughters. Your dad's dead wrong about that. If he's done that, he'll go to jail." He released her. She didn't move.

"Do your parents know that you've left home?" I broke in on

Harold.

"No, I snuck over to Cindy's. I told her I was upset about a cat of yours that had died and that I needed to come up here to see you."

"You can stay here tonight, but we should call the sheriff. In the morning we can call children's services. They'll protect you and contact your parents."

"No!" she screamed. "No one else can know! You have to help me run away! You have to!" She grabbed Harold's shirt and tugged on it.

I rushed to her and stroked her hair. "Okay, sure," I whispered. "Don't worry about that now. You're safe here. We won't let anything bad happen to you. Come on, sweetie," I said as I put my arm around her and led her down the hallway to our guest bedroom. "Let's get you settled in bed. You'll be safe; do you believe me? You'll be safe."

"Remember," she stated firmly, "you can't tell anyone about me and Dad. All I want you to do is help me run away."

"Don't worry about that now, Michelle. Get some sleep tonight. Tomorrow morning we'll talk about what to do." We entered the room. I turned back the covers on her bed and fluffed the pillow. I hugged her and asked, "Can I get you a cup of cocoa or tea?"

"No thank you, Mrs. Brown," she murmured. "Can I take a bath?"

"Yeah, sure."

"Cause my body's crawling with daddy slime," she hissed, barely audible. Her lips pulled into a tight frown, and her brow creased in disgust.

"I'm so sorry, Michelle." My face felt heated, and tears escaped my eyes.

"Do you have anything I can sleep in, and something to wear tomorrow?"

"I'll get you a nightgown and put it outside the bathroom door while you're bathing. In the morning you can pick out some clothes of mine to wear. Anything else?"

"Yes, promise you won't call the sheriff or children's services."

I hesitated. My instincts told me to promise her anything tonight, but my brain insisted that I tell the truth. "I can't promise you that," I said, "but I do promise that I'll talk to you before I, we, do anything." Michelle frowned and fidgeted impatiently. I wanted her to know that her secret was safe for the night so I said, "There's no one to tell until morning anyway. The sheriff's fifty miles away, and even if we did roust a whole bunch of people out of bed, they wouldn't come out here until morning. So you're safe, completely safe. We'll talk in the morning before anybody does anything."

She looked at me with that strange emotionless expression of hers, the one with the plastic smile. She was withdrawing from me. I got scared.

"Please, Michelle," I begged, "I would never do anything to hurt you. I want to do what's best to help you."

"Then promise," she demanded. "If you don't, I'm leaving now."

"Okay," I lied in a panic, "I promise."

"I don't believe you."

"Oh Michelle," I answered. I was crying openly.

She softened. "Don't worry about it," she said casually. "I'm going to take a bath." She went into the bathroom and shut the door.

I found a nightgown that was in decent shape for Michelle to wear. I also set out a T-shirt and some sweats in case she didn't like the other choices. I walked into the living room to talk to Harold.

He sat stiffly on the couch, flipping a wrench between his fingers. I thumped down beside him and leaned my head on his shoulder. "This is a mess," I said.

"Should we call anyone tonight?" he asked in a whisper. "I don't want to get in trouble about having her here."

I lifted my head from his warm body, and clutching his arms in my shaking hands, I looked at him intently. "I promised Michelle that I'd wait until after we talked with her in the morning. She doesn't want us to tell anyone. She repeated that she wants to run away. I know we can't let her do that, but we can wait until morning."

"Oh shit." Harold said and moaned. In one quick movement, he kissed my cheek while squeezing my shoulders and moving me to one side. He sprang from the couch and began pacing back and forth in the small space between the furniture and television.

I pleaded, "I was afraid that she'd run. She's insisting that no one can know what she told us."

"We have to call the authorities, now would be best but in the morning for sure," Harold said as he approached me and held my hands in his.

"I know, Harold, I know," I responded, my belly tightening and my heart racing.

A while later, when I saw the light go out in Michelle's room, I quietly tapped on her door and opened it. I tiptoed into her room and peered through the shadows at her small form under the covers.

"I'm fine, Magdalena. I'll see you in the morning," she whispered.

I walked further into the darkness and reached out to touch her shoulder. I felt her body stiffen as my fingers touched her. Oh no, I shouldn't have done that, I thought, as I quickly withdrew my hand. I whispered, "I'm sorry I disturbed you, Michelle. I won't open your door again tonight. I was worried about you and wanted to make sure you were okay."

"I know. Don't sweat it," she said in a sleepy voice.

"Good night, Michelle."

"Good night, Mrs. Brown, and remember, don't call anyone."

"I won't do anything until morning, until after we talk."

Harold and I slept fitfully. In the morning, we crept around the house, trying to not make any noise as we stoked the fire in the woodstove, cooked breakfast, and waited for Michelle to wake. We kept Lucy from barking and hushed Sean, admonishing him to be quiet so that Michelle could sleep.

I didn't call anyone because I'd promised Michelle that I'd talk to her first. Time limped by. I glanced at the clock for the millionth time, eight o'clock. The bus picked Sean up for school.

"I think we should look in on her," I said.

"About time," Harold said.

We tiptoed to her door. I turned the knob slowly so that it wouldn't make any noise. I pushed the door open a crack and peered in. "Oh God no!" I yelled and swung the door open wide.

"What? What?" Harold shouted as he shoved his way around me into the room.

We stared at the empty bed. "She ran," I said. "She didn't trust us not to call anyone. This is my fault, all my fault."

Harold tore about the room, lifting covers, opening the closet. He was frantic. He waved his hands wildly as he spoke, "Oh my God, I hope she's all right. I should have stayed awake and made sure she stayed here." He stared at me, despair and anger sparring for dominance.

"You wanted to call last night. I was the one who said to wait," I told him. "Come on; let's call the sheriff and children's services and anyone else we can think of."

"How about her folks?" Harold inquired; his twisted smile resembled Michelle's.

"Yes, we ought to check there first. She might have gone back home." My gut ache intensified.

"Yeah, she might have."

"Even if she has, we're going to call the authorities," I said as I dialed Michelle's number.

"No question about that."

The Beechum's phone rang. A male voice I didn't recognize answered.

"Hello," I said unsteadily. "May I speak to Michelle?"

"Who is this?" the unfamiliar voice demanded.

"Mag Brown," I answered. "Michelle works for me. To whom am I speaking?" The owner of the voice covered the phone. I heard muffled talking.

A new voice came on the line. "Mag, oh Mag," a distraught Mrs. Beechum said, sobbing. "She's dead, Mag. Whitey found her out behind Jolane's as he walked from his car for coffee this morning."

Her words slammed against my head. "She can't be dead," I said.

Michelle's mother dropped the phone, and I heard her shrieking. The phone thudded against the floor. The unknown voice returned and said, "I'm Officer Regar. When was the last time you saw the deceased?"

My mouth felt swollen and stuffed with cotton. My words lobbed out, already falling as they hit the air. "She was here in the guest bedroom when we went back to bed."

"When did she leave?"

"I don't know. She said she wanted to run away because her father sexually abused her. We thought we'd convinced her to stay until morning when we could get help." I was swimming in murky water, lost, lost, lost.

"I'll need to talk with you."

"Of course," I answered woodenly, struggling to reach the surface of that dark water.

"Is your husband at home or at work?" the voice intruded into my swampy mind.

"Here." A mutter.

"What?" Officer Regar asked gruffly.

"At home."

"I'm going to have to ask you both to stay handy for questioning."

"We'll be here." I forced myself to answer clearly.

"I'll see you in a couple hours probably. Goodbye, ma'am."

"Wait! How did she die? What happened?"

"Drug overdose, ma'am."

"She was desperate when she came her yesterday evening. She said her father had had sex with her last night. I believed her. I think she was telling the truth about her father." The words rushed from my mouth with a will of their own.

The officer didn't answer for a moment. "We'll discuss that when I get there," he said quietly. I thought he sounded suspicious of me.

"You need to check it out. She was very afraid of him." I wanted to holler at him to arrest her dad.

"Ma'am, a child has just died. We need to keep our heads about us. Don't say anything you'll regret. And don't discuss this with anyone. Hang tight until I get there." He hung up.

I set the phone down. I raged at myself. How could I have let this happen! I swung around to face Harold, gearing myself up to tell him. But he knew; his face was drained of color, his jaw slack.

Officer Regar knocked on our door at ten o'clock. Harold and I sat huddled on the couch, as we had been since we'd heard the news. Sean was still at school.

Harold sucked in a quick breath as if startled. "I'll get it," he murmured. He pried his sweaty hands from mine, rose from our warm nest, and walked slowly to the door. I heard him open it and heard the muffled exchange of words that followed.

Officer Regar and he entered the room together. Harold motioned to a chair adjacent to the couch. The deputy sat there, and Harold reclaimed his place next to me.

The deputy initiated the conversation. "You said that you two saw Michelle the evening previous to her death."

We both cringed at that word, death. Harold answered, "Yes, sir, Michelle stayed with us last night. She got here late, after we'd gone to bed. We thought she was still sleeping this morning after we'd gotten up, and we were trying to let her get her rest since she had been so upset last night. "

"What do you mean you were trying to let her get her rest?" Regar interrupted.

"You know, because she'd gotten here so late and was so upset. We figured that she needed to rest," Harold responded.

"Who went to her room?"

"I opened the door. We both were there," I said.

"And you saw that she wasn't there," he concluded my statement. "How come you called her folks to find her when you said that she was running away from her parents?"

"We thought that she might have changed her mind and gone home," I said. "We wanted to check that out before calling anyone else."

"Considering the gravity of the information that Michelle told you last night, why didn't you call the authorities before going to bed."

"Michelle begged us not to. She said that she'd run if we did."

"When were you planning on calling the sheriff?"

Harold cut in. "Sir, we promised Michelle that we'd talk to her first in the morning. We believed that we could convince her that for her own safety, we had to call the sheriff. We assumed that they would handle contacting children's services and Michelle's parents."

I said, "No matter what Michelle decided, we were going to call the sheriff in the morning. With what she had told us, there was no other choice. We wanted to keep her in the house for the night. It was so cold. I wasn't sure anyone would respond during the night anyway."

"A sheriff's deputy would have been around."

"Yes, you're right," I said. "But we didn't want Michelle on the run in the cold and dark." I had to take responsibility. "I was the one who promised her we'd wait until morning to call. She said she'd run if I didn't promise. Harold wanted to call last night."

"Mag thinks what happened is her fault, but truthfully, we were most worried about Michelle running when it was so cold and dark," Harold said. "We thought we were helping her by not calling last night, She probably would have run either way." Harold put his arm around me and briefly rested his head against mine.

Regar continued his questioning. "When was the last time you saw Michelle?"

I answered him. "I went into her room just after she'd gone to bed, about midnight, I think. I wanted to make sure she was all right, but she was very uncomfortable with my presence in her bedroom so I told her that no one would bother again and that we'd see her in the morning." I wracked my brain for clues I should have caught, clues that she would run that night. "I assured her that she was safe here and that we wouldn't call anyone until we'd talked in the morning."

I paused briefly, then demanded from Officer Regar. "Why did she run? How could she have gotten drugs at that time of night? What drugs?" I searched for answers. I hadn't noticed any signs of drug use with Michelle.

"All that we can tell now, ma'am, is that she died and that there were drugs found on her person. Do you know where she might have gotten those drugs, Mrs. Brown?"

Suddenly I realized that he suspected us or at least numbered us among possible suspects. "No, I don't," I answered, sensing my own defensiveness, "and thinking about the friends of hers that I've met, I can't even pick out anyone suspicious."

"I never thought of her as a drug user," Harold added. "She always made it to work and did a good job."

"Do either of you use illegal drugs or take prescription drugs that she could have used to kill herself?" Regar asked as he withdrew a small spiral notebook from his breast pocket and flipped it open to write.

"No, sir, we don't," Harold answered emphatically.

"Mr. Brown, I'll be blunt. You have a reputation around here as an alcoholic. Were you drunk last night?"

"I haven't had a drink in over a year. No sir, I was not drunk." Harold's face flushed, and his shoulders slumped. "I'm in AA. I don't drink anymore."

"Do you, Mr. Brown, use drugs other than alcohol?"

"No, sir, I don't."

"Have you ever engaged in sexual activity with the deceased?"

"Wait a minute!" I called out. "We tell you that Michelle came to us because her father has been raping her for years and that in fact he had raped her that very night, and you suspect my husband of that foul activity?"

"Ma'am, I'm just doing my job," Regar answered, extending his hands in a calming gesture. "I checked out the information you said that you got from Michelle by talking with a few neighbors, but to tell you the truth, the people I questioned this morning did not have one unkind thing to say about her father." Officer Regar regarded us with detached professionalism.

Harold said, "Michelle was too upset and too specific to have made up her story. What she said made my skin crawl." His hands clenched; his voice wavered. "Her father gave her religious justification for what he did. He told her all fathers had sex with their daughters, that if she didn't allow it, she would be a fallen angel."

Regar said, "Kids today pick up all kinds of information from movies and TV. Michelle could have been an unstable teenager, on drugs, who made up that story to cover her own covert sexual activity."

"Sir," Harold said, "I believe Michelle told the truth about her father. You can't shake my belief in that." He was resolved.

"Why was she out messing around with drugs if she wanted to run?" Regar countered.

"She must have been too scared," I shot back. "She must have lost faith that running away was possible. How was she going to get out of this valley without her parents finding out? She must have decided that no one could protect her from her father. As Harold said, her father had convinced her it was the will of God that he do to her what he did."

Harold's whole body shuddered. "Oh God!" he cried out. "She must have been so terrified. Why didn't I stay awake?" He paused as he struggled to control his emotions. Tears streamed down his cheeks. "I don't know where she got the drugs she used, but I suppose lots of teenagers in town could tell you who deals." He looked at Regar. "My guess is that she had the drugs on her already, as backup, in case she couldn't take it anymore, in case she couldn't run away. That she purposely took what she knew was an overdose. She must have thought there was no other way out."

"For the sake of Michelle's parents, you should keep your suppositions to yourself," Regar said, his tone cold.

"Examine her, perform an autopsy, see if there's evidence of sexual violation. Talk to that friend of hers, Cindy," I said.

"Mrs. Brown, there is no proof that what you and your husband say is true, and proof of sexual activity would not necessarily prove her father violated her, unless we have her testimony or testimony of a witness or physical evidence of her father's sexual presence in her, we have nothing. Good day Mr. and Mrs. Brown." Officer Regar touched his cap with the fingers of his right hand. He turned and headed toward the door.

"You should at least test for that evidence," I said.

Regar stopped and turned toward me.

"After what we've told you, you should at least test for her father's sperm in her. She'd taken a bath, but there might be something. Our statements should at least justify looking."

Regar tapped his pad with his pen. "Not necessarily," he said. He opened the door and left.

Chapter 27
Hiring Michelle

Michelle had started working for Magdalena in the fall, and she glommed onto Mag like molasses to bran. In fact, their union seemed as nourishing to Michelle as the grain mixture was to cattle.

From the first time I met Michelle, I noticed that she had a hungry dog look about her, but it wasn't food she was longing for. She greedily grabbed up any bone of affection cast her way, seeming to crave love and attention, like she couldn't ever get enough.

I puzzled over her behavior because when I saw her with her folks, they seemed to show her the normal amount of parental affection. They had their own ways of disciplining that I didn't quite agree with, one in particular was a bit harsh, but their intentions seemed good. For Christ's sake, her father was the lay minister of Valley View Church; of all people, he should have been one to exercise Christian compassion.

A child can get beyond control, I imagine, and need drastic methods. Leona and I were never lucky enough to have kids so I can't judge, but the thing they did that bothered me was how they punished Michelle for sassing. She had to sleep in the tack room of the barn with it locked from the outside. I worried about her getting cold or being scared, and I worried about fire. Not that there was any reason for a fire to start in their barn, but God, what if it did?

Reverend Beechum spoke openly about having to lock his daughter in the tack room. If she said anything bordering on defiance, he quietly suggested, "Looks like my little missy needs a night in the tack room." Odd thing was, he always smiled sweetly at Michelle after his threat.

When he said those words and smiled like that, I don't know why, but the hairs on the back of my neck rose up, and my stomach tightened. Something about his look and her face flushing in response was creepy. I never told anyone this because there was nothing definite to really tell, a gut feeling; that was all.

I was seeing more of Michelle now that she was earning her own money. After stopping at the bank to deposit most of it as she said her parents made her, Michelle came by my place to buy a cheap lipstick or one of them hanging from a rack perfumes. She was proud of her weekly paycheck and wanted to talk about her work.

"Me and Mag are getting a shipment ready for the Good Earth Nursery in Seattle," she explained one day, waving her hands to emphasize her exhaustion. "Sooooo many plants! One day we're potting starts. Another day we're packaging dried rose petals; the next day we're processing lavender for the oil. I'm learning how to pot cuttings and dig bulbs. I see green as I fall asleep." She laughed, happier than I'd ever seen her.

"Mag's lucky she found you to work for her," I commented as I bagged her Pouty Plum lipstick and Midnight Escapade mascara.

Michelle's expression showed genuine surprise as my compliment slowly eased its way into her brain. "Yeah," she responded, a smile stretching bigger and bigger across her face, "I guess she is. See you later, Mr. Mobley. Bye!" She fluttered the fingers of her right hand rapidly in her version of a wave and hurried out into the chilly November evening. I figured she was running home to smear Pouty Plum all over her lips and to glop Midnight Escapade with lengtheners onto her young eyelashes.

Since business was slow at the store in the afternoon, I wandered on over to Harold's for a visit. "Harold, what's happening?" I called as I walked toward him, not that he'd really know much, but what he did know he'd turn comic. He was hunched over the engine of a '79 Chevy Impala, putting a plug in. He lifted his head and turned just enough to acknowledge me.

"Howdy, Joe," he called and returned his gaze to his problem. "Not much happening here." He seemed preoccupied by more than that Chevy. He shook his head in dismay. "I don't know how Dave did it," he said, "but he managed to cross-thread each and every one of his plugs. One of those save money, home repair schemes gone bad."

"Can you fix it?" I asked.

"Oh sure," he said, "but it's a pain in the butt." We both laughed. "Anything I can do you for?" he asked.

"No, I just came by to shoot the breeze."

"Sorry I'm not better company; this job's a bitch, and, Joe, I'm sort of worried about something else." He paused. "Michelle Beechum, the girl who works for Mag. You know her?" he smiled at me, raising his eyebrows the way he did.

"She stops by the store more now to spend some of the money your wife is paying her; that's about the size of it," I hedged. I didn't want to get into no Michelle talk with Harold any more than I wouldn't want to with Mag.

"Ah, yeah." Harold's look was suspicious. He went back to leaning over the car's engine, touching a part here, jiggling another part there. "Well, I better be getting back to work. Thanks for stopping by, Joe." He slid his dolly under the Chevy.

"No plugs down there, Harold."

He laughed. "You got that right, Joe. Dave mentioned a fluid leak of unknown origin, I thought I'd have a look while I was thinking about it." That was it? No story, no funny commentary of the week's work? No detailed description of his latest work of art?

I shifted uneasily and fiddled with the change in my pockets. I knew I could give Harold more information about Michelle, and my guilty mind figured that Harold knew it too. "Ah, okay, catch you later, Harold," I said and sidled toward the door. "Bye," I said, but I thought that Harold was probably thinking, don't let the door hit you in the rear on the way out.

I was bagging Mrs. Hampton's $10.46 worth of groceries, still stewing over Harold's lack of pizzazz during my visit to his shop, when I saw Harold and Mag drive by in their pickup. Mrs. Hampton spotted them and grabbed at the opportunity to proclaim, "I heard them two is joining a Satanic cult. In fact they're taking the rights of initiation this weekend." She set her jaw; her dark eyes stared at my throat; she was a short, old woman with a perpetually stiff neck.

"Is that so?" I said. "I think your informant is misinformed. In fact, you can tell Sally to give it up already with the Satanic crap." I shook my head in disgust. Sally was too much. I'm not one to say much, but Christ, Sally had gone off the deep end on this one.

"Sally knows what she's talking about," Mrs. Hampton insisted.

"In a pigs eye!"

"Enough!" she shouted. "You don't have to get testy about it. Who's an old lady to believe these days? Goodbye, Mr. Mobley." She smiled her misaligned false teeth smile, hoisted her brown bagged groceries into her cloth handled bag, and clumped out the door, whacking the floor with her cane in rhythm with each step. The rubber end protector on that cane always left black skid marks that were the dickens to get off the floor, damn her.

My evening ruined by that exchange with Mrs. Hampton, I fussed around the store stocking shelves and cleaning, mumbling to myself. I was in a dither.

Harold and Mag stopped at the store on their way back through town. I could tell right off that Harold's mood had improved markedly.

"Hello, you two!" I called. "I better put out the word that you're back from your drive, Harold, so that our vehicles can start breaking down again."

"No need to do that, Joe," Harold answered. "I've come to believe that I emit vibes that draw decrepit and injured engines to me. The forces in control of said vibes are much bigger than all of us." He pointed to the three of us.

"I'd say by your cheerful mood that everything must be all right now. I mean, with Michelle." What in hell caused me to bring Michelle up? Damn! Now they could say that everything was not all right. I hated conflict, but more than that I hated the guilt I'd been feeling.

Mag answered, "We're working on it."

Harold reached over to hug Mag. He pulled her close and planted a big kiss on her cheek. "We called children's services, but it seems we don't have enough proof for them to get involved." He smiled a sad smile at Mag. "We don't know what else to do. We're talking about it, trying to figure something out." He shrugged his shoulders and looked at his watch. "Mag, we better get a move on; we have to pick up Sean by six." They bought chicken breasts and spinach and hurried out.

Along about November nineteenth, Portland's Oregonian newspaper sent a reporter to do a human-interest story about Harold and Magdalena. He brought a photographer with him. Folks joked that there were more important characters in town than an alcoholic mechanic and hippie plant grower and adamantly discussed who should be interviewed instead.

After one day in town though and having talked to no one but Harold and Mag, the reporter and photographer hopped in their van and drove west toward Portland. Folks shrugged their shoulders and made disparaging comments about Portland and newspapers, but nothing more was thought of the incident.

No one really expected an interview with the Browns to appear in the newspaper, but two weeks later, the front page of the Oregonian's Sunday City and Region Section featured the beaming faces of Harold, Sean, and Magdalena. They stood in front of their south-facing slope, the one that was peopled with Harold's creations. The article was long, extending to page two. It was full of welding and planting details and homey little references to the loving couple.

Personally, I think the gossipy sniping about the story was rooted in basic human resentment of the notoriety that such an article gave Harold and Mag. Whatever the cause, the result was that Halfway had a bitter brew of powerful feelings swirling amongst its residents, a brew that was waiting for an outlet.

Portlanders who'd read the article began inquiring at my store for directions to the Brown place even though the weather was getting bad. If it was a weekday, I directed them to Harold at his shop; if not, I told them where the Browns lived. I always planned on asking Harold if he really wanted these strangers to have his address, but like a lot of my intentions, I never got around to actually doing anything about it.

The Baker City News ran an article telling about the Oregonian article and exclaiming on the talents of Harold and Mag. More folks showed up at the store asking directions to the Brown place. All us merchants profited from this unexpected influx of people, but the resentful grumbling continued.

"Don't that beat all!" George exclaimed as he ate his dinner at Jolane's. Leona and I had met George and his wife at the door and had ended up eating with 'em, much to my dismay. George continued, "The prodigal alcoholic comes home and gets writ up in the paper for the litter he's spread all over the hillside in front of his house. I heard some weirdoes telling Bob that the town should put up a billboard announcing the presence of our famous resident, the artiste, Harold." He laughed derisively. "More to the point, he should get a citation for degrading the landscape." George slapped his knee. "Go figure," he added, in a disgusted tone.

Leona was getting uncomfortable with the criticism George was heaping on her pals, the lovebirds. She fairly squirmed in her seat; she was worrying so. Finally, she broke into George's monologue. "I like Harold's figures," she said.

George stared at her silently for a moment. "Is that so?" he stated more than asked.

"Yes," Leona answered firmly. She neatly placed her fork and knife along each side of her plate. She clasped her hands together in her lap, a sure sign that she was ready to do battle. "I think they're interesting and fun." She nodded my nod at George. I cringed.

"Ain't you the little art critic," George intoned flatly. His face was drained of color. I was madly trying to think of something funny to say to diffuse the situation. Marge, his wife, just kept on eating, humming softly to herself, seemingly unaware of the drama unfolding around her.

"I bet the snow melts off right early this year," I said casually. "I know it'll be near three foot come December, but I have a feeling that it's going to be an early spring."

My silly words hung clumsily between George's cold stare and Leona's back-at-ya defiance. Then Leona jumped as if someone had startled her with a tap on the shoulder. She seemed to be coming to as she shook her head slowly from side to side. She spoke carefully, "It's not worth the bother, arguing with you, George. You and I know nothing's going to change your mind." She looked sagely and pityingly at George. I had never seen Leona act quite like that before. Marge hummed on, engrossed in her meal.

Leona turned to me. She addressed my comment about spring. "I agree, Joe. I think we will have an early spring. Say, I've been wanting to try some of those winter hardy honeysuckles up by the house and maybe another cherry tree. Come March, we should go to Baker City and check out the plant situation at Hilton's nursery."

Leona rattled cheerfully on about plants and the spring that was still at least five months away. I jumped into the conversation wholeheartedly, ignoring George. I glimpsed him out of the corner of my eye; he was balled up with suspended anger and frustration. But he didn't know what to do. Any kind of eruption on his part would put him in a bad light in a public place, seeing as how Leona and I were talking civilly to him and each other. Marge hummed and forked food into her mouth.

We ended our meal with a cup of coffee, but George sat unmoving in front of his food. When the waitress asked if she should take it away, I had to tell her no, that I didn't think George was finished yet. Marge had emptied her plate and wiped it clean with pieces of her dinner rolls. She hummed to herself and smiled at us; I was beginning to wonder about that woman.

When we were ready to leave, George still sat locked in anger. We stood and said howdy to a few folks. Leona grabbed Marge's hand and bade her goodbye. Marge nodded at her and hummed to herself. Then Leona reached across the table and patted George's hand, "It's okay, dear. We'll be leaving now. It's all over. You can eat." She "tsk-tsked" to herself while shaking her head in dismay. "Come on, Joe. We best be leaving," she said. She hooked her arm under mine and steered me to the cashier.

Long about the first of December, Mag came into the store, acting all preoccupied like. She shopped slowly and had to double back many times as she remembered items in aisles that she had already passed.

When she made it to the checkout counter, I asked her what was weighing so heavily on her mind. She brought her head up real quick and looked at me like she wasn't sure she should say what actually was on her mind. She glanced around the store. Just three other folks were there, and they were engaged in conversation back by the vegetables.

She leaned in close to me. Our faces were only two, three inches apart. "Joe," she whispered, "how well do you know Michelle and her parents?"

"Just casual like," I answered, also in a hush, but them nagging hairs were up on the back of my neck again.

"I don't know what's wrong," she breathed out hoarsely, "and as we told you, we don't know enough for the children's service people to get involved, but something is wrong. Something is terribly wrong. Michelle does and says some strange things when her guard is down."

Mag lowered her gaze to the counter and braced herself on her arms. She really looked troubled. My neck hairs bristled, but I said nothing.

She smiled dolefully at me. "We don't know what to do, Joe."

"Not much you can do, 'less you know something for sure," I said.

"Yeah, I guess," she mumbled as she fished in her purse for a pen to write a check. I handed her one. She accepted it, thanked me, and wrote her check.

She scooped up her groceries. I waited for her to add one last sentence, the way she usually did. "I get this gut ache, Joe," she said uneasily. "Like my body's sending me signals. The black and white proof may not be there, but I tell you, Joe, this girl is being abused by her father. I know it."

My neck and spine were on fire; them hairs were singed. Mag had said the words of accusation out loud. They sounded awful and raw. My gut reeled like Mag's must have saying those words. A part of me agreed with her, knew she was right.

"There's no proof, Mag. You can't say something like that without proof."

"Then you've thought it too, Joe." Recognition of my knowledge flashed through Mag's brain. I saw her face flush crimson as she realized I had suspicions too. She reached over and touched my chest near my throat. I felt the power of her emotions.

"Listen, Mag," I whispered hurriedly because the vegetable group had broken up, and two of 'em were strolling toward the checkout counter. "You better watch what you say. Neither one of us knows what's going on. A gut feeling ain't enough." Phil plopped a steak and some carrots on the counter. I leaned around him and mouthed into Mag's ear, "This won't go no further than me, Mag."

She looked at me, puzzled and disappointed. "Sure, Joe. See you later," she mumbled.

"Joe," Phil called. "What the hell you two been arguing about? You look like you seen a ghost."

Mag turned, her hand poised to push open the door. "We weren't arguing, Phil, just discussing probabilities. Scary stuff, huh, Joe." Mag's piercing look collapsed my throat and set my heart to pounding.

"Yeah, scary, and so uncertain," I answered.

Mag nodded affirmatively and stood, ready to go but not leaving. Suddenly, she dropped her head, listlessly swinging it from side to side. "Probabilities and uncertainties, that's what it's all about, that and things so awful and frightening, we can only guess at them." She turned and left.

"What's eating at her?" Phil queried.

"Oh, nothing she won't get over," I answered like a coward.

Three days later, as I came to open my store, I saw two of Baker County's ten cop cars parked in front of Jolane's. I knew something big must have gone wrong. Then I got word of Michelle's death. I didn't want to think. I didn't want to show myself, sure that my blaze of yellow cowardice would show me for what I was, making evident to everyone my guilty part in Michelle's death.

Chapter 28

Michelle Is Dead

I faced a confused, angry Harold. We stood two feet apart, yet neither of us approached the other.

I worried about Sean finding out about Michelle at school. "We need go see Sean and tell him about Michelle," I said.

"Yes, we do," Harold answered. "We'll both go. I don't want to be alone right now. I might do something stupid."

"Sweetheart," I said and beckoned him into my embrace. Harold walked over to me and into my arms. He laid his cheek against mine. His wrenching sobs shook his entire body.

Harold kept in almost daily contact with his Phoenix sponsor and support group by phone, but he hadn't joined a group here. I had worried about this but hadn't talked to him about it.

As if reading my mind, Harold said, "I know I need to join an AA group here. The closest one is in Baker; I checked. I hadn't wanted to have to drive that far, but I know I need to. There's a meeting tomorrow. I'll go."

"That's a Saturday. We can all go if you'd like, make a day of it," I said.

Harold nodded. We held hands and walked to the truck. Once at the elementary school, we told the principal what had happened, and he let us use his office to meet with Sean.

I broke the news. "Sean," I said, "Michelle didn't wake up this morning because she was no longer at our house. She left sometime during the night and went to town. When she got there, something happened, and she died. We found out what had happened to her when we realized that she was no longer in the bedroom and called her parents to see if she had gone back home. We told the sheriff that Michelle had been at our house last night. He's trying to figure out what happened to Michelle after she left us. Everyone is very upset and sad. I'm sorry to have to tell you this, Son." My words had spilled from my lips in an unbroken stream. What terrible things to say to a child, so brutal and plain.

"Is Michelle really dead?" he whispered, and I imagined his child's mind configuring what he knew of death: Frieda's death, the fish he caught, dead birds, dead dear, a road-killed animal. "Is it really true?"

"Yes, it's true," I told him, not knowing what else to add. "We're all sad, but we'll have to help each other get through this. Your dad and I don't understand how this happened, but . . ," I started, then paused to look at Harold, "we hope Michelle is at peace."

"We wanted to be the ones to tell you Son," Harold said. "Would you like to come home for the day so we can be together, to talk more, or do you want to go back to class?"

Sean shrugged. His lower lip jutted out.

"You can stay in school for now if you like," I said. "But if you change your mind, you can call us any time during the day."

"Yeah," he said. "I think that's what I'll do." He looked ready to dry; I was uncertain that I should let him stay at school.

We said our good-bye's, and Principal Jones walked Sean back to class. He said he would keep an eye on him and let us know if he thought he would be better off at home. "Sometimes the distraction of school is a good thing in these types of circumstances," he said. "I'll fill in his teacher. Then I'll contact Michelle's family. We're going to have to have an assembly about it. Word will get here. Most of the kids know who Michelle is."

Harold and I went back to our truck and drove home. Harold had decided he'd go to his shop later in the day, if at all.

"We'll get through this," Harold said and hugged me as soon as we came in the house. He took a deep breath and relaxed his hold. "But we have to make this right. We have to find out if what she said was true. Her death has to matter."

I didn't say anything. I put my hand in Harold's and felt his strength; I gathered strength from knowing that I could count on him, that he wouldn't be out the door and down the drive on his way to the bar, escaping. He would be here with me. We would help each other.

"How about we have some hot chocolate," Harold suggested, "and talk?"

"Sounds good to me," I answered with a weak smile.

I stirred the heating milk while Harold got out mugs. I measured hot cocoa mix into the milk. I turned the radio on to a station that played old rock 'n roll, keeping the volume low. The phone rang.

"Don't answer it," Harold said. "We know what they're going to say. Don't answer it." His look was grim; I saw his anger growing as he realized the extent of his grief. The phone rang and rang.

"Okay, Harold," I said. "I won't answer it."

Harold took a seat at the table and gazed at his hands."

I looked over at him. His hunched body seemed heaped upon the chair in which he sat. The phone started ringing again. "Maybe I should answer it and let folks know that we know so that they'll quit calling," I said. "I'll keep it short."

"Yeah, sure, that's fine," he said. "I'm sorry. I guess I'm not being much help." He rested his face in his palms. "Arrrrrg!" he shouted into his cupped hands, but when he lifted his head, he looked calm. As I lifted the receiver, he said, "We'll get to the bottom of this."

"Hello," I said.

"Mag, it's Marge," a shaky voice said, "George wanted me to call you to see why the police were out to talk to you. What's that, George? George wants to know if Harold and you gave Michelle drugs?"

"Why doesn't George ask me himself?' I asked.

"She wants to know why don't you ask yourself." I heard Marge's muffled call to George. "Well, you could talk to her yourself," she continued. "Humph, old fart," she said, and then she must have taken her hand off the receiver because I heard her clearly. "Mag, I can't abide this old man. Usually I ignore him, but he's been yapping at me all morning to call you. Him and Sally are scheming like two old rooster-less hens. Do you have anything you want to say to him?"

"Yes, Marge, tell him no, we didn't give Michelle any drugs. We did give her a place to sleep last night, but she left sometime during the night. Goodbye, Marge."

"Goodbye, Magdalena."

I hung up the phone.

"That should stop most of the ringing. I'm sure George was making Marge keep dialing until she got an answer," I said.

Harold said. "Is that milk hot yet?"

"Yep," I answered and poured our mugs full.

We talked about the upcoming holidays for a while, whether parents were coming to us or we were going to parents; then abruptly Harold said, "We have to know the truth, Magdalena. You know that."

I felt it too, a crystal hardness. Shame over not having saved Michelle. Anger at her father for doing what he did to her. And worst of all, isolation. Sylvia and Whitey would believe us and help us, I thought, but the rest of Halfway would suspect us of involvement in Michelle's death, just as George did. They might not say so. They might not want to think it so, but somewhere at the backs of their minds would be nagging thoughts about drunk Harold and weird Magdalena and that yes, we did give Michelle drugs. If we told townspeople what Michelle told us about her father, they would say that we made it up to get out of having given her drugs.

My mind spun on, out of control with fears and suppositions. Reverend Beechum was a respected member of the community. We weren't. He was a minister, a lay minister, but a minister none-the-less.

"We have to get the truth out," Harold said.

"Get the truth out?" I echoed, noticing the slight but significant difference in what he said. "Yes, we do. I just don't know how."

"People have to know what Beechum did," he said. "He's a minister. People trust their well being with him. He may be harming other children. We can't let this be."

"But we don't know for sure," I insisted, even though in my heart I believed that I knew for sure.

"Drop the pretext, Mag," Harold said flatly. "I know what you think."

And he did know, but how would we ever get the truth out? We knew the truth. It had to be the truth. Why would Michelle lie about something like that? What could be her reasons?

"I need to call my sponsor," Harold said, and he reached for the phone.

As he dialed, I said, "Yes, good idea." I felt numb; I wanted to go back in time. I wanted a do-over of last night.

Chapter 29

Druggie or Victim, Your Guess Is As Good As Mine

What can I say about that morning? God, I'm not sure. Maybe because of the way Michelle died and the shock of it, you know, I always connect it with that squealing guitar, rock song I hear on the radio about a purple haze burning in someone's brain. I wonder if that was what Michelle felt as she died or if that was what she feared? And if I think on it too long the insides of my own skull start to crackle and seer.

The craziness started soon after I'd eased into town the back way, like I always did, so's no one would see that I was at the store and come pestering me before it was opening time. I was slithering around in the dimness of the unlit aisles, relying on streetlights to guide my shelf stocking, when I noticed red and blue lights flashing on the back wall. "What the hell?" I muttered to myself and meandered toward the front window to check out what was happening.

Two sheriff's squad cars were parked in front of Jolane's, their lights flashing. The deputies were not in sight. "Jesus Christ," I said to myself. "That's twenty percent of Baker County's sheriff's department. What the hell's going on?" I scrambled to unlock the front door and headed over to the crowd already gathered. Bill was the first one I came to.

I grabbed onto his arm and shook it a little, demanding from him, "Bill, why are these deputies here?"

He lowered his chin a bit while continuing to stare into the shadows moving along the backside of Jolane's. "Woe, settle down, man," he whispered into my ear. "I'm more likely to tell ya what's happening than not. No need to get excited." He waved me even closer with a slight flick of a crooked index finger.

Then he leaned his whole body in toward me, as if everyone but me didn't already know what he was about to say. "Joe, you know that Beechum girl, Michelle?" I nodded, fear already needling me. "Whitey found her dead out back a here when he came in for coffee this morning. That's her body under the sheets that they're putting in the ambulance. Cops are saying drugs."

I felt my face drain of color. I heard the rest of his words as from a distance, muffled-like. "Damn kids! Fooling around with shit like that, causing their folks all that grief. It's a harsh sentence, but like as not, she got what she deserved."

"What?" I asked, astounded. I came to real quick with those last words of his.

"I said that she got what she deserved." Bill pulled out a pack of cigarettes, extracted one, and lit it. A cloud of smoke enveloped his head as he inhaled frantic, short puffs. He could no longer breathe very deeply without coughing up a storm. Squinting his eyes against his self-made noxious onslaught, he nudged Ed and leaned toward him to confide. The weight of his last comment had slipped from his lips and into the airwaves without even bruising his tongue.

I was stunned. My own complicity and guilt filled my chest to capacity, as if I'd backed a mixing truck up to my mouth, rested the shoot on my lower incisors, and filled my lungs with solidifying concrete. I gasped for breath and looked around for Whitey. He sat away from the crowd on the curb. His arms hung loosely from where they rested on his knees. His chin rested on his chest. The brim of his beat up old cowboy hat bent slightly upward where it touched his chest, and the hat itself perched inches away from his head, teetering. Sylvia rubbed his back slowly. I could see her lips moving as she talked quietly to him.

I sat down next to him. "Howdy, Sylvia. Whitey." I said, nodding with each name.

Whitey nodded only, but Sylvia spoke, "Hello, Joe. Poor Michelle, so sad, so sad." She looked about to collapse into tears.

"Yeah, she was a sweet girl," I agreed. "I can't believe what Bill was saying about drugs, can you?" In my mind I beseeched them to give me clear insight into what had happened.

Whitey slung his head up; his hat wobbled uncertainly before it settled on his skull. He stared at me for many seconds without speaking, his eyes dark and grieving.

"Something isn't right with all this," he said with a hoarse voice. "I don't know what, but the whole deal's off kilter." He paused and shook his head. He reached an arm around Sylvia and hugged her. "You're right, Joe. Michelle didn't seem the type to use drugs."

I put in my two bits. "I didn't figure her that way," I said. Then I changed the direction of the conversation. "Had she been dead long when you found her, Whitey?"

"She was colder than a stillborn calf resting on March snow," Whitey said wearily. He glanced over at Sylvia and then back at me. He hesitated, as though considering his words carefully. At length, he said, "We talked to Michelle quite a few times when she was working at Mag and Harold's place. To be honest, Sylvia and I considered the possibility that there was something hidden about her, but it wasn't a drug problem that we worried about." He looked at me real intense-like. Then he asked, "You ever notice anything odd about Michelle, Joe?"

I heard the cock crow and the bell toll. I swallowed slowly before I answered him. "No, nothing definite, Whitey." My alarms went off; I wondered how much he, Sylvia, Mag, and Harold had discussed Michelle. I kept talking to fill the spaces of my omissions. "She was such a shy little thing, always buying little teenage doodads."

Whitey zeroed in on my half-truths. His choking emotions made his words erupt spasmodically from his mouth. "Yeah, nothing definite, but something. You got to admit; there was something."

He touched my chest with a long, steady index finger and then wagged that finger in the direction of the restaurant and the deputies. He rasped, "I told the deputies that she wasn't a drug user, that maybe someone was hurting her in intimate ways, that they ought to investigate. They asked me, 'Based on what?' I could only answer, 'Nothing definite, words here and there, peculiar actions.'"

"Christ Almighty." He fumed in impotent rage. "Nothing definite, and Michelle, meanwhile, is dead." His eyes drilled into mine, and pain ripped through my brain.

Sylvia patted Whitey's knee. She murmured to him, "Let's go home, babe. We'll go see Mag and Harold later, to decide if there's anything we can do. Come on, Whitey." Scooping her hands under Whitey's armpits, she rose to a crouch while gently tugging her husband up with her. "Bye, Joe. It's been a day for us already. Bye, bye."

"See you both later. Take care of yourselves," I answered. Whitey said nothing as he let Sylvia lead him away. The vulnerability of these two aged friends loomed suddenly prominent in my thoughts as I watched their tender departure. Michelle's death had made me keenly aware of life's fragile hold on us.

The crowd had grown while I'd talked to Whitey, but I didn't have the stomach to speak with anyone else. I turned in the direction of my store and padded on back. It crossed my mind that I'd left the door open and the store unattended for at least fifteen minutes. Simultaneous with this thought, I scolded myself, "How could you think of merchandise at a time like this." But I quickened my pace anyway.

A half hour later, I opened my door for business. Folks were soon shuffling inside, busy gabbing about this fresh disaster. I'll hear about this all day, over and over, I thought to myself, misery upon misery.

I saw Sally stride full tilt across the street and along the sidewalk fronting the store. When she came in, she shoved the door so hard that it banged noisily against the flimsy plywood backstop I'd rigged up between it and the magazine rack. Her purposeful ardor immediately angered me. With her hefty swing of the door, not only had she exposed the shoddiness of my handiwork; she had introduced her bothersome presence into my business. "Here comes my first earful," I complained to the cash register.

"Joe! Joe?" Sally called loudly. "Did you hear about Michelle?"

"Yes, Sally, I did," I answered. "I feel mighty sorry for all concerned."

"All?" Sally inquired icily. "Seems one dead little girl played on the wild side and got her comeuppance."

"Sally, I'm in no mood for your rancor today," I stated as calmly as I could.

"Well, I never, Joe Mobley," Sally said, indignant as hell. "There's a good portion of this town as feels the little druggie's death will serve as fair warning to other teenagers not to mess around with that evil stuff."

Sally lowered her head, and her eyes filled with tears; she looked almost like she was genuinely concerned, but she continued talking, showing that my request had no weight with her. "A child's death is always sad, naturally," she prattled on. "I feel especially sorrowful for her parents, but the Bible says you reap what you sow."

I interrupted her, "Keep that in mind, Sally. Excuse me, I have paying customers to help."

Sally wasn't affected by my rebuff. As I turned away from her, I heard her call, "Ed! George! Marge! Did you hear?" She raced over to the meat counter where Ed was busy pawing through my T-bones, which he wouldn't buy, just criticize, and Marge was looking at each and every package of chicken breasts, wings, legs, thighs, half-chickens, and whole chickens before, humming tunelessly, she would settle on one.

I'd just rung up Ed and Marge's purchase when Leona called, in tears, to find out if what she had heard was true. I knew I should have called her. As usual, my selfish self had concentrated on my own feelings. I kept this in mind as I told her, yes, it was true, and she bawled harder. "Calm down," I said. "I'll be home as soon as Beth gets here. I don't feel up to listening to everyone's retelling of events all day." I couldn't help but inquire, "Are you gonna be okay until I can get home?"

My expression of concern was enough to mollify poor old Leona, as sad and shocked as she was. Her sobbing slowed some, and she answered me through jerking breaths, "Yes, sweetie, I'll be fine. Hurry home."

"Soon as I can. Bye, Leona."

I left the store for home about eleven. Around three-thirty in the afternoon, our phone rang. It was Mrs. Rodal, demanding, "What are you going to do about it? You're friends with them. You need to help us stop them. Are you with us?"

I'd been dozing on the couch with the TV sputtering in the background. I'd only answered the phone because Leona didn't. I didn't like talking to Mrs. Rodal in person, let alone on the phone. "What the hell are you talking about?" I growled at her as gruffly as she had spoken to me.

"Your friends, Harold and Magdalena, are going around town accusing Reverend Beechum of violating his daughter, God rest her soul. We need to band together and stop them."

Oh Christ, I thought. Out loud, I said, "Mrs. Rodal, tell me exactly what they did and said and make it snappy."

"Sally said that George said that Harold and Mag told Bob that Reverend Beechum was having sex with his daughter and that was why she killed herself. He said killed herself, not drug overdose. In all my days, I never . . ."

"I'm sorry I asked," I cut in. "Call somebody else, Mrs. Rodal. I'm in no mood." I thumped the phone back into its cradle and sat there fuming. I heard the front door knob, about eight feet away, turning slowly. Leona quietly stepped into the room while peeping over the couch to see if I was still sleeping. "I'm awake," I snapped. Leona jumped slightly, startled, and walked briskly to me.

"You wanna know the latest?" she asked bluntly.

"Do you have it straight from the horse's mouth?"

"Nearly, I met Bob and Nancy on my walk. They drove by on their way to Boise for Nancy's hysterectomy tomorrow. That's why Bob called Harold, and that's why Harold came to town to pull his vehicle out of his shop," she announced, as if a riddle were now solved.

"Huh?' You'll have to fill me in a bit more."

"Bob has to get Nancy to Boise by six this evening so's she can check in to the hospital and get prepped for the operation she's having tomorrow. He needed Harold to get him his car.

"Harold did this, and in the course of their conversation, he told Bob that he figured that Michelle had killed herself because the reverend was having sex with her. Bob didn't know what to make of this shocking information so he asked George if he knew anything about the reverend abusing his daughter. George, being George, has told everybody in town.

"George, Sally, and Ed are circulating a petition to get Harold's business closed on account of he's a no good liar." Leona gripped my arms and frowned into my face. "What are we going to do, dear? What should we do? Why would Harold say such a thing about Reverend Beechum?"

I hesitated momentarily, deciding whether to get Leona involved in my wonderings, Whitey's, Harold's, and Mag's suspicions on the subject. I considered how Leona was an integral part of this town. I reasoned that I didn't want to tell her anything that might cut her off from her life's blood. I figured I was excusing my chicken-heartedness. Whatever the reason, I mumbled to her, "Beats the hell out a me where Harold gets his ideas."

Leona remained unsettled. She said, "I don't know what to think. I've always trusted Reverend Beechum, but then, I never thought of Harold as one to lie."

"Maybe he's just mistaken," I suggested.

"He must believe what he said to talk of it like that."

"Harold didn't know Bob was gonna blab to George. What the hell was Bob thinking, asking George for an opinion?"

"Yeah, but still," Leona reasoned, "Seems there's always a grain of truth in rumors and gossip."

"Michelle's dead so what can we do? It's over, isn't it?"

Leona looked at me quizzically, appearing astonished by my ignorance. "Oh, Joe, I would reckon the tragedy's only just begun."

She was right. Our phone rang repeatedly for the rest of the day and evening. Within ten minutes of Leona finishing one conversation, another person called to pump her for what she knew and to impart any rumors he or she had.

From what Leona told me, sympathy for the Reverend and Mrs. Beechum grew hourly as rumors of Harold's accusations spread.

Harold's past alcoholic indiscretions multiplied in number and grew in magnitude. The oddness of Harold and Magdalena assumed new proportions. The hillside of metal people and the tea parties in the sanctuaries loomed again as fascinating topics of suspicion. Even the old greenhouse-pot growing rumors resurfaced.

"Leona, why do you keep answering the phone?" I finally asked.

"It might be important," she answered emphatically.

"If it's important, whoever's calling will drive out here and see us personally."

"A girl is dead, Joe."

"She won't be any less dead by stirring up all this confusion and emotion."

"Folks are trying to understand it, is all."

"Folks are trying to pin it on someone, is more like it. Harold tried to pin it on the reverend, and the town gossips are firing it right back at him. Hell, by dawn, you all will be ready to ride him and Mag out a town on a rail."

Leona's face scrunched up, her preamble to tears. "I don't want to hurt Harold and Mag. I'm talking to my friends about Michelle's death, trying to understand. I keep wondering about why Harold told Bob those terrible things about Reverend Beechum, how he got such a notion." Her quivering lips firmed into a frown. "I don't understand why you're not more bothered, Joe."

"I am bothered, Leona. I just don't go blabbering my bother all over town. I have a hell of a lot of things to work out about Michelle and her dad and Harold and Mag, but I got a work 'em out in my head, not on the phone." I wondered again, though, whether I should confide in Leona. Was she strong enough to learn of my weakness, my indecision, my suspicions?

We stood facing each other in silence for a good thirty seconds. I saw reproach gain prominence in her expression. She knows, I thought. She knows I know a lot more about this than I'm saying. A sudden realization occurred to me. She's known all along that I don't confide in her. All these years as she's emptied herself of every worry and joy in her soul, she's known that I've had my own feelings but that I haven't told her any of 'em.

I risked staring into Leona's eyes, not just in the general direction of her face, as was my habit, and saw no barrier to me speaking my mind now as she had always spoken hers. But the distance from my brain to my vocal chords seemed infinite.

"Enough's enough," was all I said.

Leona looked away toward the view out our picture window. "Hmmm," she said dreamily, "you're a lonely old bull, Joe; you can't even confide in your mate."

The phone rang. "I have to talk to someone," Leona murmured. She turned to answer it. "Too bad it isn't you."

At eight o'clock, Ed called to notify us that the sheriff's department had officially ruled Michelle's death a drug overdose. Blood tests had shown she had all kinds of crap in her, plenty more than enough to kill her.

Chapter 30

Signs of Grief

Sylvia and Whitey came by the house about seven that evening. Looking near death themselves, they hugged us, asked how we were doing, and plopped down on the couch. Sylvia put her arm around Whitey. He sat with bowed head, staring at his hands, which he slid against each other in a circular motion. He was agitated in a way I hadn't seen before.

We talked quietly, mostly trying to help Sean work through Michelle's death, until Harold and I put him to bed. At his request, we left the light on in his room. He had lasted the day at school, but Michelle had been the topic of conversation all day. The principal had held the assembly about her death in the afternoon. Sean had been pretty emotional when we picked him up, making me wonder if we'd made the right decision in letting him choose to stay at school.

"Thankfully, he's exhausted and went to sleep as soon as his head hit the pillow," Harold said.

I hugged Harold close. "Yes, that is a good thing," I said. "Whitey, you don't look at all well. How are you doing?"

Gesturing only with his fingers, he explained his condition to me. "I feel guilty; that's what's the matter with me. I knew something was wrong with Michelle, and I didn't check into it. If that girl'd been a sick calf, I'd a checked out her problem immediately, traced it to the cause, and cured her. But..."

I interrupted. "Michelle's difficulties were far more complex and obscure than any problem one of your calves could have had. Michelle kept her pain to herself until it was too late for her to believe there was a way out."

Harold leaned forward in his chair. His voice was low, almost threatening. He said, "We're all mad at ourselves for what we didn't do. We agree on that, and we'll have to live with it. " He paused and gulped from his coffee mug, the same coffee he'd been nursing for an hour; it must have gotten cold a long time ago. "But what really galls me is how her dad could have behaved so perversely with his own child and yet paraded around town like a model citizen. A child, for Christ's sake, and his own kid!"

Harold breathed in rapids puffs. When he spoke again, his voice raked the air. "Beechum can't get away with this. He can't get away with playing the part of the grieving father and wallow in the town's pity. We didn't help Michelle when she was alive, but we can make her death have meaning."

The phone rang. I jumped. "Oh, oh . . . the phone," I sputtered. "I'll get it." My thoughts raced; I felt a rush of adrenaline. My hands shook as I picked up the phone. I worried where Harold's angry rhetoric might lead. "Hello," I said softly.

"Magdalena, it's me, Leona."

"Hello, Leona," I answered her, relieved; Leona was safe. "How are you holding up?"

"I'm all right, I guess. I was more worried about you and Harold, what with your feelings for Michelle and with the news of the blood test."

"What news of the blood test?"

"You haven't heard? The sheriff said Michelle's death has been determined to be accidental death by a drug overdose. She had a witch's brew of drugs in her. Amphetamines, barbiturates, all kinds of stuff. They said there was undigested stuff still in her stomach when she died. She took way more than enough to kill herself, they said. Where do you suppose she got all those drugs in the middle of the night?"

"I imagine she must have been saving them for a long time, Leona. Did you hear if the sheriff is investigating why she overdosed?" I asked.

"I think they think it was an accident, but deputies are asking around, trying to find out where she got the drugs."

"Yeah, they asked us."

"Oh my, I'm so sorry. Magdalena. Ah, there's another thing I got a tell ya, Folks are saying that Harold's causing trouble, accusing the reverend to Bob, and they're wanting to do something to stop him before he does anything else." Leona sounded nervous.

"Maybe folks should be more worried about themselves."

"They never are, Mag, but you're right, they probably should be. I just wanted to let you know that folks are talking." Leona sighed. "I really like you and Harold, and I'm trying to make heads or tails of your suspicions of the reverend. I can't say I agree, but I know you and Harold would have to have good reasons to feel how you do."

"Thank you, Leona."

"I'll do what I can to calm folks down, which probably isn't much. I just wanted you to know so's you could figure out what to do."

"I appreciate it, Leona. We don't know what we're going to do yet, but I don't think we're going to change our minds about what

Michelle told us her father did to her."

"Yes, yes, Mag, I understand your grief, but please be careful and don't act rashly."

"Thanks for your concern, friend. You get some sleep now. Good night."

"Good night."

I carefully replaced the receiver and considered how to relay this information to my edgy group. Harold seemed dangerously angry, and I worried that I might leap at a call for action. I was afraid of what I might do.

"Who was that?" Harold inquired brusquely.

"Leona. She said the blood test showed Michelle had consumed more than enough drugs to kill herself and that her death has been determined a drug overdose. She had a variety of drugs inside her. She must have been collecting them for a long time."

Whitey spoke in a monotone, "That's it then? Her dad's off the hook?"

"All Leona knew was that they were trying to find out where Michelle got the drugs. Why don't we call the sheriff's office and find out if they're checking on what we told them about the reverend?"

Harold sprung from his chair and reached the phone in one long stride. "Yeah, you're exactly right. Let's give the sheriff a jingle." He thumbed through the phone book, searching for the number.

"I think the sheriff's number is at the front somewhere," I suggested.

"Figures, so's you could get a hold of their inefficient asses quicker," he flung back at me and flipped to the front of the book.

He found the listing and punched the numbers harshly. He waited. We waited. "Hello," Harold said. "Yes, I'm calling for information on Michelle Beechum's death." A pause. "No, I'm not a family member." Another pause. "My name is Harold Brown. Officer Regar talked with me earlier today. Michelle worked for my wife." A third pause. "She told us last night that her father had been sexually abusing her, that he had abused her last night as a matter of fact. What I want to know is, will the possibility of Reverend Beechum having abused his daughter be investigated?" More waiting.

Suddenly, Harold thundered, "No, I will not wait for the newspaper article! I have a right to know now! You find out!" A short pause. "Get whomever you have to." Again, a wait. "I'll hold."

"Officer Regar," Harold said at length, "Harold Brown here." Pause. "Yes, I understand you've had a difficult, long day. I have only one question. After what we told you, will the possibility of Reverend Beechum having abused his daughter be investigated?" Long pause. "There was no evidence found to verify what we claimed Michelle said happened that evening." Short pause. "Clearly an accidental death by drug overdose?" Pause. "I see, yes, all you can do, uh huh." Harold nearly shouted his next words into the receiver, "She took a bath, cleaned herself up. That's why there wasn't any evidence. See if there's possibly more you can do to pursue an investigation. Why would she make up a story like that about her dad?" Pause. "Yeah, not my call. Try, Officer Regar, please try to check it out. Other children's welfare may be at stake."

Harold eased the phone back into place as if it were glass. He stood with his back to us, but I could see his shoulders heaving with the struggle of his angry breathing. Still facing away, he spoke quiet, spaced words, "They're not going to do one thing more."

We sat numbly watching Harold's back. No one moved.

"Crap!" I shouted. Whitey and Sylvia straightened up. Harold spun around. "Pure crap!" I reiterated and stood. Then I walked into the kitchen, grabbed the teakettle as I passed the stove, and thrust it under the spigot. I set the kettle on the stove, turned the burner to high, and faced the group, hands on hips.

"You want to know what we're going to do, Harold. I'll tell you what we're going to do," I said. "We're going to let the world know what Michelle told us. The town may not believe us, but if we don't want to remain silent, I know, what we have to do. You're right in what you said to the deputy. Other children's welfare may be at stake. Are you with me?"

All three nodded vigorously.

Whitey asked cautiously, "What do you have in mind?"

Harold cut in, "Count me in if it nails the reverend and if we can do it right away."

I was grim when I said, "We're going to go to the Beechum home and ask to speak to the reverend. If he talks to us, we tell him what Michelle said. See what he says, and make decisions based on that. If he refuses to talk to us, we send him a message letting him know that we will make Michelle's accusations public if he doesn't talk to us. If we're again refused, we go to the newspaper; if again refused, we make a sign. Right now, we need to write down Michelle's accusations of her father as much word for word as we can recall. We need to get our observations of Michelle's suspicious behavior and her suspicious questions and statements about sex and fathers written down, again as accurately as possible."

We were silent for a few endless seconds. Harold gripped his chin fiercely; the skin around his fingers whitened. He stared at me; his countenance held so much anger that I couldn't tell how he would respond. "Yeah, let's do it. Maybe the face-to-face meeting will drive him to confess. If not, I'm ready to go public."

Whitey sat glumly regarding his weathered hands. "We'll be stirring up a mess of hate toward us if we do this. You know that, don't you?"

The teakettle began to whistle noisily. I went to take it off the burner.

Sylvia cupped Whitey's head tenderly in her hands. "You're right, sweet dear, and we may be terribly wrong doing this." She paused a moment as she stroked the side of her husband's head with one hand. "But we have to let Beechum and if necessary, the town know what Michelle said."

I wrote what we recalled Michelle telling us about her father, and then we recorded behaviors and other things she said that had caused us to be suspicious. We went through her words again and decided what was firm enough to use.

Whitey glanced at his watch. "It's eight-thirty. We best be getting down to the Beechums."

"If we don't like what he says and John at the newspaper says he won't print Michelle's words, we come back here and make the sign?" I asked, as if clarity would make decisions any easier.

Like waterlogged jeans, Whitey's sadness hung on him and dripped from his features in great sagging slabs. His tragic stare bored into me, and I questioned the rightness of my hasty plan, but he answered, "If I'm not satisfied with what happens at his house, and there's no other avenue to get Michelle's words out, I'm with you." His voice quavered; I saw his eyes well with tears. "I have to relieve myself of the guilt I feel over Michelle's death. I see her cold, dead body, all huddled into itself before my mind's eye. I need to satisfy my suspicions or this image of Michelle will forever haunt my sight."

We stood and single file, walked to Sylvia and Whitey's car. Harold carried a sleeping Sean. No one spoke as we drove to the Beechum's home. As we turned the corner onto their block, we saw that every room of their house was illuminated. Cars were parked everywhere, jammed wherever the heaped up snow provided space beside the road. We parked about half a block away. Silent, we got out of the car and walked to the Beechum's door. Harold carried Sean, who slept still. Whitey reached the door first; he rung the buzzer. Sally opened the door.

We had decided that Whitey would be the best one to speak initially since he'd be the one most likely to get to talk to the reverend. He addressed her, "Hello, Sally. We would like to speak with Reverend Beechum please."

Sally called over her shoulder excitedly, "They're here. Come help me; come help me!"

Whitey moved his hands in a calming gesture and continued his quiet speech. "Sally, we want to talk to Reverend Beechum. We knew Michelle and are very upset by her death."

By the time Whitey finished speaking, five men backed Sally in the doorway. George was one of them, He said, "We know why you all are here. Get on out a here, or I'm calling the sheriff."

"Would you mind asking the reverend if he'd talk to us, or talk to just me, for just a few minutes," Whitey insisted quietly.

George sneered at Whitey's sad face and shouted, "The reverend said he didn't want to talk to any of you. He doesn't want to see you, and he doesn't want you bothering him ever. You got that?" He glared in turn at each of us. "You all got that?"

Once more, Whitey asked, "Please ask him again if he would talk with us or with one of us. We're here to talk to him peaceably. Please ask him if he could grant a few of Michelle's friends a moment."

George hollered, "You deaf or something? Ain't you been hearing what I been saying?"

Sylvia leaned forward, her arms embracing her husband. She asked, "Are you sure that's how the reverend feels? You're sure that those are his instructions?"

"Straight from his mouth. Officer Regar told him what you said, and I filled him in on the rest. Satan has possession of your souls and is making you say filth about him. The reverend said it was sad but true that poor little Michelle was a drug addict." George grabbed the door and began to pull it shut. "Come on, Sally, get yourself in here." He tugged at Sally's dress sleeve, coaxing her inside the house. Vigorously shaking his fist at us, he yelled, "You all be off a this property in two seconds, or we'll remove you."

Whitey grabbed hold of the door. "You need to tell the reverend that if he doesn't talk to us, we're going to make Michelle's accusations public. You tell him that and see if he doesn't change his mind."

"Get the hell off this property," George yelled again, and he slammed the door shut.

Without speaking, Whitey turned and strode briskly to the car; his long field-crossing lope brought him there quickly. Like chastised children, we traipsed after him. We drove home in silence.

I called John Eggars, the editor of the town newspaper. As soon as I told him who I was, he said, "No I won't publish your filth," and he hung up.

We stood in the living room, both terrified and excited. Time passed. Reverend Beechum didn't call.

"Harold, we'll need a frame to support a four by eight piece of quarter inch plywood," I said. If you make the ends of the poles spiked with supports to stand on, we can drive them into Reverend Beechum's lawn without noise by jumping on them. I'll measure and letter in pencil, and Sylvia will calligraphy Michelle's words. We need to decide what we want to have on the sign. Are you with me?"

"I'll go weld up that frame," Harold said, "as soon as I put Sean back to bed." He looked at me. I stared back, trying to think of something rational to say but so full of anger and confusion that nothing came to mind. Harold had always depended on me to be the one to make him have second thoughts in situations like these, but I was full steam ahead. No one would put on the brakes.

Harold draped sleeping Sean over his shoulder. "Let's bring some food out to the shop. Would someone be interested in going out to the shop and getting a fire started while I put Sean to bed?"

"I'm on it," Whitey said and he hurried out the door.

"Magdalena, tell me what you're thinking," Sylvia asked me as we started gathering food in the kitchen. "All of it."

"I think, in a way, that we're taking the law into our own hands." I pondered what food our tired group would eat.

"And?"

"The consequences will be enormous."

"And?"

"We're all locked into this and not one of us has enough sense to pull out." I gazed at Sylvia. It didn't seem right to involve her and Whitey in this. "Are you sure you want to be a part of this."

"I wouldn't have it any other way," Sylvia murmured.

I nodded but couldn't help adding, "Have you thought about what this sign could do to your and Whitey's life?"

"Yes, but we'll weather it. We've been here all our lives. You and Harold will take the brunt, whatever the reaction is. Our poor judgment, in the town's opinion, will be mediated by our long shared past. In fact, my guess is, that no matter what we say, they'll blame you and Harold for leading us astray." Sylvia eyed me gravely. Her voice breaking with emotion, she said, "Are you ready for that?"

"No, but the alternative is to do nothing and wait," I answered, my throat constricting and tears falling. I was afraid. I didn't want scorn or hate heaped on my family or me. I didn't want to have to move. Harold and I were doing well. I liked our life here. I walked over to Sylvia, and we hugged.

"Yeah, this is a tough one. Whatever we do, though, it isn't going to bring Michelle back, poor soul," Sylvia said, and we wept, holding each other close in a vain attempt at mutual consolation.

A sliver of moon radiated weak snakes of light over the landscape; the frozen grass crunched underfoot as Sylvia and I carried a pot of coffee, soup, and sandwiches from the house. Winter was here with bone chilling cold, no breeze at all.

When we came in the shop, Whitey was banking the fire and

Harold was welding. We set down our trays, and cradling mugs of coffee, we walked over to the piece of plywood we intended to use.

Harold spoke in a voice full of pleading. "We have to make folks feel the terror that poor girl felt." My husband's face twitched with guilty anxiousness, the same guilt we had all assumed for not having saved the life of a girl we instinctively sensed was in danger.

"You're right," I said. "Every accusation of her father from last night needs to be up there. One whole side. Suspicious, specific things she said and did before that on the other side."

Sylvia drew lines on one side of the plywood while I drew lines on the other side, the side that would chronicle Michelle's last night. Then I measured and roughly lettered it while Sylvia began her calligraphy over my penciled words. Harold and Whitey worked at designing a frame that could be quickly assembled; one that we would be able to drive into the frozen earth in front of the reverend's house.

The men finished the frame before Sylvia and I finished the lettering. Using my hair dryer, I dried the paint on the first side while Sylvia finished lettering the second. Even with the heat from the woodstove, the shop was too cold for the acrylic paint to dry quickly. The time was nearly three-thirty. Finally, Sylvia, Whitey, and Harold stood behind me, waiting as I ran the hair dryer over the last of Sylvia's letters. I turned to face them.

"Anyone have any regrets, any don't do it's, any stop and think advice?" I asked.

"Hmmm, like we'd be out here, freezing our butts if we weren't going to go through with it," Sylvia said. "Let's get moving."

"Bundle up," Harold ordered. "It's not more than ten or fifteen degrees out there. After I push the door open, Whitey and I will grab the plywood. Each of you gals grab a bundle of frame. We'll go over how we'll assemble the sign in the truck. Ready?"

"What about our son?" I asked.

"He'll be safer here than if we took him with, too cold," he answered. "You should stay back with him."

"I'm not staying back. He'll be warm in the truck if he's in the down sleeping bag," I said.

"Okay, you're right, go get him. We'll get the frame in the truck." Harold shoved open the door.

I fetched Sean, bundled him in a jacket, hat, mittens, sleeping bag, and quilt and carried him to the truck. Harold swung the shop door closed, and we drove to town.

We parked in the shadow of the reverend's church, which was on the opposite side of the block from his house. All we had to do was to carry our gear across the church parking lot and around the parsonage and set up the sign on his front lawn. Yeah, that was all. I wondered why it felt so right to do this while I felt so much like a criminal doing it.

Only two cars remained in the church lot. The utility pole light beamed down on them, setting their cracked and faded ice coated paint to sparkling. I bundled blankets around Sean and left him in the cab with the doors locked. Each crunching, crackling step we took echoed like hammer blows in my mind. We sounded so loud that I couldn't see why everyone in town wasn't sitting bolt upright in their beds and running to their windows to stare at the sign erectors.

"I'm not sure why we're worried about getting caught," Harold whispered. "We signed our names. We're intending to get caught."

"I know." I rasped back. "I just don't want to get caught here."

We made it to the front of the Beechum's house. The utility pole in the front corner of their yard beamed down its glaring white light, illuminating the entire front yard. The bare branches of a sugar locust, the only tree in the front yard, gave scant cover. Cars still crammed the roadway.

"Do you suppose all the people from these cars are sleeping inside the Beechum's house?" I breathed into Sylvia's ear.

She stared at me, either confused or stunned by my question. "Who the hell cares?" she answered at length. Embarrassed, but giddy with nervousness, I retreated.

To drive the first post into the ground, Harold and Whitey jumped on the rung they'd welded onto it, about eighteen inches from the sharpened tip. Gradually, the point of the post pierced the hard ground and each of the men's jumps eased it deeper into the earth. We slipped the plywood into the standing post's slot and set the slot of the second post up against the sign's other end. Whitey and Harold jumped on the second post's welded rung. Five minutes, start to finish, and we were slinking back around the Beechum's house and across the church parking lot. Slinking, yes, that meant somewhere inside of us we must have known that what we were doing was not the way to go about this.

"Wait a second!" Harold exclaimed, almost at full voice. "Where the hell was that little barky dog they have? We should have been hearing that annoying yap right through the walls of their house."

"All those cars and people," Sylvia retorted, "the poor thing probably lost his yap hours ago." Sylvia stopped, and the harsh utility pole light cut her face into angles of black shadow and white protuberances. Her red wig shown as a brassy halo surrounding her face. She fixed her angled black shadowed eyes on Whitey as she murmured, "Michelle hated that dog. She said that her dad held and cuddled that dog all the time. An act he perverted with her. Shit. God damn it. And now she's dead."

Brave-hearted, in-your-face Sylvia broke down. She sobbed uncontrollably; Whitey gently led her toward our truck. We drove home to eat an early breakfast and talk about what might happen in the morning.

"We're going to have to explain this to Sean," I said and nuzzled my sleeping child as I carried him into his bedroom.

"We'll tell him in the morning," Harold called after me. "No sense riling his sleep."

We ate a simple meal of eggs and toast. I was sliding into hazy fatigue and vague dread of what was to come when Whitey spoke. "We need to remember, no matter what happens, that right now, what we did tonight was what we thought we had do to. No regrets. From what we know now, we had to take the action we took. Okay then, let's go to bed." Sylvia and Whitey waved goodbye; we heard them start their car and head up to their place to sleep.

The phone rang at six-thirty, shortly after first light. Harold rose from our bed and walked into the living room to answer. From his brief responses, I couldn't tell what the conversation was about.

"Who was that?" I asked as he returned to our bedroom and slouched onto the bed.

"That was Joe," Harold answered. "He said folks began gathering in front of the Beechum's house soon after the paper boy saw the sign and ran home to tell his mom about it. He said he went over to have a look and was standing there reading it when Reverend Beechum himself came out."

Harold sighed. His face was ashen. I didn't want to hear any more, but he continued. "Joe said that the crowd fell silent as the Reverend read first one side and then the other. The longer he read the redder his face got. The color of beets, Joe said. By the time he finished reading, he was fuming so bad that you could see steam rising off the top of his bald head. He shook his fists at the people standing around in the cold dawn. Folks tried to drag him inside, talking to him real quiet.

"He went in finally," Harold said. I held my breath and prayed to every holy spirit I could think of that that was all the news. Harold lifted his head and stared straight at me. I saw his empty confusion, guilt, and fatigue. "He went in," he repeated "and shot himself in the head with a pistol he kept by his bed. He's dead, Mag."

Chapter 31

Judgment Time for Harold and Magdalena

"Mr. Mobley," thirteen-year old Justin called to me seconds before he tossed me my papers. The Halfway paper only came out once a week; I got the Baker City daily paper delivered to the store. Folks liked news every day. I sold all I got. I caught the bundle as he rolled his bike to a stop about ten feet in front of me. Puffs of steamy breath huffed from his gaping mouth as he called over his shoulder, "Have you heard the latest?"

"I just now got to town; I haven't even been inside the store yet," I answered, a feeling of dread tickling my gut. I didn't think I could take a second day of disastrous news.

"I discovered it, Mr. Mobley, and I'm hurrying on my route so's I can get done and get back over to it at the Beechum's. I want to look at it more. Mom said I had to finish my route before I could hang out there though, and I could only stay until it's time to go to school."

"I don't reckon that the Reverend and Mrs. Beechum feel like having people around this early in the morning, Justin. What with their tragedy . . . ," I began.

But Justin cut in, "That's what I was gonna to tell ya, Mr. Mobley. Mag and Harold Brown and Whitey and Sylvia put up a sign in the Beechum's front yard last night. You got a go read what it says about the reverend. I got a go. Bye, Mr. Mobley." He swung his right leg over his bike and sped away, skidding crazily on the icy pavement as he rounded the corner of the store.

I watched Justin as he disappeared from view. Then I looked at the front page of the top paper, but I couldn't focus on the newsprint. All I could think was, dear God, what in hell have Harold and Mag done?

I debated on whether or not to join the crowd around the sign. My curiosity wiggled alongside that tickle of dread inside me. What was on the sign? If I didn't get over there right away, Beechum or one of his relatives would come out a the house and pull the thing down. Then I'd never know for sure what had been on it. All I'd have was fifty different versions from fifty different memories.

Well, toss me in Satan's bin along with Harold and Mag. I was hooked. I had to go see that sign. I hotfooted it the three blocks over to the Beechum's house. I could see a small crowd around the sign from a half-block away. Folks were moving in slow motion as they read and wandered from one side to the other.

I got close enough to recognize some of the people milling about, and goddamn it, old lady Hampton had beat me. How in the world she had found out and toddled over before me, I'll never know, but there she was in the twenty-some degree cold, hobbling around with that black rubber tipped cane of hers, her black eyes squinting up at that sign.

I began reading. Michelle's words of accusation about her father, made on her last night alive, were brushed in eloquent strokes of red across one whole side of the four by eight piece of plywood. Her words assaulted my eyes with their plainly stated, harsh reality, a reality, the sign said, Michelle had begged Harold and Mag to assist her in escaping, somehow, to anywhere. My own suspicions crawled up my spine and slithered into my throat and mouth. I felt queasy.

I finished reading one side and walked around to the opposite side. I saw John standing there, front row, center, reading and sipping from a steaming cup of coffee. All of a sudden, I wished I had a cup of coffee and almost asked for a sip of his.

He acknowledged my presence with a nod and continued his reading. Without shifting his gaze from the sign, he said, "What do you think, Joe?" He swallowed a mouthful of coffee and turned toward me. I said nothing. He continued, "Sylvia and Whitey put in their two bits too. Sylvia's judgment could be questioned, but Whitey's?"

I finished reading the last of the foursome's statements and was about to answer John when the Beechum's door banged open. The reverend himself burst through the opening and stomped toward the sign. He was wearing an aged, white T-shirt and gray, wrinkled work pants. He had shaving cream smeared over half his face. His hands were fisted and his brow knotted.

The crowd of thirty-some people fell completely silent, waiting. Beechum huffed up to within reading distance of the sign, an arm's length from me. He muttered the words to himself as he read. I could hear his rapid, shallow breathing.

He cursed several times, mostly saying, "God damn 'em! God damn 'em!" I tried to determine if these utterances indicated his guilt or innocence, but I couldn't decide. I focused my attention on the back of his head. The bald spot visible to me gained color with each syllable he read. Beads of sweat appeared, and steam rose from his crimson pate. As he read the last word of the last statement out loud, Beechum shook his fist at the billboard; then he headed toward the other side.

Just then, old lady Hampton came wobbling 'round from that direction, her scrawny head bent low, keeping sight of her feet. She and the reverend were pretty much on a collision course unless one of 'em veered. I took a step forward and reached out, as did three or four others. Beechum gave Hampton a not too gentle shove with the back of his left hand.

The old bird teetered, and her arms flew out for balance. Her cane waved wildly in the air as if seeking firm ground. She grabbed the signpost with her flailing right hand and held on. The plywood swooshed to and fro as the metal post she hung onto flexed under the weight of her body.

John and I reached Mrs. Hampton at the same time. "Are you all right?" I asked.

"What the hell happened!" she exclaimed. "Was there an earthquake, or did I hit a slick patch?"

"You ran into the word of God," John said, smirking, "and He wasn't happy."

"What? What's that, you say?" Hampton squeaked.

John patted the old woman's back. "That was just someone in a hurry, Mrs. Hampton."

"Humph! Kids these days never watch where they're going," she said and proceeded on her way.

John and I stayed where we were. From our new vantage point, we could see the reverend's face as he read Michelle's words from her last night on Earth, and for some perverse reason, I really wanted to see his expression as he read those words.

Now, I wished I hadn't seen it; the image of Beechum's face, twisted in rage, haunts me even more than Michelle's death. As he read each line, he swore. "Damn Magdalena and Harold Brown for perverting my daughter! Satan take them all for uttering these lewd, hateful words!" He screamed at the four by eight piece of plywood with red letters painted on it.

From the neck up, his skin was the color of beets. His T-shirt was drenched in sweat. He paced back and forth in front of the sign, shouting at it. Relatives and supporters surrounded him, cajoling him to come into the house.

He broke from them and stood as if to preach to the assembled group. He swung his arms wildly and proclaimed, "Michelle curses me in her death, the wanton woman child! The sinful daughter of Satan, unabsolved of the burden of her sex!" Beechum wheeled away from George and Ed and almost knocked Sally and his wife down as he sought to continue his preaching.

"Go sinful daughter, go! Go to Satan! Go in death as you lived in life, sinful! I tried to save you! I tried!" Six men surrounded him; two were his brothers. They forcefully dragged him toward his house. Mrs. Beechum sobbed noisily while Sally comforted her as she followed her husband toward the front door. Beechum continued to holler out his sermon even as the last of his shaking fist and rage red head were pulled inside.

The door thudded shut, and it was quiet. I looked at John. He was staring at me. "I'll never know what to make of that," he remarked hoarsely. "Christ," he whispered and shielded his eyes with one hand. I was sure that I heard him weeping. I reached my right hand over and uncomfortably rested it on his back. I felt considerably light headed myself. We stood there, stupidly staring at the spectacle before us. Folks started to drift away; most were pretty shook up.

Ka-boom! I heard a shot, then frenzied screaming. George came tearing out a the front door, yelling, "Reverend Beechum's shot hisself! Make way for the ambulance! Make way!" And he galloped full speed toward the volunteer fire department building two blocks away, where the ambulance was housed.

John and I locked eyes. Terror flooded his tear-soaked face. He leaned against the sign. I didn't move.

A minute or two later, the local nurse practitioner, Mark Jeffries, swung his Honda sedan full speed around the corner, balls to the wall, and skidded to a stop in the middle of the Beechum's lawn. He flopped his door open, letting it stay swung wide, and grabbing his black doctor bag from the passenger side of the front seat, he dashed toward the open front door and a frantically gesturing Sally.

He had hardly disappeared inside the house when George and the ambulance careened into view. George stopped abruptly in the middle of the street and stuck his head out a his window. "Get out a the way!" he ordered. John and I stood where we had been, not catching any reference to us in his mad waving and yelling. Finally, he barked, "Get out a the goddamned way, you two old farts!" and we moved.

George backed the ambulance onto the lawn, and he and Ed unloaded the gurney and an emergency bag of equipment. They rushed inside. The ambulance idled out front, its powerful engine throbbing, ready to take Reverend Beechum to Baker at breakneck speed.

No one came out. Minutes passed. At last, a blood spattered Mark Jeffries emerged from the wide-open front door. "Holy shit!" I breathed. John wavered woozily. I sort of held him up with my arm around his back.

Mark waited for everyone to pay attention and for George to silence the idling ambulance. Then, in a loud, clear voice, he calmly explained, "About five minutes ago, Reverend Beechum shot himself in the head with a 32 caliber pistol that he kept by his bed." Terrified exclamations arose from women and men alike.

Mrs. Hampton croaked, "What'd he say? What'd he say?"

Someone filled her in as Jeffries continued, "The loss of blood and damage to his brain were immediate and immense." Jeffries wiped his face with a clean, gauze-like cloth he held in his left hand. He gazed from face to face. "The reverend is dead," he announced.

He turned and walked back inside. Someone unseen reached a hand out and shut the door behind him.

John and I hunkered together like the two old men we were. We watched as the grief and shock of the people around us turned to cries for vengeful action. With the grip of strong hands on each rung, they pulled the sign's posts out a the ground. The unsupported plywood flopped over, hitting the frozen lawn with a whomp as the air rushed out from under it. From somewhere, axes appeared in hands, swinging. Angry men splintered the wood; I worried that someone would get hurt from an errant ax.

Phil revved up his chain saw, and that racket was added to the bedlam building around the nearly destroyed sign. Men, women, and children heaped the sign's chips and splinters into a pile. Someone doused them with gasoline. Little Justin tossed on a match. A sucking poof and a massive wave of heat whooshed up immediately.

John and I watched it all. John no longer tried to hide his tear-streaked face. Feeling old and helpless, I'm sure we looked as confused and scared as we felt.

More folks gathered as time went by, lots of kids; I wondered if school had been canceled. As the sign and its words turned to ashes, the group began to focus on Harold and Magdalena. They seemed to have forgotten all about Sylvia and Whitey's part in the sign.

"Who the hell appointed Harold and Magdalena Brown judge and jury?" one man shouted, mad as hell.

"Yeah, look at their lives, an alcoholic and a hippie. Who are they to judge?" a woman blasted angrily.

"But Sylvia and Whitey had words up there," some poorly advised soul had the nerve to observe.

"Come on, like you believe they actually had anything to do with this? Well, Sylvia maybe. But old Whitey? Never. Get your head out a your ass, man. It's them Browns that's behind this."

"I say we go out to their place an' beat the living shit out a Harold!" sneered a skinny young man whom I recognized as the one who'd been trying unsuccessfully to charge beer at the store lately.

"Yeah, and get yourself arrested for assault while you're at it. Their sorry asses aren't worth getting arrested over."

"Harold's shop," one man stated simply.

"Yeah, I could use me some good tools," chortled another, catching his drift.

"Never can tell how tools have a mind of their own. Just up and walk off," suggested a third fella.

"As I see it, Harold Brown ain't doing no more business in this town anyway," the initiator of the tool stealing scheme added.

"Harold and Mag are holed up at their house. They'd never know what storm blew in and swooped up them tools."

"A good man should be using those tools, not the likes of Brown," exhorted a man old enough to know better than to get involved with the tool-stealing mob.

The rabble rousers bounced inflammatory remarks off each other another minute or two while John and I stood still as statues, saying nothing. Finally, a huddle of six men left to ransack Harold's shop, and I let 'em go.

The remaining crowd members began their own dance of vengeance. "I say we burn 'em in effigy on that slope of theirs. Their images burning would fit in with all that unholy crap they have strewn around," a woman announced. I couldn't clearly swear who said them words, but it sounded like Sally.

The group was mobilized. "Yeah, and let's put up a sign at their house, telling them to get their Satan loving butts out a town!" Phil suggested fiercely. "How many are with me on this?" he asked the crowd. Hands shot up all over.

"We'll all help," Sally said. "We'll rid Halfway of the Browns.

They've gone too far this time."

Echoes of "Yeah!" and "Damn straight!" and "They got it coming!" came from the group. Sally marched to the road, and swinging her right arm in a wide arc, commanded her troops, "Follow me! We'll make the sign and effigies in my garage and then march to the Brown's." I considered that she would remember this as her finest hour. I also wondered if this group was fired up enough to be crazy enough to walk the four miles out to the Browns. Not a one of them had suggested using vehicles.

Mrs. Hampton tottered off after her departing cohorts. Puffing, she called, "Wait up! God damn it, wait up!" to their rapidly vanishing backs.

John and I were the only ones left on the Beechum's lawn. The last of the plywood smoldered, flicking weak flames into the frigid morning air. Horrendous sobbing came from within the Beechum's house. Mrs. Beechum, I guessed. Their little dog yowled and yipped along with her sobs.

John stirred. "I need a beer," he announced "Let's get out a here."

"I'm with ya," I answered, the only thing I could manage to say. "Let's go to my stockroom. I don't want to talk to anyone." We walked toward my store. "Leona," I remembered, sadly anticipating that exchange. "I'll have to call Leona and go home to see her," I told John, "but first, a beer."

We reached the back door to the store. I felt a hundred years old. I thought how I didn't need to be seeing or knowing any of this. "What next?" I asked John as I turned the key in the lock.

But I knew in my heart what had to be next. I had to take a stand whether or not it hurt my business. I had to tell what I knew, what I believed. There was no telling what that mob of yahoos might do if they made it all the way out to the Brown's place. "I'll have to skip that beer," I told John. "I need to take a ride on out to the Brown's place." Then I remembered. "But first, I'll call Leona."

Chapter 32

Making Amends

Moments after Joe had told Harold of Reverend Beechum's death, we heard a soft knocking on the front door. I hesitated to answer, fearing who might be outside and what they might say. Then, without my assistance, the doorknob turned, and Sylvia peeked into the room. "Hon, can we talk to you two?" she asked. Her mascara drizzled down her cheeks; she'd been crying.

"Sylvia, of course, come in," I called to her. Relieved that she was our visitor, anxious joy overwhelmed me, and I hastened to reach her, nearly stumbling over a toy truck Sean had left in the center of the living room. I hugged her as if we'd been parted many years; tears welled in my eyes, and I didn't want to release her.

Head bowed and hat in hand, Whitey stepped into the room as I clung to Sylvia. "Morning," was all he said.

Sylvia gently pushed me from her. "Hon, we have to talk," she stated firmly. "I take it that you've heard the news." She glanced from Harold to me.

"Yes, Joe just now called," Harold answered her.

Sean wandered into the room, bleary-eyed and holding a teddy he hadn't clung to in years. "What's everybody doing?" he asked, his voice sleepy and small.

I let go of Sylvia and latched onto Sean. "Son, we're talking about Michelle and her father and a sign we put up last night," I said, as I stroked his head and caressed his face, "and we're wondering what we should do now. More bad stuff has happened."

"Oh, no," he said and yawned. He slumped onto the couch, curled up, and closed his eyes,

"We'll talk quietly. You go ahead and try and sleep," I told him.

Sean nodded, and a tear slipped sideways down his cheek. I rested my hand on his back.

Harold offered Whitey and Sylvia coffee. He made hot chocolate for Sean, but he was already asleep.

"We should eat something," I said.

But no one really wanted to eat. I knew we had to respond to this new tragedy but had no idea of what to do.

"Well," Harold said. "What should we do?"

"I don't know," I admitted, "but I'm thinking." I sat on the couch between Harold and Sean and sipped my coffee. "We can't undo what we've already done, and even with what's happened, I don't want to. Never in my wildest dreams did I think Reverend Beechum would harm himself, much less shoot himself, over our sign, but he did, and we have to deal with it. We'll never know whether his actions prove his innocence or guilt, and that's what I wanted to know."

"Yet everyone in town knows that we think he was guilty, and they think that our accusations drove him to kill himself, fast on the death of his daughter," Whitey pointed out, "and they're going to want their pound of flesh from us."

"Are you suggesting that one of us off himself so that folks around here feel vindicated?" Harold asked, a stunned look on his face.

"No, no, no," Whitey assured him, "I mean that we have to come up with a response that affirms the sincerity of what we did and the grief we feel over its outcome." He gazed at Harold, fatigue and stress emphasizing the frailties of his age.

"What could we possibly do that would placate folks?" Sylvia asked.

"I know," I said, standing, getting an idea, and with it, becoming animated. "We have to give them the sanctuaries, but not the sculptures. I wouldn't give them up, and anyway, they won't burn."

"What do you mean, give them the sanctuaries? Why? How will that help?" tumbled from Harold's lips all in a breath.

"We give them the sanctuaries in a giant pyramid of everything that's in them, the poetry signs, the furniture, everything, down at the bottom of the drive, right next to the road. We stack everything up, invite folks out, and set the whole thing on fire."

"Lose the sanctuaries and the tea parties? But why, Mag?" Sylvia asked, her eyes wide with distress.

"Because they've been a major issue of suspicion and a bone of contention since we started them. Folks here don't like the outsiders who hang out in them. They don't like that local teenagers hang out in them. They suspect them of being subversive influences. They set us apart, and to a lot of people, they show our contempt for what the town believes and wants."

"My sculptures do that too. There's that whole Satin rumor going around. The sanctuaries won't be enough," Harold said. "They'll want more."

"Your sculptures are fine," Whitey told Harold. "Mag's right, it's the outsiders and teenagers hanging out that bugs folks more than anything."

"I don't know. Some people around here think they're evidence that I'm in league with the devil," Harold said.

"If you eliminate the sanctuaries, outsiders and teenagers will continue to come to see the sculptures, but they won't be hanging out, hidden, in the woods," Whitey said. "That's the thing that really arouses suspicion."

Harold looked pretty shaky. "I hope so. I put my heart into those hunks of metal." He rubbed his face. "Are you sure you're willing to give up the sanctuaries, Mag?"

"All but the first one we made and the one Sylvia and Whitey made for themselves, and they'll be by invitation only, for local folks, adults only." I looked at my group. "We need to make another sign or two. And we'll need to talk to folks. We'll say how sorry we are for the deaths, how we wish we could have stopped Michelle from taking her own life, and how we never imagined that Reverend Beechum would harm himself. We'll admit that we handled things badly and that the signs weren't the way to make our views known. But we'll tell everyone that we wrote what we did because we believe what Michelle told us, that we were overcome with grief, and that we want to make her life and death have meaning. We don't say we were mistaken in what we said. I won't say that," I said.

Sylvia wiped her smeared eye make-up from her cheeks. "I'll letter some new signs with those very words on them."

"Well, if we're going to do get the sanctuaries down the hill," Harold said, "we'll need to hurry."

"Hurry, why?" I asked.

"Because Joe said that the group outside of Beechum's was headed up this way, maybe on foot, maybe in vehicles."

"And you're just now telling us?"

His voice wavered. "I didn't know what to do. I was hoping they'd get too cold and never show up."

"No time to waste," I said, "for they will most likely come. We probably have less than an hour left. We'll gather the sanctuary fixings and haul them on down. We may need sledge hammers for anything left to weather for these items might be frozen in place. Harold, do you have some pieces of wood big enough for Sylvia to write on?"

"Yeah, I'll get you set up," he said. He nudged Sean. "Son, would you help Sylvia in the shop while your mom and I gather a whole mess of wood for a big bonfire?"

"A bonfire?" Sean said sleepily, sitting up. "I need to get dressed."

"You don't have to come outside if you don't want to," I said.

"I want to," Sean said and hurried to his room to dress.

"I'll call the Baker AA group as soon as this is over," Harold told me as he shrugged into his coat. "I'll see if I can meet with someone tomorrow."

"Good," I said.

We bundled up for the cold and headed outside to our tasks. I was bone weary and knew Harold, Whitey, and Sylvia had to feel the same, but Whitey was right, we had to make peace with Halfway, or we wouldn't be able to live here anymore. I hoped what we planned would be enough. If it wasn't, I wondered what the approaching crowd might do? Maybe Sean shouldn't be present. What if the encounter became violent? Violence, oh no, no, no.

My mind raced with thoughts of doom as we tore through the sanctuaries, throwing frozen tarps from stacks of furniture, grabbing the tables and chairs beneath, knocking board after board of poetry from trees and yanking boards and chimes from frozen twine. As soon as we'd filled our pickup, Harold headed down the slope to stack his load, and I helped Whitey load his truck. Harold soon returned and helped. Whitey's truck loaded, he headed downhill. Harold and I started tossing stuff into the bed of our truck again. My feet were numb, and my fingers ached, from cold and cuts. Finally, except for the two sanctuaries we were saving, we could find no more signs, no more tarps with crazily painted furniture beneath, no more wind chimes or flags.

"I guess it's time to see if Sylvia's ready," Whitey murmured. Snow had begun to fall. The day had grown colder, and the flakes were tiny, barely wisps of crystal water, each minuscule, but falling fast and accumulating.

As I stepped into the shop and the warm air hit me, I almost fell asleep standing up. My bones seemed to melt, and my eyelids, rock-heavy, hung low over my bleary pupils.

"Take 'em on out," Sylvia said all too soon, pointing to her new signs. "They're finished, and they're dry to touch."

We leaned the two four by four pieces of plywood Sylvia had painted against each other, teepee like, in the back of our pickup. We climbed into the cab and headed down the slope. Whitey held Sean.

I hadn't seen the stacked sanctuaries until this moment and was astounded at how high a pile Whitey and Harold had made. They must have climbed the stack and dragged stuff up to get it as high as it was. "Was there that much hidden in the forest?" I whispered.

Sylvia was equally impressed. "I do believe this ought to make a statement," she said as she climbed out of the pickup next to the heap.

As we unloaded the signs, we heard voices coming from the direction of the road, the speakers yet unseen. We looked at each other. "Maybe I should head up to the house with Sean," I told Harold. I was about to drop my end of the plywood, grab Sean, and hightail it, whether or not Harold agreed.

"Help me get this set up first. Then we'll talk," he said. " I don't think people would harm Sean, whatever happens, but we'll talk in just a minute."

"There isn't a minute left," I begged, my maternal instincts screamed at me to take my son and run, yet I held onto my end of the sign. We set this new sign on a ledge that Harold and Whitey had made as they'd stacked, and we stepped back to look at the two signs and the stacked furniture and words of poetry. Tiny flakes of snow fell all around us, muting the words of the crowd now closing in on us.

A car we recognized as Joe's came racing up the road. He honked as he made his way through the crowd and turned into our driveway. He parked his car next to our truck and jogged over to us. "I have to talk to you all," he said, panting. "I was suspicious myself. I'm going to tell folks that. I'll tell them how you tried to help Michelle and how I failed to help her, even with what I knew." Joe blinked back tears. "I'll tell them I wish I'd a done something to help her with all I knew and feared. I'll tell them I'm going to feel guilty for the rest of my life for not helping her. Let me talk to folks first, before anything happens. They can choose not to belief me, us, but they have to understand how much we believe Michelle."

I threw my arms around Joe. Harold shook his hand and then turned to me. "Did you remember to toss some fire starter in the back this last trip?" he asked.

"Yeah, right here," I answered and pulled a gas can from the bed of our truck, setting it on the ground next to us.

"Let me pull the pickup off to the side, and I'll be right back," Harold said.

Joe moved his car next to our truck.

I stood next to the stacked sanctuaries. Sean circled the pyramid and called to Harold and I, "This is going to be a big fire."

The crowd came into view around the bend. Harold rushed to Sean and scooped him up into his arms. "Mag," he called, "That's a bigger group than I thought it would be. I think you ought to head up to the house with Sean after all." He held Sean to him, sheltering his head with his hands as from blows that were to come.

"No, I think we all need to be here," I said, "and there isn't time to take Sean to the house. Besides, he'd probably be scared up there, with this happening down here." I put my arm around Harold's waist and kissed Sean and him lightly on their cheeks. I saw Harold's fear, but I also saw stern determination.

"We've made it this far, and we still believe what Michelle said was true," he said. "We can weather an angry mob." We smiled at each other, and facing the town's people now walking the road in front of our slope, we waited.

Joe said, "Later, I have to tell you what the reverend said after he'd read the sign. There was something major askew with that man." He looked me in the eye. "You were right in your fear for Michelle."

I was instantly overwhelmed and fell to my knees, sobbing. "We must give Michelle's life meaning," I said as I glanced from our group to the people trudging uphill. "This is only a beginning."

Sean watched quietly.

"Don't worry," I told him. "It'll be all right. These folks will probably say some angry things to us. We'll try to make them understand why we did what we did, that we know we should have done things differently, and that we never meant for the reverend to hurt himself. We'll light the fire and hopefully, over time, everything will be a little better. All right?"

Sean's lower lip stuck out, and his face contorted in readiness for tears as he looked from Harold to me. "It'll be okay, Son," I told him. "I'm sure of it." For suddenly, gazing at the pyramid of sanctuary clutter, I knew it would be.

We would never be wholly a part of Halfway; no one who hadn't been here for generations was, but loved or hated, we would be accepted. The exposed, jumbled remains of our poets' sanctuaries showed us for what we were, our frailties and our strengths. They revealed us to the approaching crowd as completely as if we stood naked before them. We waited, huddled close, arms around each other, ready to face the crowd, ready to accept responsibility for what we did and didn't do, ready to give meaning to a meaningless tragedy.

Made in the USA
San Bernardino, CA
03 June 2017